"YOU OWE ME AN APOLOGY!"

Laura's face grew flushed with anger. "I do not!"

Dusty's touch was gentle as he pulled her into his arms. "You do. I would never take advantage of you, Laura. Never."

"Oh." She looked away. "I . . . I'm sorry about that remark. I was letting my feelings get the best of me. It won't happen again."

"Of course it will. You won't be able to help it. Just like I won't be able to play the total professional all the time." He dipped his head and kissed her, parting her lips with the tip of his tongue. At first Laura resisted, then slowly gave in. When he finally released her from his tender embrace, she was having trouble catching her breath.

This is insane! he told himself. What had made him get involved with this alluring but cantankerous female? Had he listened to reason—or his libido? Whichever, he made a vow to himself that no matter how terrific she looked, he'd bail out on her and shoot her down if their partnership got too complicated— or too hot to handle.

QUANTITY SALES

INDIVIDUAL SALES

STAR SPANGLED LOVER

Linda Vail

A DELL BOOK

Published by
Dell Publishing
a division of
Bantam Doubleday Dell Publishing Group, Inc.
666 Fifth Avenue
New York, New York 10103

The trademark Dell ® is registered in the U.S. Patent and Trademark
Office.

ISBN: 0-440-20310-4

Printed in the United States of America
Published simultaneously in Canada
July 1989

10   9   8   7   6   5   4   3   2   1

KRI

The age of virtuous politics is past,
And we are deep in that of cold pretence.
Patriots are grown too shrewd to be sincere:
And we too wise to trust them.
—WILLIAM COWPER

STAR
SPANGLED
LOVER

1

"This is all your fault, Mom." Laura Newton pulled her twelve-year-old Toyota off onto the shoulder of the narrow strip of heat-baked asphalt, watching as the first puffs of vapor from beneath the hood turned into a steady rush of sweet-smelling steam. "You're the one who wanted a doctor in the family."

Had she been there to defend herself, Laura's mother would have taken great umbrage at such an accusation. What she'd wanted was a surgeon, not a Doctor of Philosophy. And if Laura hadn't rebelled against that desire, she would be tending the sick in some plush office instead of nursing a cantankerous radiator across the barren wastes of Southwest Colorado.

But Laura had to blame someone else for a change. She'd given herself so many swift kicks that her ego was black-and-blue. Since early spring, not a day had gone by when she didn't either wake up in a cold sweat or go to bed in a deep funk.

Besides, it *wasn't* her fault. Not really. Granted, she did seem to have a talent for attracting the wrong sort of attention. As far back as Laura could remember, her curiosity and burning desire to break new ground had gotten her into one scrape after another.

To this day, her former high school chemistry teacher started each semester by directing his students' attention to one wall of the classroom. There, preserved for posterity, was a mottled purple blotch known far and wide as "Newton's Stain," the result of an explosive chemical reaction caused by Laura's eagerness to stray from standard methodology. Fame at fifteen—as a negative example.

Then on to college, where she'd gained notoriety as the first student in the history of her alma mater to be allowed to change majors four times. In one year. There was a small plaque in the freshman lounge to serve as a reminder of this feat, as well as a framed letter from the dean advising that "Newton's Record" would never be surpassed. Or else.

To the great relief of her parents—not to mention her guidance counselor—Laura settled down in her sophomore year, having at last found an area broad enough to encompass her bright mind and variety of interests. Anthropology. The scientific study of human beings and their physical, social, material, and cultural development. But as that study was usually restricted to primitive peoples, and Laura could never abide restrictions, she managed to leave the infamous Newton mark there as well, especially in postgraduate work.

From the very instant she had her bachelor's degree in hand, Laura predictably chose the unbeaten path. Ignoring the advice of mentors and friends, she headed off to blaze new trails, expanding the limits of her chosen field into the closely aligned territory of sociology. And she did it well, earning the coveted Ph.D. Unfortunately, she also earned a name for herself. A very unflattering name.

Laura's doctoral thesis concerning the effects of ultraviolet light on criminal activity throughout history caused quite a stir among her colleagues. It also thrust her into the limelight of the sensationalistic press, which debated what she'd intended as pure theory with persons of limited education and vast imagination. She came away looking like a loony alarmist, a rogue scientist crying wolf. The most admired talk show host in America branded her an eccentric. Her staid peers had another word for it.

Dr. Laura Newton. Flake.

But it wasn't really her fault. The concept was sound, her work impeccable. If it hadn't been a slow news day, her research would have gotten the notice it deserved and then found a quiet academic niche somewhere. Instead it ended up splashed on tabloids under the headline "Newton's Folly." Blame, therefore, could be placed squarely on the shoulders of the media. Having someone to point a finger at, however, didn't take any of the sting out of Laura's embarrassment.

Rather than face the laughter and in some cases open hostility of her colleagues, Laura decided a sabbatical was in order—one she'd as soon extend forever if she couldn't repair her damaged reputation.

Somehow she had to come up with a research project that would make everyone take her seriously again, one so soundly professional they would forget the media circus she'd stirred up with global crime and the greenhouse effect.

So there she was, on the side of a desolate stretch of road, watching her radiator boil over for the third time in as many hours. And for what?

For the merest hint of a lead: a collect phone call from a dimly remembered acquaintance who offered no information, just the vague promise of a fantastic research opportunity and an urgent request to make due speed. As even her dim memories of him were bad, that Laura had bothered to listen to Carl Flemming in the first place showed the true measure of her desperation.

A former classmate and would-be lover, Carl would be hard-pressed to find his own backside with both hands, let alone the sort of suitably important topic she needed. During their brief association, of which the absolute pinnacle was a simply dreadful one-night stand after a boozy post-finals bash, Carl had displayed only one real talent. He could lie, cheat, or force his way into bed with any woman he fancied—and he fancied a lot of them—while making it seem as if they had begged to be taken advantage of.

Laura's car gave a final, belching gasp. She reached into the backseat for the five-gallon water jug she'd wisely purchased after the first boil-over, put on her straw safari hat with its bright floral band, and smeared some more sunblock on her face. Thus ready to face the overheated engine and broiling sun, Laura stepped outside, wondering if late June was always this hot around these parts. Probably not.

"It's a sign," she muttered, carefully opening the hood of her car. "Maybe I should take the hint and crawl into the desert to die."

As she began the by-now-familiar ritual of dribbling water over the radiator cap to cool it, Laura heard an equally familiar sound. First a rumble. Then a distinctive hiss, followed by the squeal of air brakes slowing a behemoth semi to a stop behind her little car. Amazing.

Now *there* was a phenomenon worthy of scientific study. What was it about a woman standing in front of a car with the hood up that attracted every horny truck driver within a hundred miles? Plus two subtopics: Why did they, *one,* assume she was desperate for their help, and *two,* assume that upon receiving that help she would throw herself upon them and offer her body out of abject gratitude?

"Hey, honey! What's the problem?"

Laura gritted her teeth. "Shit. Here we go again." Three breakdowns, two propositions. Maybe she could cut this one off at the pass. "Oh, I've got it under control," she said in a firm but friendly tone. She stuck her head out from under the hood. "But thank you for stopping. You guys . . ."

"What a cute hat!"

"You're a woman!" Laura spluttered.

The truck driver looked down at the prominent bulges beneath her own shirt and gasped. "My God! How'd that happen?"

Laughing, Laura said, "Sorry. It was just such a

surprise. A pleasant one, I might add. You wouldn't believe how many times I've been hit on today."

"No? Try stepping out from behind the wheel of a rig like mine and into a crowded truck stop sometime. Believe me, you don't know the meaning of the word pressure." She pointed to Laura's engine. "But it looks like your car does. I take it this is a chronic problem?"

"Wolf Creek Pass took its toll, I'm afraid. Thermostat. I should have had it fixed, but I'm in a hurry."

"Out here, being in that much of a hurry can get you in a lot of trouble," the other woman advised, then took a pair of thick leather gloves out of the back pocket of her jeans, using them to remove Laura's radiator cap. "Fill 'er up."

Laura did so, then replaced the cap and closed the Toyota's hood. "Is it far to Teec Nos Pos?" she asked.

"About another thirty miles." The lady truck driver arched her eyebrows. "Strange place to be going in such a hurry with a wounded car."

"I'm meeting someone there, and he said I had to get there before dark today no matter what."

"Sounds like an asshole."

"As a matter of fact," she said, "he is. Or was. I haven't seen him in a very long time."

"In that case," the truck driver told her, "I'd do two things if you manage to make your appointment. Get your car fixed, and kick your friend where it'll hurt him the most if he doesn't offer to pay for it." She started back to her truck, shaking her head. "Good luck!"

"Same to you."

Thirty miles and one boil-over later, Laura arrived at her destination, just ahead of the sunset. She was hot, tired, frustrated, and feeling almost as degraded as on that fateful day last winter when she was made to look like Chicken Little in front of the television viewing public. The studio audience had laughed her into the commercial break and booed when she'd abruptly left the stage.

There was a service station up ahead on her right as she came into town—closed, naturally—where she was supposed to meet Carl. He was there, waving, a big grin on his face. Laura had to fight the urge to run him over.

When he came up to her she practically bit his head off. "You shit! This better be worth the hell you've put me through today."

"Hey!" Carl objected mildly. "That's not any way to greet an old friend. Especially one who's going to do you such a big favor."

"Keep talking." Her radiator was starting to steam again. Laura knew exactly how it felt. She got out of the car, slamming the door behind her. "And it had better be more than the line of crap you've given me so far."

"Sorry. Really. I didn't want to talk about it over a public phone. It's kind of a touchy subject around here; you can never tell who you might offend." He put a finger to his lips. Then he asked, "What put you in such a nasty mood anyway? Didn't you enjoy the scenic drive?"

She laughed bitterly. "Scenic drive? Ha! After I got out of the mountains all I saw was yucca, dust, and lizards. And the side of the road. My car boiled over four times on the way down here."

"Really? Gosh, that's a shame, Laura." Carl put his arm around her shoulder for sympathy. He also let the tips of his fingers dangle on her left breast. "Tell you what. We'll leave your car here with a note on the windshield. The station owner's a friend of mine. He'll have it all fixed for you when we get back tomorrow."

"Tomorrow?" Laura asked, frowning.

He gave her a hug and added quickly, "Meanwhile I'll take you out to the excavation site. We can eat, maybe have a drink, and relax while we talk over old times. There is beauty to be found out here if you know where to look."

Carl was leading her toward a beat-up truck that looked as if it was on its last legs. Laura stopped walking and shrugged off his arm, glaring at him.

"You haven't changed a bit. Same oily bastard you were in college," she said with utter disgust. "Get this through your thick skull, Carl. I don't like you. The only reason I came down here is that I'm desperate, and you know it. If you've got something for me, hand it over. Fast. Otherwise they'll be making an excavation to put you in! Understand?"

"Temper, temper! Don't get bent out of shape, Laura dear. It's not my fault that you got your cute butt kicked in the press. I'm the one who's going to aid you on your return to grace, remember?"

"For which you imagined I'd repay you physically, no doubt. Well, you can forget it. I'm not *that* desperate."

Carl held his hands up in a placating gesture.

"You've got me all wrong, Laura. I'm just happy to see you, is all. Here it is coming on nightfall, you've had a rough day, and your car's on the fritz. And what do I get for offering you the hospitality of my camp? Accusations!"

Laura didn't believe for an instant that his wounded tone was genuine. Good old Carl had something up his sleeve. But she'd known that the moment she picked up the phone and heard his smooth, wheedling voice. She would be forced to accept his so-called hospitality for the same reason she'd just driven hundreds of grueling miles; if there was a chance in hell he had the sort of research topic she needed, she had to check it out.

"Can the crap, Carl," she told him. "I'm not an imbecile. You're not doing any of this out of the kindness of your heart. Mainly because you don't have one."

"That hurts, Laura. It really does."

She sighed. "Right. Come on. What's the price tag?"

"Well . . ." He had to squint to see her face, as the sun was just over her shoulder now. "I'll admit that I'd hoped to be included in the project. You're not the only one with reputation problems, you know."

Carl's problems had to do with rumors that he was selling some of the artifacts he'd found rather than turning them over to the university funding his dig. Yet another reason Laura should have her head examined for even talking to him.

But she was encouraged by his admission. It meant he really might have blundered onto something after all. "You said this concerns Indian ruins and the work going on around here. Physical anthropology isn't my thing. You know I've been concentrating my efforts on modern man; I haven't cracked a book on Native Americans or been in this area since my senior year. So if you've got a viable topic I'll probably need your assistance in any case, for which you'll get due recognition."

"That's all I want."

He was apparently relieved by her understanding. But again, one could never tell with Carl Flemming. Even his body language was tricky.

"And I really am glad to see you," Carl continued. "I thought as long as you were here we could kick back and visit before we got down to work. What's wrong with some innocent conversation with a colleague? It gets pretty damned boring out here, Laura." He started to put his arm around her shoulder again. "Lonely too."

She backed away and pointed a finger at him. "I told you to cut that out! You want to be included? Fine. If it works out, that is. Right now *I* want a hot bath, some food, and one hell of an explanation."

"Sure." He grinned and held the battered truck door open for her. "But you'll have to settle for a shower. We've managed to make the site pretty comfy considering the conditions, but I'm afraid a bathtub is too much of a luxury for an archaeological dig."

"That'll be just fine." She got into the truck. It was filthy. Then again, she didn't exactly smell like a rose herself. "Oh, wait! The note."

Carl reached past her and got some paper out of the glove compartment. "I'll take care of it."

"It's the thermostat." She handed him the keys to

her car. "And get my duffel bag out of the trunk, will you?"

He grinned. "Right. Don't you worry about a thing, Laura. You're in my territory now. All you have to do is sit back and enjoy the ride."

2

The Four Corners region—the only point in the nation with four state corners in common—attracted hordes of fascinated tourists and dedicated scientists alike. Whether sightseeing or conducting research, both flocked to the great number of Indian ruins, geological formations, and fossil beds to be found on the sprawling Colorado Plateau. It was an area rich in history, steeped in tantalizing mystery.

This particular segment of it was also dry and windswept, two factors that—when combined with a hot, dusty ride in a dilapidated truck—had caused a large amount of topsoil to be deposited on Laura Newton's skin. She felt like a walking dirt pile by the time she arrived at Carl's camp.

The shower he had promised was an ingenious device, fed by a tank that used the sun's rays to heat water. Laura could have lingered beneath its warm, gentle spray for hours. Unfortunately, though there had been plenty of sun that day, water had to be trucked to this remote excavation site and was therefore under strict rationing. She was lucky to get all the soap out of her eyes before her allotment ran out.

Still, she was clean. Which was more than could be said of the rudimentary bathroom facilities Carl shared with his two student assistants. Laura stepped out of the tin shower enclosure and wrinkled her nose at the mess. Used towels littered the wooden floor along with dirty, unidentifiable pieces of clothing. There was dried shaving cream on the small mirror over the plastic washtub-like sink, where whisker remnants floated in an inch of gray water above a layer of sandy mud clogging the drain.

Trying not to touch anything, Laura combed her unruly mop of curly brown hair, did the best job she could with her makeup in the dim light of a single overhead bulb, then pulled on a clean pair of jeans and a University of Southern Colorado sweatshirt. It was a relief to get out of the place. The air outside was dry, fresh, and a bit chilly now that full dark had descended.

Carl was waiting for her. He was wearing baggy white pants, a white muslin shirt, and a sly grin that made Laura wonder if there was a peephole in the shower. On his feet were black leather boots and around his waist a ludicrous red silk sash. His teeth flashed in the light of the half-moon overhead.

Combined with the four army surplus tents that served as research facilities and sleeping quarters for the excavation site, his attire made her feel as if she'd stepped into the middle of a bad remake of a Rudolph Valentino movie.

The idea made Laura distinctly uncomfortable.

"Hungry?" Carl asked.

"That depends," Laura replied, thinking of the awful state the bathroom had been in, "on who does the cooking."

"We take turns. Tonight it's *FYO*. Find Your Own. The students went to town for their weekly pizza fix. I whipped us up a little something we can nosh on in my tent while we chat."

Town was more than twenty-five miles away via a series of tortuous dirt roads and barely discernible paths that had left Laura completely disoriented. If the students went for pizza, they also went for beer, and probably wouldn't wander back till very late—if at all.

She was alone with Carl. In the middle of nowhere. And he had just invited her into his tent for a nosh and a chat. Laura was liking this situation less all the time.

"Pizza sounds good," she said. "Why don't we join them?"

"We have important things to discuss, Laura. And like I said, the project I've come up with for us is a touchy subject around here. It's best we're alone." His grin broadened. "Besides, they took the only vehicle that's running at the moment. I'm afraid we're stuck."

"Shit. Carl . . ."

"Come along, Laura dear. Our steaks are getting cold."

He turned and led the way to his tent. Laura followed, motivated by the thought of bright light, food—and a sharp steak knife to fend off what was starting to look like a carefully planned seduction.

That impression grew stronger when she saw the inside of his tent. It was small, what Laura would have called cozy under other circumstances, with only two main pieces of furniture: a table, covered with a white tablecloth—upon which Carl had set out a candlelight dinner complete with fluted champagne glasses, and a bed. Not the sort of folding cot she had expected—but a real bed, covers turned back and pillows fluffed, ready for use.

The lights weren't bright, but soft and romantic. And the steaks he'd mentioned were done shish kebab style, cut into bite-size pieces. Nary a knife in sight.

Perhaps she could fork him to death. "Why do I get the feeling you do this sort of thing all the time?" Laura asked with heavy sarcasm.

Carl pulled a chair out for her, the picture of gentlemanly innocence. "No, potluck is the norm for us hard-working archaeologists," he told her. "But special visitors deserve special treatment."

"Uh-huh."

She took the seat he held for her, the back of her neck prickling until he moved around the table and sat down across from her. It was obvious what Carl was up to. Ply her with a meal and champagne, then move in for the kill. Nevertheless, the food did look good, sirloin done to a turn and accompanied by grilled peppers and onions, all atop a bed of fluffy white rice. And after the day she'd had, a glass or two of wine was too tempting to pass up. Laura dug in without further ado.

"More wine?" Carl asked.

"Please."

"You still have a healthy appetite, I see."

"And I see you still think you're going to get me in there tonight," Laura said, looking pointedly at his bed. "If we're going to be working together—and you have a lot of convincing to do on that point—we'd better get something straight, Carl. Just because I slept with you once doesn't mean I'm anxious to do so again. In point of fact I seem to recall it being the absolute pits."

Carl bristled, his dark eyes flashing. "Oh, really?"

"Yes, really. I was plastered. I barely knew what I was doing, much less possessed the strength to fight you off. You took advantage of me, and I've always hated you for it."

She could see she was pissing him off. It probably wasn't a wise thing to do, considering he had yet to tell her about this mysterious research project he wanted to embark upon with her. However, a full stomach and the start of a pleasant buzz had robbed her of both wisdom and the last ounce of her dwindling patience.

"But I'm relatively sober now," she continued, putting her wineglass down beside her empty plate with a thump, "and a hell of a lot tougher than I used to be. You'd be well advised to keep your distance. So why don't we stop fooling around and get down to business?"

Carl carefully folded his napkin and dabbed at the corners of his mouth. Then he looked her straight in the eye and said, "You've really turned into a bitch, Laura."

She chuckled, albeit without much humor. "You're damned right I have."

"I was just trying to show you that *I'd* changed. I know I have a lot to make up for before you'll trust me." He glanced at the bed, turned back to her, and then looked down at the floor. "I'm sorry. I guess I thought maybe I could show you I'm a different man as well. Tender. Gentle. All this was supposed to prove that I don't force myself on women anymore."

"Carl . . ." Laura trailed off with a sigh. He was genuinely hurt. "Damn."

It was unfair to judge him this many years later solely on his antics as a rash, randy college student. And after all, he hadn't raped her, just caught her at a moment when her defenses were down and her mind fuzzy from alcohol. True, honorable men did not behave the way he had, but how many twenty-year-old males could even be considered men, let alone honorable?

"I know I've been harping on you from the word go," she told him, "and I'm sorry. But you have to understand what's happened to me. I've been laughed at, sneered at, badgered, and verbally abused. My name has been dragged through the mud and my reputation as a scientist held up for public ridicule." Laura put her hand on his. "I'm not interested in being wined and dined, Carl. All I'm interested in is regaining my credibility. Okay?"

Carl looked up at her and smiled. "Okay."

"What do you say? Think you can help me turn myself from a serious bitch into a serious scientist again?"

"Piece of cake," he replied, taking her hand. "Step this way. I have something I want to show you."

He took her outside, leading her along the mesa's edge to an escarpment that looked down over the ragged hills below his excavation site. In the wan moonlight, the vast, empty land stretched out like a sea that had formed in a pocket between mountain ranges, which were now only black shadows in the distance. Dark fingers meandered across this forbidding landscape, marking arroyos and deep, yawning canyons.

When her eyes had had time to adjust, Carl pointed to one of those distant canyons. "See that light?" he asked. "Scarcely more than a glow, really. Look hard."

It took her a moment, but then she saw what he meant. Or thought she did. "Sort of. What is it? Another dig?"

He laughed. "In a way. It's one of them. I mean, it could be an intrepid tourist, or even a Navajo—this is part of their reservation, after all—but I doubt it. I'm pretty sure it's one of them," Carl repeated.

"Them what?"

"A grave robber. Looting an Indian ruin. I've even heard them called 'amateur archaeologists' on occasion, but it's tongue-in-cheek. There's no scientific method to what they do, no record keeping or careful marking of what they find where. They just dig up as much as they can, as quick as they can without risking breakage, and get the hell out before someone catches them."

"That's what you called me about? Looters? I don't believe this!" Laura cried. "Carl, people have been digging stuff up around here and taking it home or selling it for ages! For that matter, someone at *your* university has accused *you* of being a looter, selling the stuff you find instead of studying it."

Carl shifted uncomfortably in the dim light. "Well, I had to do some research on it before I called you in, didn't I? Just to see how it was really done."

Her eyes went wide. "Oh, God! That's what this is all about, isn't it? You wanted me to cook up some flashy project to add credence to whatever lies you've been telling the people at the university. Shit!" She kicked a rock over the edge of the escarpment, wishing it was his head. "How could I have been so stupid? You didn't want to help me. You wanted to use me again!"

She was advancing toward him, fists clenched at her sides. Carl backed up. "Okay, so I got into a little financial bind and sold a few artifacts. It was no big deal compared with some of the real professional operators at work around here. But the university got suspicious and—"

"All that crap about changing, being a better man. Christ! You haven't gotten better. You've gotten worse!"

"Now, Laura . . ."

"Bastard!" Laura took a swing at him, barely missing his chin. "I don't have any time to spare on a wild-goose chase, dammit. You knew I was desperate. You knew!"

She swung at him again and he ducked, then moved in beneath her next wild punch and wrapped his arms around her waist. They both went down in the sand, Carl maneuvering himself atop her.

"Would you just listen for a minute?"

"Get off me!"

"Not until you calm down," Carl told her. He tried to pin her arms to her sides, couldn't, and settled for protecting his face with his hands. "It's *not* a wild-goose chase. I have changed, or at least I want to."

Laura was bucking like a wild animal, pummeling his arms and hitting him in the back with her knees at the same time. "Bullshit!" she cried. "Get off!"

"Ouch! You have gotten tougher!" At last he managed to grab her wrists. It didn't stop the abuse his back was taking, but now he could look at her face. She was livid with rage. "Listen, damn you! I made a mistake. Now I want to make amends. And I can, with your help. This is a chance for both of us to grab some glory, Laura."

She made one final try to get out from under him, then lay still, puffing and panting. But she wasn't giving up. All she was doing was gathering her strength for another attack. In the meantime maybe she could put him off guard.

"All right. I'm listening. But this better be good."

"It is." Carl wasn't fooled; in a moment she'd be fighting like a wildcat again. So he talked fast. "I know this has been going on for a long time. And why not? Looters are hard to catch and even harder to prosecute—unless you happen to have a university breathing down your neck like I do, that is. They're sending someone here tomorrow to give me the third degree. I'm under the gun too, Laura."

"So what am I supposed to do about it?"

"You were right. I need a cover story. There's too much competition for grant money to expect a second chance, no matter how sorry I tell them I am. They'll just replace me and probably set the law on my tail to boot."

"It's what you deserve," Laura said through clenched teeth. "I'm not going to lie for you, Carl. In the first place I'd love to see you get your name smeared. And in the second I'm too busy trying to find a way to repair my own reputation to fool around with this nonsense."

"That's what I've been trying to tell you. It isn't nonsense." He sighed and let go of her wrists. "See? A good-faith gesture."

"Fine. Now get off me before I black your eye."

"Not just yet. I want you to see it my way first, the way I've planned it all out. I really am sorry for what I did, Laura."

She uttered a short, derisive laugh. "Sure you are."

"I am," Carl insisted. "But it did give me an inside track on these guys. What they're doing, how they go about it, who their customers are. It's getting worse, you know."

"I repeat, what am I supposed to do about it?"

"Start thinking like a scientist again, for a start," he replied. "American Indian burial grounds are being pillaged for commercial gains, Laura. The history of this great and glorious nation is being destroyed and valuable information on primitive societies lost forever, all for the sake of a few unprincipled collectors who have created a thriving black market for these illegally obtained artifacts."

Laura let her head drop back into the soft sand beneath her. "Lord," she groaned. "You sound like one of those boring documentaries Professor Tompkins used to force us to watch."

"Maybe so. My theme papers always did read like shit." Carl leaned forward so his face hovered above hers. "But yours were brilliant. You could always take the oldest, most completely debated topics and find a fresh slant, a new angle."

It was true. She was never satisfied with the standard arguments. To Laura, the old ways weren't the best ways, they were just more accepted—sometimes to the detriment of the whole topic. Then again, thinking like that was what got her publicly roasted.

"What's *your* angle, Carl?"

He smiled down at her. "With my knowledge of the area and the way the looters operate, and your talent for sniffing out the best way to approach a project, we can't miss."

"Get to the point, you ass!" Laura yelled in exasperation.

"Tompkins always said to start with a question. Try these on for size, Laura dear. Would you like to vindicate yourself in the eyes of the academic community by bringing public attention to bear on these greedy criminals? Would you like to prove that black marketers are no match for an intrepid student of man?"

"I . . ." Laura blinked.

The man sitting astride her may have been a lousy lay and an even worse student, but no one could fault his sales ability. Somewhere in the inner workings of her mind, a set of gears that had been spinning uselessly for far too long suddenly meshed. He was onto something.

"It's been done. Or tried. The newspapers run a piece every now and then. Most people don't care, and those who do haven't had much luck convincing anyone else."

"Aha!" Carl exclaimed. "I see I've managed to pique your curiosity at last. A golden opportunity to restore your good name is within your grasp, Laura, and you can help a pal out of a jam in the bargain. I can cover up a grievous mistake for which I am truly repentant, while you can use that sharp, rebellious mind of yours to accomplish what the government and those laughing, sneering fuddy-duddies you call your peers haven't been able to. Sound good?"

It sounded good. Very good. Her toes were tingling, and Laura didn't think it was the result of Carl's weight cutting off the circulation in her legs.

"How?" she asked, though she wasn't really asking Carl. She was asking herself. "It can be done. It *needs* to be done. But how?"

"That's my girl."

They hadn't gotten along very well in school—especially not after that one night—but he knew her well enough to see she was hooked. Completely and truly hooked. That pleased him. So did the feel of her body beneath him. He had to admit he'd gotten pretty excited when they were struggling.

But now was not the time. She was hooked but not totally immersed in the idea. Later, when she had wrapped her tenacious mind around it and made it her own, he could press his advantage.

Carl got off her and stood up, offering her his

hand. Laura didn't appear to notice, seemingly in a daze. "Come on," he prompted. "Why don't you sleep on it? You must be bushed after the day you've had."

"Huh?" Laura looked up at him. "Oh. Right."

She took his hand and allowed herself to be led back to his tent. Only when she saw the bed did Laura emerge from her mental fog. "Wait a minute. I told you no, Carl."

"Relax. It's all yours," Carl assured her. "I'll bunk with one of the students."

Laura kept an eye on him while he lowered flaps over the tent's mesh windows, blew out the candles, and moved a gas lantern to a bedside table. He did glance longingly at the bed, but then he sighed and moved to the door.

"Get some rest."

She touched his arm. "Carl?"

"Yes?"

"Thanks. For the meal, the wine, and the use of your bed. Alone. As for the idea, I don't know . . ."

"You will. It's a good one." He smiled. "Pleasant dreams, Dr. Newton. I'll be nearby if you need anything."

When he was gone, Laura sat down on the edge of the bed, letting her mind wander as she pulled off her hiking boots and jeans. The sweatshirt would stay on against the chill of a high-plains night and the possibility that Carl had second thoughts.

She doubted she'd be sleeping much this night in any case. Her head was spinning. It *was* a good idea. Carl Flemming, screw-up and total bastard, had actually come up with an answer to her problems.

A *possible* answer, she told herself curtly. It would

take a lot of thought. As well as a lot of digging around in an area she'd only visited a few times on brief field trips, talking to people who could conceivably take her questions the wrong way—even violently. This wasn't going to be easy.

Nor would Carl's involvement make it any easier. He knew his way around, but his very presence could cast a dark shadow over the entire project. Perhaps afterward, when and if she accomplished what she'd set out to do, Laura could tell a little white lie and get him out of trouble.

But not until then. True, the whole thing was his idea, but what good would it do him if he ruined it? There was too much at stake to let him take part. For both of them.

Laura knew she couldn't stop the looting—and subsequent destruction—of the burial grounds. At least not entirely and certainly not without more public concern and legal support. But that was what had her so excited. She was damned sure she could do a better job of telling the story and attracting attention. Attracting attention was her strong suit.

This time, however, she would make sure it was the right sort of attention, with the best possible results. To be taken seriously again. It was the stuff pleasant dreams were made of, all right. For the first night in a very long time, she could have gone to sleep without dreading the following day.

Could have, that is, except for one thing. Tomorrow she would have to tell Carl his project had fantastic possibilities. And that she was going to take it and run, leaving him to twist in the wind until she could bring it to a successful conclusion.

3

Laura did manage to fall asleep. Only to awaken a short time later with a fuzzy mind and a half-naked man sitting beside her on the bed.

"What the hell?" she muttered.

"Sorry to wake you. I just couldn't sleep, thinking about this thing. Have you made a decision yet?"

Laura sat up. Either she'd inadvertently left the lantern burning or Carl had relit it, because she could see him clearly in its soft glow. There was a lot of him to see. He was clad only in a brief pair of boxer shorts, his masculinity a clearly defined bulge.

She cleared her throat. "Um, Carl—"

"I have to know," he interrupted. "Those bastards are going to fry me, Laura. I have to know if you're going to help me." Carl took a drink from a half-pint bottle of bourbon, then offered it to her. "Want a swig?"

Laura couldn't help noticing he'd put on a little

weight, most of it around his waist. But there was muscle as well, too much for her taste. As he held the bottle out to her, the veins in his arm stood out beneath his taut skin. Carl had taken up weightlifting.

"Uh, no, thanks." Laura waved the bottle away. "And maybe you'd better hold the celebration for a bit too. I've been thinking. It's a great idea. A really great idea."

He raised his fist in the air and shook it, shaking the bed as well. "All right!"

"But after careful consideration, I've come to another decision as well. A rather painful decision."

"Such a powerful mind." Carl grinned, his attention captured by the tempting mounds her breasts made beneath her sweatshirt. "In such a nice package."

He was practically sitting on top of her, close enough for her to feel the heat of his body through the bedcovers. For Laura, however, trying to wake up and find a way to break the news gently, his leer seemed nothing more than high spirits.

"Carl, I know I promised you recognition, and if this comes together you'll get it," she assured him earnestly. "I'll put in a good word for you at the university. But surely you realize you can't get involved? The rumors and accusations . . . Repentant or not, your name on this in the beginning could blow us out of the water before we start."

His smile didn't waver. "But the idea has promise?"

"Oh, yes." She nodded. "I'm very excited about it."

"And you're definitely going to pursue it?" he asked.

"Definitely. As I've been telling you, I'm desperate, and I feel certain this is just what I've been looking for."

Carl took another drink, then set the bottle on the bedside table. "I'm glad. I had a hunch you'd get so hot to trot you'd make a crusade out of this. I see I was right, and that's good, because now that you have I'm going to make sure you stick to it."

At first Laura wasn't sure she had heard him correctly. Then she decided he was only adding his own solid conviction to hers. When she saw the odd, flinty gleam in his eyes, however, she realized she'd made a mistake. A big one.

"I don't understand," Laura said, starting to get out of bed on the side opposite him. "I just told you—"

His hand shot out and he grabbed her roughly by the arm, stopping her. "Sure you do. Bright girl like you. I'll do anything to get the university off my back, Laura. *Anything.* And you're going to help me. From now on we're going to be inseparable." Carl pulled her against his chest and kissed the nape of her neck. "Who knows? You might even learn to like it."

"Damn you!"

She started to hit him. Carl grabbed her other arm, showing a great deal more strength than he had out on the sand earlier. "Careful! You'll also have to learn when your old chum Carl is playing and when he's serious. I'm serious now. Do you believe me?"

Laura nodded, her heart thumping in her chest. It had been a game. She may have gotten tougher, but

Carl had gotten stronger. He took her wrists in one hand and held them easily behind her back, while his other hand roved across the front of her sweatshirt.

"Carl, please!"

"You've developed into quite a woman!" he exclaimed. "These used to barely fill my hand, now they barely fit!"

Struggling, Laura could feel his manhood hard against her bare thigh. He'd gotten worse, all right. Before, he enjoyed forcing himself upon helpless women. Now he enjoyed it more if they fought back. She should have aimed more carefully and decked him when she'd had the chance.

Laura tried to stay calm and use her head. It wasn't easy with his rough touch upon her breasts. "This really isn't necessary Carl. I'll help you. I—"

"You're damned right you'll help me!" he bellowed. "Did you think I'd just let you steal my idea? You're going to whip up a project that'll dazzle them all. And while you're at it, I'll be making more contacts. You find ways to stop them, and I'll find ways to fill their shoes." His lips brushed her cheek as he whispered in her ear. "We're going to corner the primitive-artifact market, Laura dear."

That did it. Whatever debt she felt she owed him for letting her in on this took wing. As for any sympathy over his plight with the university, that turned into a desire for vengeance.

"You're right about one thing, Carl. Demons from hell couldn't stop me from looking into this now. Because if it's at all possible, I'm going to make sure you get your comeuppance, right along with the rest of the grave robbers."

"I'm giving the orders here, bitch!" He moved his hand from her breasts, down her stomach to her thighs, pushing the bedcovers aside. "You always did have such lovely legs. Good, strong thighs. It's nice to see you've kept the muscle tone, though, otherwise you might have gotten hippy. And that ass! Every man's dream!" His fingertips touched the lacy edge of her panties. "Now, let's see what other changes have taken place since last time."

"Let me go, Carl. I mean it."

He laughed. "Don't you get it? I've been playing you for a sucker all along. Working on your sympathy, luring you in. Even got you to apologize for thinking bad things about me. I knew I could get you to listen to me, enough to light up that brain of yours and find out if I had a winner with this idea. But don't kid yourself, Laura. I just pretended to lose that fight earlier."

"No, Carl," she told him. "You just didn't give me enough of a reason to win. Now you have."

She jabbed him sharply in the rib cage with her elbow. Carl cried out in pain and let her go. She skittered out of bed, but he jumped up and caught her, wrapping his arms around her from behind so she couldn't use her elbows again.

So Laura resorted to other weapons. His first yell was just a peep compared with the one he let out when she brought the heel of her foot down on his instep. Then she raised that same heel, fast and hard, straight up into his crotch.

Suddenly Carl didn't feel like yelling anymore. He

sank to his knees, whimpering and gasping for breath. According to the karate instructor she'd dated for a while, some men recovered from such a blow quickly, others took several minutes. Laura didn't plan on waiting around to see how tough Carl was. She grabbed her jeans and boots and headed for the door, plucking up her duffel bag as she went. But she couldn't resist a quick glance over her shoulder.

Carl was getting unsteadily to his feet. "I think I'm going to be sick," he said in a strained voice.

"The pain goes away. Or so I'm told. But I warned you to keep your distance, didn't I?"

He nodded, his eyes squeezed shut. "Yeah."

"I still am. Don't try to follow me."

"Follow you? Where? There's nothing around her for miles, Laura."

"I'll find something."

"Don't bother." Carl groaned. "I've learned my lesson. Shit! My balls are busted! And I think you broke my foot too."

"Poor baby," Laura said without the slightest trace of sympathy. "What did you expect for attempted rape?" She reached for the door handle.

"So you're going, huh? Just like that. What about me?"

"Don't give me that pitiful routine! I'm not buying it anymore. The only thing I owe you is a piece of advice. Stay here and wait for the university investigation, Carl, and take your punishment like the man you say you want to be. Or run and hide. But don't you dare try to get in my way again."

"I won't have to," Carl told her. He started to take a step toward her, but it brought on a fresh wave of pain, so he leaned against the table and glared at her. "I'll be right here, waiting for you to come to your senses. There's nowhere for you to go. And even if there was, you can't do this without me, Laura, and you know it."

Laura smiled. "I wouldn't bet on that if I were you."

With that she turned and made good her escape before he could regain any more of his mobility. Stopping at the edge of camp to put on her jeans and boots, however, she realized Carl was right about one thing. She didn't know where to escape *to*.

Which direction was town? She wasn't sure. As a matter of fact, after the confusing ride here, she wasn't even sure which of the four states she was in. Colorado? Utah? New Mexico? Arizona? On the way down she'd passed the monument where their corners met, but she didn't have any idea which direction that was now, either.

Think! The sun was at her back when they left town. That meant she had traveled east. But only for a few miles. Then Carl had turned off the main road onto another. A right turn, she thought. She'd been too mad to notice. That would be south. Maybe. From there, however, it was turn after turn, rutted trails, and what felt to her travel-weary buns like nothing more than animal paths.

Laura looked at the sky. The sun wouldn't be up for hours yet. The moon was still out, and plenty of stars, but in the first place her knowledge of orienteering was not that sharp and in the second it didn't matter anyway. Even after she determined which direction she was headed, she still wouldn't know if it was the *right* direction. There were other towns of course, and Navajo villages too, but wandering around on these desolate plains, hoping to run across one of them, could take her farther into the badlands. And into deep shit. She was on foot, with no food and no water.

Water. To hell with food, she had to have water.

Without realizing it, she had already run some two hundred yards away from the dig. Carl didn't come after her, perhaps because he was still hurting, but she thought it more likely he was just so damned arrogant he expected her to come crawling back and beg for forgiveness. Could she go back, get a canteen, and take off again without alerting him to her presence? She had no choice but to try.

Just as she was turning that way, however, she heard it. The sound of an engine in the distance. The students were back! Her heart soared.

Then fell again. How did she know they weren't in cahoots with Carl? Evidently there was money to be made in Native American artifacts, and a college student was no more immune to temptation than anyone else. Besides, they had left him alone, knowing he was under suspicion for theft. Either they had no loyalty to their school or they were screwing it too. Laura didn't want to risk finding out.

The engine noise grew louder, coming from somewhere off to her right. She ducked behind a rock and let them pass, then got up and started running again, taking advantage of the shield of dust they raised, to put some more distance between her and the camp. At least she now knew which of the many rutted paths to take out of there. With any luck, she could follow the fresh tracks of the truck back to town.

Forty minutes later the camp was out of sight, far behind her. As far as she could tell there was no pursuit. That, however, was the least of her problems.

Country like this got broiling hot during the day, but at night it rapidly gave all that heat back to the open sky. For a while the effort of hiking across the rough, rock-strewn ground kept her warm, but once her energy started to flag she had to slow down lest she turn an ankle. Her own perspiration became a chilling enemy. Laura was cold and tired, and simply because she didn't have any water, her mind had convinced her she was already dying of thirst. But at least she could still see fresh tracks.

Then the wind started to blow.

4

She was asleep when he found her, curled up amid a small outcropping of rocks, using a navy-blue duffel bag for a pillow and a thin windbreaker for a blanket. The sun was just peeking over the horizon. It had been a nippy night for late June. But there she was, sleeping like a baby.

Douglas Cantrell had roamed over a fair part of the planet earth in his forty years. He had rubbed noses with Maori in New Zealand and elbows with Hindu fakirs in India. He'd spent months on end in the snake- and bandit-infested jungles of South America and a near fatal summer in the Sahara. Experience had taught him never to assume he'd seen everything, but he had certainly seen quite a bit.

This, however, was one of the strangest damned things he had ever come across. A woman, with no camping equipment whatsoever, in one of the loneliest, most desolate parts of northwest New Mexico, snoozing peacefully on a pile of rocks.

Good-looking too. Very. Out of sheer professional habit he proceeded to mentally catalog her every attribute, enjoying himself immensely.

Mid to late thirties. Roundish face with high, fairly prominent cheekbones and an even, honey-colored complexion. Lush brown lashes. Her hair, also dark brown, framed her face in soft curls. Being a man given to making such distinctions, he would say the overall effect was vaguely Hawaiian, though he'd seen plenty of good old mainland-America melting-pot girls with the same basic bone structure and coloring. He imagined her eyes would be brown too.

Nice hips—a personal preference of his—curved into what looked to be strong thighs beneath her faded denim jeans. Good calves. And some common sense at last, sturdy hiking boots on her feet, about a size six. It was hard to tell, all curled up and turned half on her side as she was, but he judged she'd probably stand about five five or five six. The rest of her was hidden by the windbreaker draped over her upper body, but there was a promising swell beneath it that suggested a womanly fullness there as well.

All in all, a very pretty female, the sort one did not expect to see unaccompanied much of anywhere, and certainly not out here amid all this nothingness.

She was a puzzle. Douglas "Dusty" Cantrell loved puzzles, had in fact spent most of his adult life chasing after one kind of mystery or another. He was also particularly fond of women. Having almost literally stumbled over both at the same time, Dusty had no choice but quietly to take the small day-pack off his back, have a seat on a nearby rock, and wait for this one to wake up.

Which she did momentarily. Her eyes opened with a flutter of those curved lashes and then focused on him, wide open and confused. Dusty smiled, congratulating himself on his deductive powers. Big, brown, beautiful eyes.

He said, "Good morning."

She let out a scream that nearly knocked him off his seat.

"Whoa! That's a god-almighty powerful set of lungs you've got there, lady!"

Laura scrambled to her feet, looking around for some kind of weapon. Spotting a fist-sized rock, she picked it up and took aim. The man dove for cover.

Had she found her first looter? Or was he just a common bandit, vagabond—or worse? From the brief glimpse she'd had of him, he appeared washed, well-groomed, and dressed like a hiker, but what sort of man sat watching a stranger sleep? Then again, what sort of violent type said good morning and hid behind a yucca plant when threatened?

"What the hell are you doing?" she demanded.

Dusty raised his head up, but only a fraction. She was still holding a rock in her hand and seemed quite willing to bean him with it. "Getting ready to duck!" he yelled back. "What the hell are you doing?"

"Getting ready to split your head open if you don't answer my question. Why did you sneak up on me like that?"

"Sneak?" His head came up a bit farther. "Hell, lady, I damn near tripped over you. I was just walking along, minding my own business, when what should I find but a blue-ribbon idiot parked in my path."

"That doesn't explain why you were sitting there watching me sleep, like some kind of blue-ribbon pervert!" Laura hollered. "Why didn't you either move along or wake me up, like any normal, decent human being?"

"Damn." He rose up until she could see his shoulders. "You've got a point there. I was just so surprised, I guess, and figured that anybody who could conk out on top of a pile of rocks needed her sleep. Besides, I could see you were in some sort of trouble."

Slowly he emerged from the pitiful cover of the yucca. Laura hefted the rock. "Stay where you are."

Whatever he was, he wasn't making any sudden moves. And her first impression had been correct. His jeans, though faded like her own, were clean and without holes, as was the matching denim coat he wore over a blue chambray shirt. In fact, the only disreputable thing he had on was his extremely well-worn hiking boots.

He was a big man, six feet at least, with powerful-looking hands and thick, strong limbs. But his face had a kind appearance to it that diminished the menace of his size. Laugh lines marked the tanned skin at the corners of his eyes, and those eyes, a startling shade of green, were bright with good humor and intelligence. The longish hair capping his head, though in need of a trim, she noticed, had that just-washed fluffiness. It was brown like her own, but lighter; he obviously spent a lot of time in the sun.

He was, in other words, what some women would classify as dishy. A hunk. Old-fashioned or not, Laura preferred the term ruggedly handsome.

But she still didn't let go of her rock.

"Trouble? What makes you think I'm in trouble?" she asked. "Maybe I'm a hiker, just like you."

The man laughed. "No pack. No sleeping bag. Good boots, I'll give you that, just the brand I want to buy when I get a chance. But they don't mean squat without the rest. What on earth are you doing out here?"

"All you've got is a dinky backpack," Laura pointed out. "What are *you* doing out here?"

"It's all I need. I was just starting out on a day trek," he explained. "Whereas it looks to me like you've come quite a ways, and this is where you collapsed. Nobody in their right mind would spend a night out here without the proper equipment. Unless they had to, that is." He smiled at her, evidently pleased with himself. "No, you're in trouble, all right."

"I am not!" She was, and she knew it, but didn't think it wise to tell him just yet how badly she needed his help. This handsome stranger seemed genuinely concerned, but she didn't know him from Adam. Admitting she was in trouble might give him the idea he could do whatever he wanted with her. "I just got off track, is all, and had to make do."

"Off track?" He tilted his head back and laughed again. "That, lady, is a major understatement. You don't have the slightest idea where you are, do you?"

"Of course I do."

He was still chuckling. "In that case, do you mind telling me where you're headed?"

"Teec Nos Pos," Laura replied, pointing north. "Not that it's any of your business."

"Teec Nos Pos? What state do you think you're in?"

He had her there. "Arizona?" Laura asked.

"That way." He pointed west. "Care to try again?"

"New Mexico!"

"Nice to see you at least know your geography."

Smiling, he bent to his pack and took out a map. But when he stepped toward her, she backed away, brandishing her rock. "Thanks for your help, but I can take it from here."

"Lady, I've never been the sort to force my company on anyone, but other than me, a few Navajo, and some sheep, you're not likely to run into anything else around here for quite a few miles. Do you like to hitchhike?"

"Uh . . ."

"Good. Then keep heading north. That way you can't miss Route 504, where you can thumb a ride. Maybe you'll get lucky and whoever picks you up won't be a serial killer. If you make it that far in the first place," he added. "Rough country. Lots of snakes. Dry too. How much water do you have?"

Laura's face was turning red. "All right, dammit!" she yelled, throwing her rock toward the sunrise. "You've got me! I'm in trouble! Satisfied?"

The man sighed and bent to his pack again. For a horrible moment, Laura feared he was about to take out a knife or a gun. She opened her mouth to scream.

He tossed her a canteen. "Drink some. Just a little to start. From the looks of you, I'd say you're probably dehydrated."

She looked at herself. Her clothes were covered with dust and she felt gritty. With all the wind last night, her hair was probably a mess too. And she had been worried about *his* appearance? No wonder he could tell she was lying.

"I had a rough night," she said, then tilted the canteen to her lips. Saved! The water tasted so sweet, trickling down her parched throat, that it brought tears to her eyes. But she was definitely not crying. No way.

"Want to tell me about it?"

Laura swallowed and glared at him defiantly. "No."

"Still don't trust me, huh?"

"Why should I?"

"Mainly because you have no choice," he replied. "But let's see if I can't find a way to convince you I'm really an okay guy." He looked at the sweatshirt she wore with University of Southern Colorado printed on it. "Student?"

"Once upon a time."

"And now?"

She decided to let him know he wasn't dealing with some airhead. "Teacher. I have a Ph.D. in anthropology."

"No shit?" He burst into laughter. "All this dancing around. We're colleagues, lady!"

"Excuse me?"

"Douglas Cantrell. My doctorate's in archaeology," he said, extending his hand. "But my friends call me

Dusty. Because I'm usually up to my earlobes in dust. Get it?"

"*You* have a Ph.D.?"

He frowned. "I don't think I care for your tone."

"It's just that . . . You don't look . . . Why didn't you just tell me who you were instead of scaring me half to death?" Laura spluttered.

"It's a bit hard to introduce yourself with some crazy woman aiming a rock at your head," Dusty said sarcastically. "Not that I see your reasoning. Your degree didn't stop you from behaving like a homicidal maniac. Why should mine prevent me from being a rapist?" He looked her over again. "And I wouldn't go pointing fingers on the basis of appearance if I were you, either."

"Be that as it may," Laura returned, patting some of the dust off herself, "it still might have saved us both an adrenaline rush. And why didn't you wake me?"

Probably wouldn't put her at ease any to tell her he'd been studying her ass. "Right. As if poking you with a stick would have put you in a better mood."

Laura closed her eyes and blew out a deep breath. Then she opened them, holding out her hand. "Okay. Let's start over. Pleased to meet you, Dr. Douglas Cantrell."

"Likewise. But call me Dusty."

"If you insist." They shook hands. "My name's Laura. Laura Newton. Thanks for the water, Dusty. And the orientation lecture. Now, if you would be so kind as to help me get to the nearest . . . What's wrong?"

Dusty was frowning. "Newton. I know that name."

Now she'd done it. Why had she told him her name? Out of reflex, she supposed, or maybe stubborn pride. Then there was the fact she'd only had about four hours sleep in the last twenty-four. It was too late now in any case.

"Well, of course you do." Laura released his hand and gathered up her things, fighting a familiar, sick feeling in the pit of her stomach. "It's a cookie. And then there's Sir Isaac. No relation that I'm aware of. Now can we—"

"No," he interrupted, "it's not figs or gravity. I'm sure I've heard that name. *Your* name. Dr. Laura Newton." Dusty pondered in silence for a moment, then shrugged his broad shoulders. "You'll have to excuse me. I spend a great deal of my time cut off from civilization. Hard to keep up with the present when your nose is buried in the past."

Laura held back a sigh of relief. At last, her luck had turned. Not only had she been found, but found by an apparently decent man who didn't know who she was. Not yet anyway. She could tell he was working on it and would probably connect her with "Newton's Folly" eventually.

If her luck held out it would take him a while, at least until he helped her get to a phone or a place with some sort of transportation other than her feet. After walking most of the night, she was not looking forward to putting in however many more miles that might take, but it would be enough of an ordeal without a sarcastic comment accompanying every step.

"I wouldn't worry about it," Laura told him. "I've published, naturally, but nothing of any consequence. I'm sure the things you've done are much more interesting than anything you might have read of mine."

"Gosh! Do you really think so?"

"Sure. Why, I'll bet—" He was laughing at her again. Maybe they weren't going to get along that well after all. "What's so funny?" she asked.

"Now I'm really going to rack my brain to figure out who you are. You've got to be hiding something, otherwise you wouldn't resort to such a female chauvinist trick."

"I beg your pardon!"

"I know some men won't shut up once they start talking about themselves. I am not among them, and I resent your assuming that I am."

Laura looked away. "It wasn't an assumption. It was a conclusion based upon empirical data. To my knowledge you silly saps come in only one flavor. Pompous."

"Ouch! You're pretty sharp, Laura Newton. In more ways than one."

"Can we stop fencing and get to a phone or something?" she asked, turning back to face him. "I have work to do."

"Oh, really? And pray tell, Laura Newton, precisely what kind of work is it that gets you stranded in the badlands, forcing you to take help from strange, pompous men?"

"None of your business. And stop using my full name like that! It's irritating as hell."

"Is that a fact?" He yanked the canteen out of her hands. "Laura Newton."

She clenched her fists and placed them on her hips. "Honestly. You men can be so childish."

"And you women can be so cheeky," he complained, ruefully shaking his canteen. "Drink half my water and repay me with insults. That's not nice, Laura Newton."

"Would you stop that!"

"Only if you'll tell me who you are. Repeating things helps me remember why I filed them away in the old memory bank," he said, pointing to his head. "Baked through and through, you see. Months at a time, jungles and deserts, sorting the detritus of ancient civilizations. Alone as often as not. I talk to myself, Laura Newton. And I answer myself too. You'll just have to get used to it." Dusty gave her a winning smile. "Unless you tell me."

Great. Her savior was a fruitcake. "No."

"Why not?"

"Because I don't want to!"

"Fine," Dusty said. He picked up his pack, shouldered it, and started walking west. "Come with me, Laura Newton. I wouldn't want to keep you from your secret mission."

She stood her ground. "Where?"

"If you can have secrets, then so can I. Hurry up."

Muttering under her breath, Laura followed him, though she wasn't at all sure she wanted to go anywhere with a loon like this one. Unfortunately he was right. She didn't have any choice. Dusty had water, some sort of base camp, and an apparently thorough knowledge of the area.

As she was tramping along behind him, an urgent message flashed across her mind, a thought both hopeful and disheartening at the same time. He was an archaeologist, evidently doing research of his own in the region, and would no doubt have knowledge of the digs—legal and illegal—that were going on around there. Then there was his expertise to consider. Laura needed the input of someone better versed in primitive man than herself; Dusty might very well fit the bill.

She could use him. But could she stand him?

"Laura Newton."

"What?" she asked irritably.

"Nothing. Just talking to myself."

Lucky for him she had fallen several steps behind while deep in thought. Otherwise she would have hit him with her duffel bag. She hurried to catch up.

The steadily rising sun was warm upon her back, taking the chill out of her bones and some of the ache out of her muscles. Jagged rocks did not make a good bed. But again, Laura hadn't had a choice. She had indeed collapsed there, too exhausted to go on. Now, though still tired and stiff, the movement of her arms and legs seemed to get easier with each passing minute.

Not bad recuperative powers for a thirty-four-year-old more accustomed to giving lectures than making long-distance treks. The daily stretching and thrice-weekly workouts must be paying off. However, the calories of last night's dinner were nothing more than a memory. She was ravenous.

And thirsty. "May I have some more water, please?"

"Sure," Dusty replied, handing her the canteen.

"Is it much farther?" Laura asked.

"To where?"

She gritted her teeth. "Your camp."

"Camp?" He glanced at her. "You mean, like a tent with a little ring of stones for a fire in front, sleeping bags, dried food, and a hole behind a tree for a bathroom?"

"Something like that."

He shook his head. "Don't have one."

"But you said . . ."

"I said I was on a day hike."

"I assumed that meant you had a camp and a four-wheel drive or something. You know, all the equipment and stuff you so snidely pointed out I didn't have," Laura said.

"Oh. I see. Natural assumption, I suppose. I only meant that *you* shouldn't be wandering around without stuff like that," Dusty explained. "I certainly didn't mean to imply that *I* would resort to anything so primitive. I've put in too much time sleeping on the ground and watching bugs crawl across my toes to put up with such nonsense unless it's absolutely necessary."

Laura was on the verge of screaming at him. "If you tell me there's a motel over that rise ahead of us," she said quietly, "I'll kill you."

"No reason to get violent again, Laura Newton," he chastised. "There isn't a motel or any other permanent structure of any kind around here. Oh, a few Navajo hogans. And some camps, as you call them, where our hard-working peers are busy rooting around in the ruins. I figure that's about the only place you could have come from, in fact. One of those digs. Am I right?"

"You're baiting me, Dusty."

He smiled, green eyes sparkling. "As a matter of fact I am, Laura Newton."

"Damn it! What's over that hill?" she demanded.

"You'll see." Dusty continued walking. Laura stopped and bent to inspect the ground at her feet. "What are you looking for?" he asked.

"A nice big rock."

"Okay! Over the hill there's a road," Dusty said quickly. She straightened, her eyes narrow slits. "Not much of a road! Honest! Little more than a seldom-used trail, really. But fairly flat and passable. And parked beside that little bit of an almost nonexistent road is my RV."

"Your RV."

"Recreational vehicle. Beds. Bathroom. Fully stocked refrigerator. Citizens-band radio too. But I might not be able to remember where I put my keys if you hit me with that boulder you're holding."

Laura dropped the rock, her mouth agape. "You travel around in an RV? What the hell kind of archaeologist are you?"

"A smart one," Dusty replied, "with a share in a gold mine some friends and I stumbled on."

"Stumbled on." She walked past him and stood on the crest of the hill, looking down. It wasn't much of a road. But the RV was something else again, a sturdy, bus-shaped behemoth gleaming in the morning sunlight. "How does one just stumble on a mine?" she wondered aloud.

"Easy," he replied. "I stumbled on you, didn't I? And while you may not be a mine of information, you're certainly a treasure, Laura Newton."

She turned to study his face and caught him intently studying the rounded curves of her buttocks. Laura sighed. "If you're quite finished, I am in desperate need of that bathroom you mentioned."

"Hmm?" Dusty looked up. "Oh. Terribly sorry. You see, I'm working on a theory about female posteriors. I've found evidence to suggest that the size, firmness, and other characteristics may have some correlation to an individual's intelligence quotient. What's your highest score to date?"

Laura crossed her arms over her breasts and glared at him. "Of all the half-baked excuses for leering at women I've ever heard, that takes the cake."

"They scoffed at Einstein too," Dusty returned. "Based on my observations thus far, I'd say your top IQ score is in the one-forty range, but that's just a ballpark figure. Closer inspection is required for any real accuracy."

"Closer inspection!"

"In-depth research, so to speak." Dusty walked around her in a circle, peering at her derriere. "This may take some time. One must be thorough."

"Stop ogling me, damn you!" Laura spun on her heel and trudged down the hill, muttering under her breath. "Rear ends and intelligence indeed. Smart-ass."

Dusty followed right behind, continuing his research. "Funny, I was about to say the same thing about you," he remarked, admiring the swaying motion of her hips. "Yes, indeed. That's what I call a truly smart ass."

5

Dusty's home on wheels was everything he said it was, and then some. The refrigerator was not only stocked, it had an ice maker. To one side was a propane range and convection oven, while on the other sat that ubiquitous modern convenience, a microwave. All three were a matching shade of avocado.

Behind the complicated-looking driver's compartment was a sort of living room, with a plushly upholstered couch that unfolded into a bed against one wall and two large swiveling captain's chairs near the other. Just behind and to one side of that was a breakfast nook, which could also convert to sleeping quarters. Then came the kitchen, or galley, as Dusty called it, and past that was the bathroom.

For Laura, the tour ended right there, but a quick peek down the short hallway beyond gave her a glimpse of Dusty's nicely appointed bedroom. He had a lot of books in there, she noticed, some in wall units, some in piles on the floor.

The RV had draperies on its gently curved windows and a curtain separating the living room from the driver's compartment, all of which could be drawn for complete privacy. Thick carpet. Rich paneling. And everything was color-coordinated in airy, space-expanding tones, with green predominant, from a luscious pale mint to a restful deep forest. It was nicer than her own home, and this one, completely self-contained, could go almost anywhere Dusty's heart desired.

Laura hated him.

"Time's up," he called through the bathroom door. "I'm sure it feels good, but we're not connected to the city water supply, you know. Leave us some to drink, Laura Newton."

"Damn." What she wouldn't give for a shower without water constraints. "Where are the towels?"

"Compartment above your head. Would you like orange juice with your breakfast?"

"I hate to sound picky," she said, "but you wouldn't happen to have any tomato juice, would you?"

"Salted or unsalted?"

"I should have known," she muttered. "Salted's fine."

"And coffee or tea?"

"Tea, please."

"Wise choice. I prefer tea myself, mainly because my coffee sucks. Food in five minutes."

"I'll be out in three."

Laura decided she could get awfully used to this.

Dusty was, as he had promised, an okay guy—when he wasn't being totally bizarre. He was a bit of a wiseass and couldn't seem to keep his eyes off *her* ass, but he was smart, strong, and knew his way around this part of the country, attributes that could be invaluable to her in the personal crusade Carl had inadvertently started her on.

She still didn't know if Dusty possessed the knowledge she needed, although it seemed likely. And even if he knew his ruins by rote, that didn't mean he would have the time to assist her. Or would want to if he did. If she could convince him to take her to Teec Nos Pos for her car, they would have the opportunity to talk it over.

But for now, breakfast. As this was supposed to have been a quick trip just to check out Carl's story, Laura had packed light. Two pairs of jeans, one of which she had worn on the way down and would as soon not put on before a good washing; the other too filthy from her desert sojourn last night to even consider. Three T-shirts, two sweatshirts, a halter top, and one good blouse, but only those two pairs of pants. And a tight pair of khaki shorts.

In view of Dusty's predilection for posteriors, it was with no little hesitation that Laura emerged from the bathroom, wearing those shorts. She left the tail of her pale blue T-shirt out in an effort to minimize the display.

It didn't work. "That's more like it!" Dusty exclaimed as she passed by the kitchen. "Now I can continue my research without having to imagine my way through all that denim."

Laura ignored him, taking a seat in the breakfast

nook. Her tomato juice and a pot of hot tea were already on the table. She had downed the juice and was sipping at her tea by the time he joined her. He placed a plate of steaming hot whole-wheat pancakes between them and a jar of strawberry preserves.

"Dig in," Dusty invited. "Sorry there's no syrup. I forgot to buy some the last time I stocked up."

"At last, something this rolling mansion doesn't have." Laura spread some preserves on a pancake and tried a bite. He made a mean flapjack. "This is great, Dusty."

"Thanks."

He seemed embarrassed by her praise. Laura found it an endearing quality in a man who had so much going for him. With his good looks, material wealth, and intelligence, she would expect him to be stuck-up. But he wasn't. Every bit as eccentric as the media claimed he was, perhaps, but not pompous and over-bearing as she'd first concluded.

"I mean it," she continued. "This is really nice of you—beyond the call of duty, so to speak. I'm sorry I've been such a bitch."

He smiled. "That's all right. I assume you have your reasons. Setting off alone and unequipped in this part of the country is an act of either desperation or insanity. And since you apparently have most of your marbles, I figure you were escaping an alternative you deemed even worse."

"It was. I . . . I accepted an invitation from an old acquaintance who hadn't changed as much as I'd been led to believe. The situation became intolerable and so . . . Well, here I am," Laura said with a shrug. In time she might tell him the whole story. At the moment she had other things on her mind. "I'm very lucky you found me, Dusty. Sorry to take you away from your research this way."

"Actually," he told her, "I'm between projects at the moment. I'm trying to get permission to excavate a site about ten miles from where I found you, but it's not as easy as it used to be. Thanks to a few insensitive scientists and greedy artifact collectors, Native Americans have taken a pernicious dislike to people who disturb their ancestors."

"Even for the purpose of genuine academic research?"

"Some consider the whole lot of us nothing more than grave robbers; and in fact there are plenty of those around messing things up as well. As a result, most new digs these days are conducted only as a preliminary to construction," he told her, "so I've got a lot of tightrope walking to do before I can get a project sanctioned."

Laura nodded thoughtfully, but inside she was burning with excitement. Dusty had just answered two of her most important questions. He had the knowledge, and he was between projects. Things were looking up.

Dusty misinterpreted her reserved expression. He shook his head ruefully. "After all I said about not running off at the mouth, here I am boring you silly. For all I know, you're as well-versed on this as I am."

"No," she assured him. "I've, uh, pursued a different line of study from most of my colleagues. While you've had your nose buried in the past, I've been poking mine into the present and future."

"I see," Dusty said, nodding. "One of those modern anthropologists edging into sociology, right?"

"Yes. But as a matter of fact, I've recently developed an interest in this area and am toying with the idea of a project of my own down here. I'm afraid I'm not up to the task, background-wise." Laura paused to sip some tea. Then she grinned. "So, at the risk of being accused of stroking your ego *and* getting some free tutoring, do go on. I find it fascinating."

Dusty cocked his head to one side. "A project, you say?" he asked, curious. "Concerning what?"

"The grave robbers you mentioned," Laura replied.

"Looters?" His eyebrows shot up. "You want to conduct research on looters?"

"Precisely."

"Why?"

She hadn't expected the question. But it was a good one. Why indeed? "As an anthropologist, I'm glad to have the body of knowledge people such as yourself have accumulated. And I appreciate the need to excavate ancient graves for the purpose of furthering that knowledge."

"Personally," Dusty said, "I'm of the opinion all human remains should be reburied after they're studied. Not that Native Americans exactly like doing reburial ceremonies, but it's a necessary compromise, and one hell of a lot better than displaying these things in some museum for tourists to gawk at."

"Quite. I'm not sure I like the idea of *my* bones or even any personal possessions buried with me ending up on an examination table, mind you, much less on display. But I am sure of one thing: The thought of their being sold for a profit to adorn some collector's mantelpiece is totally appalling," Laura said vehemently. "So let's just say I've decided to wage war on anyone who seeks to make a commercial venture out of pillaging Native American graves."

"A noble cause," Dusty said. But he was frowning. "I detect, however, a note of personal vengeance in your voice."

"I am very excited about the project."

"Uh-huh." He was studying her face. "That invitation you mentioned. Was it by any chance from Carl Flemming?"

Hearing his name gave Laura a start. To have it come from Dusty's lips completely flustered her. "Well . . . I . . . ."

He held up his hand. "Don't bother. It all fits. I heard via the grapevine that he was suspected of dabbling in just such a for-profit venture. His dig, I believe, is southeast of here, and about as far away as you could have come on foot with no water. Besides, you said you were escaping an intolerable situation; I have met Mr. Flemming and found him to be a rather intolerable fellow myself."

"You know Carl?"

"Hardly. He was at a professional function I attended a year or two ago, spouting off and goosing the waitresses. The allegations of theft against him don't particularly surprise me. Are they true?" Dusty asked.

Laura shrugged. "Apparently. I didn't see business being done or anything. But he led me to believe he had sold some things and was interested in selling a lot more."

"You were researching him for your project?"

"No. I was . . ." She paused. If she told him she had been desperate for a topic, he would want to know why. Dusty would undoubtedly figure out who she was soon enough without handing it to him on a silver platter. "I've been between projects myself for a while," Laura continued. "I took a leave of absence to find one, but the right topic kept eluding me. Carl said he might have something, so I came to talk with him. What he wanted me to do was fake a project on looters to cover up his involvement with them."

Dusty was staring at her intently. "Instead, you have decided to conduct a real research project, with the intention of roasting Mr. Flemming on a spit. Is that right?"

"No!" Laura exclaimed. Then she sighed. "Well, I'll admit the thought crossed my mind. But the project has merit, and I'm committed to it whether Carl roasts or not. That was his intention, you see; he got me interested in it before he divulged his true intentions, knowing how persistent I am about things once I get involved."

"I have noticed a stubborn streak in you, Laura Newton." Dusty said with a grin. "And you're right about the project having merit. How are you going to go about it?"

"I haven't exactly had time to develop the thesis yet."

"No, I suppose not. Surely you have some idea as to the main thrust, though."

Perhaps it was time to draw upon some of his expertise and maybe draw him into the project as well. He already seemed more interested in it than she had expected.

"I am apparently in very knowledgeable company," Laura replied. "Any suggestions?"

Dusty leaned back on the breakfast-nook bench. "That would depend," he began, "on what you hope to accomplish, whether your goals are academically or socially motivated. Do you see yourself as a defender of Indian rights?"

"Not really."

"Good. That arena is pretty full at the moment. There are some fine people involved, and some not so fine. It's all too easy to get lost among the crackpots," Dusty informed her. "I take it, then, that you're more interested in the damage being done, the things we will never have a chance to study because some fool dug them up and carried them off."

"That's right," Laura said. He was already proving how valuable he could be to her, by giving her idea more focus. She would have to give serious thought to asking him if he'd like to go beyond tutoring and actually participate in the project. "As you said, some people consider the whole lot of us grave robbers. But there is a distinction. We're talking about primitive man, in most cases; the research is necessary. Putting artifacts on display is something I'll leave for others to debate. But selling them without regard to either moral or research considerations can't be tolerated."

"I happen to agree with you. I hope, however, that you realize you can't stop the looting; it's going on all over the country, and a lot of the time it *is* tolerated."

"I'd say you've just defined my goals, Dusty," she told him. "I intend to raise some hell."

He laughed. "Set a wolverine loose among the

weasels, huh? Good luck. You and I are concerned, as are most in our professions and even a handful of politicians. But even with all that concern and the laws already in place against looting ancient ruins, you'd have to defeat one of the most powerful forces in humankind to make any difference."

"What's that?" Laura asked.

"Public apathy," Dusty replied. "And as long as I'm playing professor, I should warn you it's been tried. The subject barely makes the travel section of the Sunday papers."

"I know. I also know I can do it better."

"You're pretty sure of yourself, Laura Newton."

"I have reason to be. I'm good at getting noticed."

Was she ever! But in a strange way, she was almost glad about it now. Her previous notoriety would give her an inside track to the media few of her peers could even come close to achieving. That was her edge.

It was, however, a very keen edge, and it could slice her to the bone if she wasn't prepared for it, as she had found out that day on national television.

Dusty seemed to know at least part of what she was thinking. "In order to get as much attention as you'll need, you'll have to really raise a ruckus. The public has an odd way of looking at scientists who do that. Rather the way the mob outside Frankenstein's castle looked at the good doctor. Standing out in the crowd can be hazardous to your reputation."

"I'm aware of that," Laura told him.

"If I were you, I'd just do some solid documenta-tion on the problem, then write a biting article for one of the professional journals. Settle for the notice and kudos of your peers, Laura," he advised.

"I can't!" she exclaimed irritably.

"Can't?" Dusty leaned forward, resting his elbows on the table. "Why not?"

Because she wanted more than praise. Because she had to prove herself not just to her peers, but to the media and to all the other people who had laughed at her as well. It had, she realized, become an obsession; and she doubted Dusty would understand, even if he did know what had happened to her.

But he didn't. And she didn't want to tell him. For the past few minutes he had been treating her like the serious scientist she needed to convince everyone she was. It felt so good to talk like this, one on one, as an equal rather than a disgrace. Laura couldn't bear the thought of losing that feeling.

"That's a very determined look you have in those beautiful brown eyes," Dusty said. "Are you trying to make a name for yourself or something?"

"Yes." In truth, all she wanted was to return to the calm academic life she'd chosen for herself. But in order to do that she would have to make a name for herself all right. A better name. "That's exactly what I'm trying to do and the reason I can't settle for the virtual anonymity of a two-page article in a professional journal."

Not that the media would let it go at that anyway. Dr. Laura Newton was on the hot list now. Anything she did would be held up for public scrutiny. That's why it had to be the right sort of project, and it had to be better than great.

"I'll be damned," Dusty muttered. "A crusader."

Laura lifted her chin to a defiant angle. "You don't approve?"

"Like most careful scientists, I reserve judgment until the final results are tallied. But based on what I've seen of you so far, it's quite possible you'll kick ass."

"You better believe it."

They'd finished the pancakes and an entire pot of tea during their discussion. Laura was full but still felt thirsty. Any moment now all the liquid would catch up with her; she'd probably have to pee all the way to Arizona. But since they were in an RV, thus eliminating the need for potty stops, she decided she could risk a bit more juice.

Without thinking, she stood and reached to the counter for the can, causing her T-shirt to ride up and giving Dusty an excellent view of her buttocks, tightly encased in thin khaki.

"Whoa!" he exclaimed appreciatively. "You're smarter than I thought! One-fifty?"

"Would you shut up about that silly theory?" she demanded, hoping he'd think she was turning red with rage rather than embarrassment. "The size of my tush has nothing to do with my intelligence."

"It's not just the size. It's the fullness, the tilt, the overall roundness of the curvature. I'll bet I'm getting close, aren't I?"

She turned away, blushing furiously now.

"Aha!" Dusty exclaimed. "I am!"

"Go fall in a hole."

"That's a terrible thing to say to an archaeologist."

"A deep hole. Filled with snakes. Now, if you don't mind, could we discuss what you're going to do with me?" Laura frowned. "I didn't mean that the way it sounded."

"I kind of like the way it sounded," Dusty said, his green eyes dancing with mischief. "And in the same spirit, I was thinking about showing you my bed."

"Excuse me?"

"Relax. I assume you still want to go to Teec Nos Pos?"

"Near there, yes. I left my car at a service station to be fixed. But—"

"I know the one. Phil's. It's not far, as the crow flies," Dusty said, "but I have to take it real easy with the RV until I get to the highway, and that's a fair distance. In the meantime, I think you should go on back to my room and get some sleep. You look beat."

"Oh." The power of suggestion. She yawned, suddenly realizing how very tired she was. Food and stimulating conversation had kept her going for a while, but now she was in desperate need of rest. "That does sound good."

"Then it's settled. You go sack out. I'll wake you when we get there. Okay?"

"Okay." She ambled down the hall toward his bedroom, self-consciously aware of his eyes upon her. "Does this door lock?" Laura asked him.

"It does," Dusty replied, smiling to himself. "But I'm not going to attack you while you sleep, Laura Newton."

"I didn't mean to imply—"

"I'll be too busy driving."

6

Laura expected a polite knock on a locked door. What she got was a poke in the ribs from a man standing right beside the bed. These rude awakenings would have to stop.

"Cut it out!" she complained, taking the pillow off her head so she could glare at him. "What the hell is wrong with you?"

Dusty glared right back. "You have some explaining to do, lady." He held a magazine in front of her bleary eyes. It was folded open to a page that had her picture on it. "Or should I just call you the Ultraviolet Wacko?"

"Shit," Laura muttered, covering her head again.

"I want some answers." Dusty yanked the pillow away from her and threw it on the floor. "Now."

She had fallen asleep on her stomach atop the covers, fully clothed, thank goodness, or he would have really gotten a good look at the subject of his bizarre research. Laura turned onto her side so she could see his face.

He was angry. "All right!" she said, knocking the magazine out of his hand. It fluttered to the floor beside the pillow, her photo staring up at her in mute accusation. "So you figured it out. Does that give you the right to barge in on a sleeping woman?"

"It does when it's my bedroom, and when that woman is a damned liar!" Dusty exclaimed heatedly.

"I didn't lie!" she objected. "I just didn't tell you."

"That's not what I'm talking about and you know it."

"You're not talking, you're yelling, and I haven't the slightest idea what's making you act like such a creep!"

Dusty thumped the bed with his fist. "Lucky for me I had all those miles of desert to drive through. It gave me time to concentrate on where I'd seen your name before. Otherwise, who knows how long I would have gone on thinking you were a reputable scientist."

"I *am* a reputable scientist, damn you!" Laura rolled off the bed and stood up, her nose practically touching his. "And look who's calling the kettle black! You're not exactly a straight arrow yourself, Dr. Douglas Cantrell. Asses and intelligence quotients. Ha!" She kicked the magazine across the room. "You're flakier than they say I am!"

"I don't give a damn what they say you are," Dusty informed her. "It's what you say you are that pisses me off. All that bullshit about waging war against looters and making a name for yourself. The only crusade you're on is one that'll get your name in the papers."

"That's not true!"

"Crap!"

Dusty turned and stalked out of the bedroom. Laura stayed right on his heels. "I do want to help put a stop to the looting, or at least get the public as angry about it as we are," she said. "I really believe in this project."

He stopped abruptly in the middle of the kitchen and faced her again. "Well, you can forget it, lady. This is *my* bailiwick. I'm not going to allow some underqualified, overzealous flake to go running around frothing at the mouth, trivializing a serious subject in her quest for fame and glory."

"Fame and glory? You stupid ass!" Laura cried. "Did you even bother to read that article? They broiled me! Do you seriously think I want that to happen again?"

"As a matter of fact, I do," he replied. "I think you like the attention. I think you prefer it to the anonymity most of us live with. I think you're a grandstanding, self-important neurotic who can't stand to be ignored, even if the only reaction you can manage to get out of people is laughter and scorn."

Laura was so mad her hands were shaking. "Is that so? Well, I think you're an asshole!" She backed away from him to avoid wrapping her fingers around his neck and strangling him. "Do you know what it's like to walk into a classroom and have your students laugh at you? Have you ever had the humiliation of hearing your fellow professors whispering behind your back, or worse, had them come right up to you and tell you what a disgrace you are to the profession? Is that the sort of attention you think I like?"

Dusty frowned. "I didn't know—"

"What? Didn't know? I thought you were a know-it-all! Let me round out your education, Dr. Cantrell, describe to you exactly what that fame and glory you say I'm after has already done for me. I had to take a sabbatical because I was no longer effective as a teacher. Who listens to a crackpot? Most of my friends turned their backs on me for fear the adverse publicity would rub off on them. And you think I planned it this way?"

"But you did pick a controversial subject."

"Which I was prepared to debate in classrooms and university auditoriums, not in front of television cameras." She closed her eyes, groaning at her naïveté. "Did I stop to wonder why they were interested in such a scholarly topic? No. I was actually flattered by the invitation."

It all came back to her in a rush. Days fretting over the right attire so she would look professional but not too snotty; the attack of nerves she had in the studio waiting room; her panic when she realized the charts and graphs she'd brought to illustrate her theory wouldn't show up well under the bright lights.

And then the sheer horror when she at last understood it didn't matter. "It took a minute for me to figure out what was going on," Laura continued. "Three minutes after that I was ruined. The host and 'panel of experts' hadn't even read my work. I was there for only one reason: comic relief. So people could point at me and say, 'There she is, folks! The Ultraviolet Wacko! Step right up and see the flake!' "

She opened her eyes and looked at him. "That was my moment on the grandstand, Dr. Cantrell. And you have the gall to suggest I enjoyed it?"

Dusty was clearly flustered by her outburst. But he was angered by it too. "Don't rant and rave at me! If you've had a hard time of it, I'm sorry. But whether you asked for the reputation you have or not, the fact remains that you do have it. This is a sensitive subject. An important subject. Given the sort of sensational attention you've attracted in the past, your involvement could further irritate those Indians who are antiexcavation and threaten my bid for a sanction to work in this area. And that, lady," Dusty told her, "is one thing I will not allow."

"I *know* it's an important subject," Laura returned sarcastically. "That's why I chose it. I need to restore my credibility and get people to take me seriously again."

"In my opinion, you'd be better off waiting for them to forget all about it before you try to rebuild."

"And do what in the meantime?" Laura asked. "Join an advertising firm and do demographic research for underarm deodorant? I'm a scientist, Dusty. I like studying mankind, and I'd like to think I can make a viable contribution to it."

"Then stick to what you know. Go back to your modernist philosophy, pick a more mainstream subject, and prove yourself that way." He leaned against the kitchen counter and eyed her suspiciously. "Because quite frankly, Laura, I doubt your ability to handle this one properly. You admitted you weren't up to the task as far as background is concerned."

"You didn't have that many doubts a few hours

ago," she pointed out. "And you seemed quite willing to help me fill in the gaps in my knowledge too."

"That was before I had reason to question your motivation."

"Damn you!" she cried. "Why am I standing here talking to you when you're not even listening? You still doubt my motives? I don't give a shit! And all this garbage about how you won't allow this and can't allow that—I don't need your permission to pursue an independent research project. This may be your bailiwick, but you don't own the damned place!"

Laura stomped back down the hall to the bathroom, grabbed her duffel bag, then turned around and headed for the door. Dusty was still in the kitchen. "Thanks for everything, Cantrell," she said. "It's been a load of laughs." She slammed the door behind her.

Dusty stood there for quite some time, letting his anger subside into confusion. Had he misjudged her? Maybe. But he didn't have any doubts about her determination. Laura was not going to stop what she was doing just because he told her to. Breathing a deep sigh, he pushed himself away from the counter and went after her.

Laura's car was right where she'd left it. Exactly. It hadn't been moved, let alone fixed. She read the note Carl had left on the windshield and discovered why.

"Phil. Don't know what's wrong with it, but no rush. Won't be back for it till sometime next week. C. Flemming."

"Damn!" She crumpled the note up and ground it

under her foot, pretending it was Carl's private parts. "Take that!"

A young man had emerged from the service station and was watching her curiously. "Help you?" he asked.

"Can you fix my car?"

"Don't rightly know. The note says—"

"I know what it says!" Laura said, trying not to shout. "It's the thermostat, and I don't need it next week, I need it now! Can you fix it?"

"Thermostat, you say?" He approached her—rather warily, she noticed—and took a closer look at the car. "Sure. Old model though. Have to go to Shiprock for parts."

"And how long will that take?"

"About an hour. Hour more to do the job. But Phil's on vacation, so I'm the only one here today. Come back tomorrow about noon, though, and I should have her ready to go."

Laura shook her head. "I can't wait that long." She unlocked the car and tossed her bag into the backseat. "Thanks anyway," she said, somehow managing a polite smile.

The mechanic smiled back. "Tell you what. If you were to get the part, I could fix her right up for you."

As tired and angry as she was, that almost made sense for a moment. Then she sighed and told him, "Tell me something. Providing I can make it to a place that has the part I need, with my car in this condition, and assuming there will also be another service station there, why on earth would I drive back here so you could install it?"

He shrugged and started to walk away. "Suit your-self."

"Just a minute." She pulled her water jug out of the car. "Is there somewhere I can fill this·up?"

"Out back," he replied, with a brusque jerk of his thumb.

Laura carried the plastic bottle around the side of the building and located a greasy garden hose attached to an equally grimy spigot. Her hands were filthy when she finished, so she went to ask the now thoroughly discourteous attendant for a key to the washroom, where she found only a tiny sliver of soap. So by the time she returned to her car, lugging the heavy five-gallon bottle, Laura's temper was as close to boiling over as her poor car would soon be.

It didn't help matters at all that Dusty was waiting for her. "What the hell are you doing here?"

He smiled wanly. "That's about the way our first conversation started, isn't it? No, on second thought, it started with you screaming at the top of your lungs."

"Which is exactly what I'm going to do right now unless you leave me alone," Laura promised. "Now get out of my way. And stop following me!"

Dusty took the jug from her and hoisted it into her car. "Can't do that, Laura Newton. We have to talk."

"I think we've said about as much to each other as we need to. In your opinion I'm crazy, incompetent, and out to make a big mess of things. In my opinion you're a dipshit with delusions of godhood. What more could we possibly have to discuss?"

"For a start," Dusty replied, cheerfully ignoring her hostile attitude, "we should really discuss our partnership. They can be delicate things at best, and I'd like to set the rules right off the bat. First—"

"Partnership!" Laura started laughing. "That's rich! I wouldn't form a partnership with you if you owned the only ice cream franchise in hell!"

She shouldered him aside and got into her car. Dusty held her keys in front of her face and jingled them. "You left them in the door, Laura Newton."

"If you don't stop using my name like a cattle prod, I'm going to do what I should have done the moment I woke up with you ogling my behind."

"And that is?"

"Kick you right in the—"

"Please! That wouldn't be a very auspicious beginning for our joint venture, now would it?"

"There isn't going to be any 'joint venture.' For one thing I don't need any help, and for another even if I did I wouldn't take it from you. So fuck off!"

Dusty arched his eyebrows. "My goodness! I'm glad I'm seeing this side of you now. That way it won't come as a nasty surprise to me later."

"Listen, Dusty," she said through clenched teeth, "I am not going to be your partner, and there isn't going to be any later. If I never see you again it'll be too soon. Got it?"

"I'm afraid my situation is much too sensitive and this project much too important for me to give you a choice, Laura. We're going to tackle it together whether you like it or not."

Laura looked skyward. "There you go with your little tin-god routine. Should I get down on my hands and knees while you issue your edict, master?"

"Nice position," he replied, "one of my favorites,

in fact, but totally inappropriate for the moment. Why don't we go back to the air-conditioned comfort of my mobile abode and talk like regular people?"

"No."

"Very well. We'll do it your way." Dusty came around the car and got into the passenger seat. "Now. You *are* going to be my partner, and we *are* going to conduct this project as a joint venture."

"Just because I'm in your territory, marshal?" she asked in an exaggerated western drawl. "What are you going to do if I tell you to stuff it? Call me out at high noon?"

"Nope. What I'll do, ma'am," he drawled in return, "is call the nearest television station with a network affiliation and tell them what you're up to." He smiled at the shock on her face. "They'll be all over you like a cheap suit, hounding your every step and bringing your past back to haunt you just when it had started to fade from public memory. And that, Laura, will put an effective end to your project before it even starts."

"You wouldn't."

"I would," he assured her. "But I don't want to."

Laura was staring at him incredulously. "You really do have baked squash for brains. Why should I take your threat seriously if you admit you don't want to carry it out? Give me one good reason not to call your bluff."

"Now who isn't listening? I said I want to form a partnership. That should prove to you how much I want this project to be done. But you'd better believe I'll bring it to a screeching halt if I think it's not going to be done right. Why don't you just admit you need my help so we can stop arguing and get on with it?"

"Because I don't need your help, that's why!"

"Come on, Laura. We both know your only hope for success is to stay out of the limelight until you put enough solid work together to prove you're serious. That's going to be hard enough even if I don't squeal," Dusty said. "By teaming up with me, you can save valuable time. Right?"

Laura pursed her lips and frowned, refusing to answer or look at him.

Dusty shook his head and sighed. "This is like pulling teeth. Am I right or not?"

"Stick it in your ear."

"I'm right and you know it. The logic is inescapable. So is the fact that even with all the preparation in the world, the very people you need to impress will still take everything you say with a shaker of salt," Dusty continued. "I'll come in handy on that score too. I may be a tad eccentric, but it's a private eccentricity. My participation in the project will lend you some much-needed credibility when the time comes to face the media wolves."

As he said, the logic was inescapable. That didn't mean she had to like it. "Fine," Laura said curtly. "You've convinced me I need a credible research assistant. That does not mean I'm convinced you're the one for the job."

"Not an assistant, Laura. A research *partner*. And just how many people with my credentials do you suppose would be willing to take the risk of associating with you?"

Laura smacked the steering wheel with the palm

of her hand. "All right, damn you! You've made your point. But you've raised an interesting question as well," she said, finally swiveling in her seat to face him. "Why are *you* willing to take a chance on me?"

"Make no mistake about it, Laura, I still don't trust you. Whatever went on with Flemming, it obviously wasn't pleasant. You might only be after his hide. Or you could find your back against a wall halfway through and settle for whatever sensational attention comes along."

"How dare you!"

Dusty rather liked the way her eyes flashed when she was mad. There were a lot of things he liked about Laura Newton. If they could get past this initial phase and start working together, they might become friends—with any luck, even more than friends. But he had to make his position clear to her first.

"Oh, you impressed me with your tale of hardship. But others have made successful careers out of pursuing crackpot ideas. Object all you like, but you can't tell me it hasn't crossed your mind," Dusty said. "Most probably when you look at your bank balance."

Laura turned away and morosely studied a small crack in the upper corner of the windshield. "How many times are you going to make me say it, Dusty? I'm sincere. I don't just want this project—I need it."

"If it helps you accept the situation, I'm inclined to believe you are sincere. That's why I don't trust you. Anybody who has as much to prove as you do can't be counted on to behave in a calm and orderly manner," he told her. "It's also the main reason I'm being so heavy-handed, because I know you'll go ahead without me, hell-bent for leather, if I don't force you to take me along."

Laura sat there, scowling. Dusty didn't interrupt her silence. But she knew he wasn't waiting for her to make a decision; he was waiting for her to come to grips with the fact that he'd already made the decision for her.

She didn't have a choice. Again. "Are you coming along to help," she asked at last, "or just to keep me in check?"

Dusty fought a triumphant smile. "Believe me, Laura, I'm as serious about this as you profess to be. I'll do everything I can, hold up my end of the partnership to the utmost of my ability. But if you don't do the same, if you start to conduct yourself in a less-than-professional manner, I will do my best to further discredit you before I'll let you jeopardize my own goals. Understood?"

Laura blew out a deep breath. Then she took her right hand off the steering wheel and held it out to him. "What the hell. If you don't mind being seen with a flake, why should I mind being seen with an unmitigated bastard? It's a deal, Dr. Cantrell."

They shook hands.

"But I get top billing," Laura added.

Dusty was smiling again, back to his usual pleasant self. "Agreed, Dr. Newton. You know, together I think we might just be able to pull this off."

"We'd better," Laura muttered. "And we also better start figuring out how we're going to go about it."

"Excellent idea," he agreed. "But can we do it someplace other than the front seat of this car? I'm frying."

7

Laura sat in one of the well-padded swivel chairs, soaking up the cool air of Dusty's RV. It felt good to be out of the sun. Although she was not particularly thrilled with having to accept this ultimatum, it also felt good to know the project would soon be under way.

She was not, however, at all happy with Dusty's first suggestion on how they should proceed. "No," Laura said, glaring at him across what she had come to think of as the living room. "Absolutely not."

"You're being illogical again."

"I am not! I'm being . . ." She trailed off, searching for the right word. "I'm being prudent."

"Prudent? Try prudish!"

"I am not going to share this RV with you, Dusty, and that's final!"

Having him as a partner was bad enough; sleeping in the same vehicle with him could quite possibly give her a nervous breakdown. He was just weird enough to whip out a ruler and measure her rear end while she slept.

"We'll be traveling all over the place," Dusty objected, "asking questions and viewing sites that have been looted. Most of the time we'll be in areas that aren't exactly set up for tourists, while those that are will be booked solid. And we can't waste time finding you a motel room every night, in any case."

"Fine. I'll sleep in my car."

"I thought you said it was broken."

"I'll get it fixed. And I'll buy a sleeping bag so I won't get cold. Satisfied?"

"No," he replied. "This is just plain stupid. Why are you being so difficult?"

"Why are you being so insistent?" Laura returned. "I thought you were concerned with keeping a professional image. How is it going to look if we end each research day by stepping into an RV together?"

"Don't be silly. You won't be the first person who's shared it with me for the comfort and convenience it provides when doing research in remote areas. That's why I bought the thing!" he exclaimed in exasperation. "It sleeps six in complete comfort, ten if you don't mind the floor. There's plenty of room, we can eat whatever and whenever we like and stay where the action is without having to sleep in bags like human hot dogs."

"I still don't think—"

"Damn, you're stubborn!" Dusty interrupted. "Let me put it this way. We're traveling along, me in this nice, air-conditioned vehicle and you following behind in your hot, broken-down old car. Suddenly, you have to go to the bathroom *really* bad. We're miles from the nearest rest stop. You blink your lights, but I don't see them. Are you going to sit there and tell me you actually like peeing in the bushes?"

"You bastard!" Laura closed her eyes and sighed. Then she said, "Excuse me for a moment."

When she returned from using the bathroom, her mind was made up. "All right. We'll travel together. But I get the bedroom—and all the keys to the door."

Dusty scowled. "Why should I give up my bed for you?"

"I don't care about the bed. I want the lock."

"Oh, all right," he muttered, and threw her a key. "That's the only one. Jeez! I'm not going to pounce on you, Laura."

"Pouncing I can handle," she informed him, pointing to the toe of her hiking boot, "if you get my meaning. What I'm afraid of is waking up in the middle of the night with a tape measure wrapped around my ass."

"I wouldn't do that!"

"No?"

"No," Dusty assured her. "I use calipers. They provide a much more accurate reading."

Laura slumped in her chair and groaned. "Lord. This is going to be a long, long project! Just keep your calipers to yourself, Dusty. And everything else. Concentrate on holding up your end of things and we'll get along fine."

"I doubt that," Dusty said. "You can be pretty damned annoying yourself, you know. Why bother with this tough-cookie posture? If you're as mean and nasty as you think you are, I don't see why you're worried about little old me."

Little? Over six feet of broad-shouldered brawn and a powerful brain to match. Laura couldn't afford *not* to keep a defensive posture. "I'm not worried," she lied. "I'm just letting you know the facts. That's what this meeting is all about, isn't it?"

"Then before we move on to less trivial subjects, I have a requirement of my own concerning the sleeping arrangements," Dusty said. "The couch is comfy, but it has to be made up every night. My bed doesn't. So you're going to help me."

"I'm not your maid!"

"No, you're my partner. Everything fifty-fifty." He grinned. "That includes the cooking. I'll take breakfast, you take lunch, and we'll flip a coin for dinner. The cook doesn't wash dishes. The rest of the housework we'll divvy up according to who's the biggest slob."

"That'll be you, I'm sure. I've never seen a man yet who didn't have a high tolerance for dirt."

"For a supposedly serious scientist, you certainly make a lot of generalizations. I," Dusty told her, "happen to be a very clean person."

"Right," Laura muttered. "Everything except your mind, that is. Okay, that settles the housekeeping arrangements. Now, what should I do about my car?"

"Personally, I'd pay somebody to haul it off," Dusty replied. "But I suppose, like most of the women I've ever known, you even have a pet name for it. So I propose we leave it at Phil's. I'll arrange to have them keep an eye on it. Not that anyone would steal it."

"I want to make sure it's fixed before we leave too."

"Why?" he asked. "You won't be needing it for a while."

"I can't leave Pooky sitting there all broken!" Laura exclaimed in horror. Actually, the only attachment she had to the rusting bucket of bolts was as a means of escape, should Dusty's interest in her buttocks become more than academic.

"I knew it!" he exclaimed. "But *Pooky?* What the hell kind of name is that for a car?"

"Don't! You'll hurt Pooky's feelings!"

Dusty sighed. "Okay, I guess it might come in handy if we have to split up for a while or something. Getting a rental car at this time of year would be tough. Did they tell you how long it'll take to fix?"

"An hour. If we go to Shiprock for the part ourselves."

"We can't waste time running parts!"

"It won't be a waste," she informed him. "While we're there, I have a couple of other priorities. First of all, I want to wash my clothes and pick up some more. Something thin and cool that will protect me from the sun. I don't intend to run around ruins and digs in shorts and a T-shirt."

"Damn! There goes the only pleasant prospect of this entire venture. You really know how to ruin a guy's day."

Again she directed his attention to the hard toe of her hiking boot. "Yes, I do. And before you make any more sly comments about favorite sexual positions or pleasant prospects, you'd do well to remember that."

He held up his hands. "Just trying to keep it fun."

"I'm not interested in fun, Cantrell. I'll be too busy working. And so will you." Laura counted off her mental list on her fingers. "So, we'll get the part, do the wash, find something more serviceable for me to wear in the desert, then come back here to make sure the car is fixed." She frowned. "Am I forgetting anything?"

"The research project?" Dusty suggested sarcastically.

"No, we'll discuss where to start on that while we're getting all this piddly stuff done. Let's see . . . Oh, yes. Somewhere along the way we're going to a shoe store too."

"What now? Some high heels to impress the rattlesnakes?"

"Boots," Laura replied.

"You have boots."

"Yes, I do. Nice ones. And I do not intend to be seen next to someone with a pair that look like they should be given a decent burial." Laura stood up and peered into the driver's compartment. About the only thing that looked normal was the steering wheel. "This trip will also give you a chance to teach me how to drive this thing."

Dusty shook his head. "No way. I'll run errands with you, wash clothes with you, I'll even buy some new boots, since you insist. But I will not let you drive."

"What happened to fifty-fifty?"

"It goes for everything," he replied, "except driving. Nobody touches that wheel but me."

"Now who's being stupid? I can handle it," she

assured him, though she wasn't at all sure that was the case. "It's just a house on wheels."

"Shh! You'll hurt her feelings." Dusty gave the wall of the RV an affectionate pat. "What should we expect from someone who would name a car Pooky? But we forgive her. Don't we, Scheherazade?"

8

It was four in the afternoon by the time Laura had dragged Dusty through all their errands. They had a late lunch in a Mexican restaurant where the specialty was something called a Navajo taco, consisting of puffy Indian fried bread filled with spicy meat, lettuce, diced tomato, and grated cheese. Laura ate two. Then she had another one for dessert, without the filling and sprinkled with cinnamon sugar. Dusty was quite amazed.

"You always eat like that?" he asked her as they climbed back into the RV.

"I have to keep up my strength," she replied, "to put up with you. I don't think I've ever seen anyone take an hour to choose a pair of shoes before."

"I happen to be hard to fit, okay?" He looked down at his new hiking boots. "Neat. A little stiff though."

"What do you expect? From the looks of them, I'd

say you'd been wearing those old ones for fifteen or twenty years."

"There's still some life in them."

Laura chuckled. "Right. As doorstops."

"Fine. Ignore my comfort. As long as your delicate sensibilities are no longer offended by my footwear, I'm happy," Dusty said. "The least you could have done in return is consider the effect those pants will have on my research."

"I like them just fine."

They were all-cotton, taupe in color, with a bellows pocket on each thigh and plenty of room to move. The drawstrings on the cuffs would discourage any unwanted desert creatures from crawling up her legs—and the roomy seat would discourage Dusty's constant perusal of her behind.

She liked her new shirt, too, so much so that she'd bought the red one she had on and another in a jazzy shade of teal. They were also cotton, soft as a pajama top, and had long sleeves and button cuffs. With the shirt worn outside her desert-ready pants and the two-inch-thick, black leather belt she'd purchased at the same store buckled around her slender waist, Laura thought she looked like an intrepid but fashionable explorer.

Dusty did not agree. "I can't see anything."

"That, Cantrell, is precisely why I like them."

He sighed heavily and got behind the wheel of the RV. At least her shirt had a V neck. When she sat down in the passenger seat, the front of it gapped open just enough to give him his first real glimpse of her breasts, creamy white and full, tantalizingly hidden by her thin, lacy bra.

Perhaps he should give some serious thought to changing the direction of his research. If a woman could have a smart ass, could she not therefore have smart knockers?

"I wonder . . ."

"What do you wonder?" Laura asked.

Dusty cleared his throat. "I wonder if there's a supermarket around here? With your appetite, we'd better replenish our supplies."

After a stop at the market, they headed back across the Arizona border toward Teec Nos Pos. Dusty hadn't changed his mind about letting her drive. That was fine with Laura. Though his display of affection and pet name for the vehicle were undoubtedly a put-on—Scheherazade indeed!—it was quite obvious to her that piloting this road monster took some skill. She would as soon sit back and enjoy the ride.

"I've been thinking about the project," she said.

"About time! Come up with anything?"

"A couple of things. First, I think you're right about the main thrust being documentation. I'm not that familiar with the legitimate work being done around here, let alone the looting. Are you?"

He took one hand off the wheel for a moment and waggled it. "Some. I can take us to a few places that have been vandalized. Others we can find by asking around. But I'm glad you agree," Dusty said. "We have to know what's already been done before we can proceed to the present."

"Or peek in on the future," Laura added.

Dusty glanced at her. "Somehow I knew that was

coming. You have it in mind to try and actually watch some looters in operation, don't you?"

"Eventually. Not with the goal of jumping out of the bushes and stopping them though."

"Thank heaven for small favors," Dusty muttered.

"I see it as a vital part of the research. I want to be able to personally attest to the crudity of their methods. Just rewriting someone else's account won't do."

"We have to find some to watch first."

"And before we can do that we have to know what to look for," Laura said, "to make sure we get the sort of professional we're really after. I don't want to waste my time on some tourist digging for arrowheads. The way I see it, one of the biggest mistakes others have made on this is offending collectors."

He smiled at her. "Glad to see you're as sharp as I thought, partner. You're right. The general public isn't interested in thrashing people who just happen to have an old pot on their coffee table. Everybody collects things or knows someone who does. Who wants to bring the law down on Uncle Harold?"

Laura wasn't sure how to take his praise. It felt good, but so, in a way, did his covert study of her figure; taking either too seriously could lead to trouble.

Dusty was a handsome, witty man, and even though their relationship was not what she could call amiable, she was certainly as aware of his strong, healthy body and charming green eyes as he was of her feminine curves. The project would be hard enough, and the desert hot enough, without adding any male-female heat into the equation.

She settled for a professional nod of acceptance and continued. "It's sort of like the drug situation. Most folks agree that the key is education, teaching the evil of the stuff, and at the same time going after the source," Laura said. "In our case, we have to educate the public on the harm looting does to our knowledge of history, without sullying the legitimate collectors and archaeological hobbyists the same way we hope to smear the thieves and vandals."

"Right. Our target is some good old American outrage, and we're not going to get it unless we aim very carefully. The dealers and buyers are a problem, no doubt about it. They provide the market. But it's the looters who provide the stolen goods—the source of the 'drugs' in your analogy. Educate and go after the source." He grinned. "I like it!"

"I'm so glad," Laura said, pretending she couldn't care less. "Now you'd better watch the road or they'll put *you* in jail for speeding."

In fact, she was quite pleased by Dusty's approval. After all, he wasn't some rube who was trying to curry favor and maybe get into her pants. The man had a doctorate in archaeology, was committed to the project, and had made it quite clear he would squash her flat if she didn't live up to his standards of professionalism.

That didn't mean he wasn't also trying to get into her pants. But it did make Laura accept his praise without worrying about ulterior motives. If he approved, she was on the right track; this whole partnership idea might not be such a bad one after all. She could certainly use an emotional life raft about now.

"I do believe you're smiling, Dr. Newton," Dusty observed.

"I have reason to, Dr. Cantrell. I think I've just come up with the perfect place to start. It'll knock weeks off our background research."

"Where?"

"Carl Flemming's dig."

They had arrived at the station. Dusty pulled the RV in next to her car and switched off the engine. Then he turned in his seat, eyebrows lowered in an expression that foretold a coming storm.

"No."

So much for him being on her side. She'd have to watch this stupid tendency toward optimism. "Yes. There's supposed to be someone from the university there today to question him and delve into his activities."

"And you want to go make sure they get him securely trussed up on a spit, I suppose?" Dusty asked. "Laura, I warned you about making this some kind of revenge thing on Flemming, didn't I?"

Laura looked at him. Although his bossy manner made her want to split his lip, she was still smiling. "I don't know enough about what he's done to add anything to the university's case. But he does. And once they start to toast his tootsies, he'll tell them. I want to be there to hear every word."

Dusty's expression cleared and his eyebrows shot up in surprise. "You think he'll tell them his contacts? Who he sold the stuff to and such?"

"Carl was never good under pressure. It's a good bet he'll spill everything in an attempt to save himself. But even if he doesn't, I just remembered something he told me last night." Her smile grew broader still. "He took me out onto the mesa and showed me some flickering lights in a canyon not too far from his dig. Said he was pretty sure a looter was at work there."

"You said he was trying to lure you in," Dusty pointed out. "Maybe he made it up to lend his story immediacy."

"Maybe. But maybe not. It takes one to know one and all that. One way or another, I think it's as good a place to begin as any," she said. "And I freely admit I wouldn't mind seeing Carl forced to do something he doesn't want to do for a change."

Dusty didn't like the sound of that. "I'm warning you, Laura. If you show one little sign that getting back at him is more important to you than this project, I'll use this CB to call the reporters in. Got it?"

"Dusty," she said as she got to her feet, "you amaze me. Just when I think you really might be an okay guy after all, you jump right up and prove what an asshole you are." She grabbed the thermostat she'd bought. "I'm going to arrange things with the station attendant. In the meantime, why don't you make yourself useful and find somebody who knows the way to Carl's dig?"

She stormed out the RV's side door, muttering all the way. Dusty sat there for a moment, deep in thought. Then he reached under his seat and pulled out a plastic bag that contained a couple of items he'd picked up while Laura had been busy at the clothing store.

One of them was a magazine that had an article on archaeological activity in the Four Corners region.

He opened it to a map pinpointing the various sites currently being excavated, circled the Flemming dig with a felt-tipped pen, and placed it on the passenger seat.

The other item in the bag was a book of selected anthropological papers and essays. One of them suggested the role a certain type of vegetation had played in the development of a primitive culture. Another described the relationship between various ancient and present-day ceremonial rites. Fairly dry material, but Dusty never bought a book without reading it from cover to cover; he would eventually peruse all of this one too.

But for now he thumbed through it until he came upon the one standout in the otherwise standard fare. "Global Crime and the Greenhouse Effect," by Laura M. Newton.

What did the *M* stand for? Mary? Martha? Millicent? Mean, Monstrous, or Malevolent, most likely, he said to himself. Dusty started to read but kept an eye on the door so he could hide the book when she returned.

Her derriere indicated a high IQ. And though his secondary theory was still in its infancy, she certainly possessed what looked to be a very smart pair of breasts. From all indications she was indeed an intelligent woman. But if he was going to be spending time with the Ultraviolet Wacko, he'd better find out if she was the certifiable flake everyone said she was—or a certified genius.

The trip to Carl's dig filled Laura with an unpleasant sense of dread. Most of it was caused by the prospect of seeing him so soon after the incident last night; even though she had emerged the victor, his attempt to take advantage of her mentally and physically was still razor-sharp in her mind.

But the rest of her uneasiness was the result of the odd way Dusty had been behaving toward her from the moment she'd stepped back into his RV. As they drove along, every now and then he would look over at her and give her a strange little smile. Perhaps he was only waiting for her to compliment him on finding a map to the dig. If so, he'd have a long wait; he already seemed pleased enough with himself as it was.

For some reason, though, Laura had a sneaking suspicion he was up to something. So this time around she made careful note of every turn and change of direction. If whatever evil plan he was hatching involved another display of his "private eccentricity," she wanted to know the exact route back to her escape vehicle—which she had also made sure was in working order before they'd left town.

It seemed to take them forever to get to the dig, what with the care Dusty used in driving over such rough terrain. But she appreciated the difference between Carl's old rattletrap truck and the RV. Laura was sure she would appreciate it even more when it came time to bed down for the night—although she was anticipating that event with uneasiness too.

When at last they arrived at the ragtag grouping of tents surrounding the excavation site, however, Laura's unease and suspicion had to take a backseat. Something was going on. There were people everywhere, and none of them was Carl Flemming. Evidently the university team had arrived.

A young woman came over to them as they emerged from the RV. "Excuse me," she said. "You can't park that here. This isn't a campground, you know."

"We're not campers," Laura informed her. "Could you direct us to the person in charge?"

"That'd be Professor Jenkins." She looked them over. "You're not, um, *friends* of Carl Flemming's, are you?"

"Decidedly not," Laura replied. "My name is—"

Before she could introduce herself, Dusty stepped in front of her and extended his hand. "Hi! I'm Dr. Cantrell. This is my associate, Dr. Violet. And you are . . ."

"Cindy Blake. Are you going to be a part of the

team, Dr. Cantrell?" she asked. The sparkle in her eyes indicated she definitely hoped he was.

"Afraid not."

"Darn!" Cindy exclaimed. "My first field trip as a senior and everybody around here is either married or old as dirt."

"Gee," Dusty said. "That's a shame, Cindy."

Laura elbowed him aside. "Would you be so kind as to take us to this Professor Jenkins?"

"I guess so," the student told her. "But he's a very busy man. What's this all about?"

"We'd like to speak with him about Carl Flemming."

Cindy stuffed her hands into the pockets of her tight blue denim jeans and shrugged. "Okay. But I don't think it'll do you much good. He's just in charge of the team taking over the dig. The people who are looking into the allegations against Flemming have already left."

"Left?" Laura asked. "Left to go where?"

Another shrug. "Back to the university, I suppose."

"I would have thought they'd have questioned him here," Dusty said. "At the scene of his crimes, so to speak. Or did he confess to everything and get it over with quickly?"

"Oh, he was gone when we all got here. Just abandoned the dig," Cindy replied. "Can you imagine that? I mean, he was a creep, for sure."

"For sure," Laura agreed, although without the shapely young blonde's valley-girl twang. "So Jenkins wouldn't have much to tell us, is that it?"

"Well . . ." She moved closer to them—or rather,

closer to Dusty—and whispered, "The old fart has a lot to say about him and the condition of the dig, if you don't mind blue air."

Laura sighed. "I don't think epithets are exactly what we have in mind, Cindy. We'll pass. Thanks for your help."

She was halfway back to the RV before she noticed Dusty wasn't beside her. When she turned around to see what was keeping him, her mouth dropped open. Cindy was bending over to tie her tennis shoe. Dusty was standing right behind her, examining her assets.

"Shit!" Laura muttered. She strode back to his side. "We really must be going, Dr. Cantrell."

He smiled at her. "One twenty-five."

"What?"

Cindy had finished tying her shoe and was looking at them curiously. "Something else I can do for you?"

"No," Laura replied, tugging on Dusty's arm.

"Yes," Dusty said. "What was your most recent IQ score?"

She thought for a moment. "One eighteen, I think. Why?"

Laura couldn't help laughing. "It's just some stupid theory. And it looks like he's full of—"

"But that was in high school," Cindy interjected. "I've probably picked up a few points since then."

"Wouldn't surprise me a bit." Dusty shook the young woman's hand, then walked past Laura to the RV, whistling through his teeth. "Come along, Dr. Violet. We have work to do."

Cindy looked at Laura and asked, "What kind of project are you two conducting anyway?"

"I'm researching digs," Laura replied, "while Dr. Cantrell is digging himself an early grave." If her eyes could shoot arrows, Dusty would have had two of them sticking out of his back. "Have a nice field trip, Cindy."

"Thanks! You have a nice day!"

"Impossible."

When she returned to the RV, Dusty was back behind the wheel, studying his map. He didn't look up when Laura entered and sat down in the passenger seat.

"Charming young woman," he said. "Smart too. But not as smart as you."

"You're disgusting!"

Dusty finally looked up. "Cindy didn't seem to think so."

"She doesn't know you like I do. And what the hell was that Dr. Violet crap?"

"We agreed we don't want anyone to know what we're doing just yet," Dusty replied. "And we certainly don't want them to know the Ultraviolet Wacko is involved. It seemed like an appropriate alias to me."

"Very funny." But he was right about not using her real name, at least in the beginning. It didn't make her any less angry with him though. "We don't want them to think an ass-grabbing pervert is involved either," Laura told him. "So keep your mind on the project next time."

"Just trying to prove my point. And I was darn close too, wasn't I? Just like I am with you."

"The only thing you're close to is a fat lip, buster," Laura warned. She grabbed the map out of his hands and looked at it to get her bearings. "Well, this was a wasted trip. Have you figured out where we should go next?"

"I see. Now that you can't watch Flemming squirm, the trip was a waste." He gazed at her suspiciously. "I thought you said there was a looter at work around here."

"Dammit! I said there might be."

"You also said you saw lights," he reminded her.

"I did! But there are a lot of canyons and arroyos out there." Laura swept a hand through the air, indicating the horizon beyond the windshield. "I just barely saw what Carl was trying to show me. Without him to pinpoint the spot for me, we're just wasting our time. I think we should head for a place we know for certain the looters have been and get this show on the road."

"It's going to be dark soon," Dusty said, studying the sky. "Maybe we'll be able to see something then. If you didn't make the whole thing up just to get me to bring you here, that is."

"I'm getting pretty damn tired of your accusations."

"So let's stick around to see the lights and you can prove me wrong."

"There probably won't be any lights, you idiot!" Laura objected. "That's why it's a waste without Carl here to show us where they were. What makes you think they'd be stupid enough to work the same spot two nights in a row, especially with all the activity up here today?"

"You never know. They're a pretty greedy lot." He yawned elaborately. "Besides, we won't get very far before we have to stop for the night anyway. I've been driving all day and I'm tired."

"Then let me drive."

"On a long stretch of open highway, maybe," he said. "Just maybe. But over rough country? Ha!"

"You make me so damned mad!" Laura fumed. "If you were planning to stay the night here no matter what, why did you bother to harass me about the lights?"

"Just to hear your explanation."

"Why you . . . For the last time, I don't have any ulterior motives!" she said. Then she smiled bitterly. "No, scratch that. I have one now. I'm going to make a success of this just to see you eat crow!"

Laura got up before she belted him one, heading to the kitchen for a glass of water to wash down her anger. As she was coming back up to the driver's compartment, Dusty abruptly started the engine and the RV lurched forward, making her spill water all over herself.

"Jeez-us!" she cried. "What the hell are you doing?"

"Moving us away from the dig. That ridge over on the other side of the mesa should give us a nice view and shield us from curious eyes at the same time."

"Why should we care if they can see us?" she asked warily. "We're not going to be doing anything."

"Probably not, damn it," he mumbled. To Laura he said, "We're keeping a low profile, remember? I don't want anyone from the university team to come visiting."

"Not even little Cindy?" Laura taunted in a sugary-sweet voice. "I'll bet she'd let you see her IQ."

Dusty laughed. "Don't worry. A bouncy coed is no match for you, Laura. You have my undivided attention." He took his eyes off the rutted road ahead to glance in the rear view mirror. She was standing behind him. The water she'd spilled had plastered the front of her shirt to her breasts. "Especially right now."

Her eyes narrowed. "The only attention I want from you is on this project, Cantrell, so that had better be what you're talking about."

"Not exactly. Shall I turn off the air-conditioning?" he asked. "You look cold."

Laura looked down at herself. Her nipples were hard, clearly defined points pressing against the damp material of her cotton shirt. She wrapped one arm over her breasts and extended the other to pour the rest of her glass of water over Dusty's head.

"Hey!"

"You'd better turn the air-conditioning *up*," she advised. "Your imagination is overheating."

"That wasn't my imagination. That was all you."

"But you're dreaming if you think you'll ever see any more." Laura turned and went to change her shirt. "Just get us parked so we can start dinner," she called out from the bedroom. "I'm hungry."

So was Dusty. In more ways than one. But this was their first night together, so he supposed he'd have to behave himself. For the most part.

"Me too. What are you fixing?"

"Me? I thought we flipped a coin?"

"It's only fair," he replied. "We ate lunch out."

"But I paid."

He finally jockeyed the RV into the position he

wanted. They were hidden behind a sandstone ridge that lay some ten miles across the mesa from Flemming's dig, but they still had a good view of the canyons to the south. Dusty turned off the engine and flipped a switch that automatically leveled the vehicle. It was suddenly very quiet.

Laura emerged from the bedroom wearing her freshly washed sweatshirt. She almost laughed at the disappointment in Dusty's eyes. "Well?" she asked. "Who fixes dinner?"

"We've got wine and frozen lasagna. I'll pop the cork and defrost, you chop a salad. Deal?"

"You're on."

They ate outside under an awning Dusty rolled out from the side of the RV. He had also produced a folding table and chairs from an outside compartment so they didn't have to dine picnic-style. The sunset that accompanied their meal was reddish-pink and glorious.

So was the wine. But Laura only sipped. There was something about having a pleasant dinner in these beautiful surroundings—with a handsome man she scarcely knew and didn't trust an inch—that made her light-headed enough already. The landscape was surreal, like a brilliant oil painting, and added to the strange feeling that they had separated themselves from the rest of the world somehow.

Indeed, it was a lonely place. There was life around, to be sure, and not just at the dig ten miles away or at the more populated areas to the north and south where all the tourists were. Odd, to be in America and yet, in a way, to be in another country at the same time. Though national highways ran across this land and there were national monuments upon it, this was a reservation. Federal laws notwithstanding, Laura was of the opinion that she and Dusty were here by the grace of the Navajo people, as were the other scientists and all the tourists as well.

"How do they really feel about us being here, I wonder?"

Dusty chuckled quietly in the deepening shadows. "About the way you'd feel if someone was camping in your backyard at home, I imagine," he replied. "Seriously, though, this is just like any other part of the country. If you act like an asshole, they'll treat you like one. It never ceases to amaze me how many tourists think they can just barge right into a hogan or kiva as if it were public property or a museum. What would they do if a total stranger strolled into their house to see how the average suburbanite lives?"

"Scream for the police, what else? Unfortunately, a lot of people think of Native Americans as living relics."

"And the possessions of their ancestors as fair game," Dusty said. "Looting *is* illegal, but the laws protecting archaeological resources are weak and hard to enforce. There's too much territory to police effectively, even if you could make people care."

Laura stopped watching the sunset for a moment, not liking the tone that was creeping into his voice. "You make it sound as if we're defeated before we start."

"Hell, Laura, they're better at finding artifacts than we are. And it's self-limiting, you know. Once all the sites worth looting have been cleaned out, the theft will stop." He sighed and sipped at his wine. "Are you sure you wouldn't rather pick a war you can win?"

"You know the answer to that," she replied curtly. "Before those limits are reached, a lot of information will be lost."

"Just making sure you know the odds."

Laura turned her face back to the setting sun. "I'll find a way," she told him. "I have to."

"For the sake of history? Or your reputation?"

"Both."

"Laura . . ."

"Would you stop probing?" she demanded.

Abruptly, Laura pushed away from the table and went to stand by one of the poles holding up the awning. It was better with her back to him. That way she didn't have to look at his face and wonder if it was concern or suspicion she saw in those intelligent green eyes.

"I didn't pick this topic for the flash, okay? I told you I was waiting for the right one to come along. In fact, I was desperate for it," she admitted. "But it had to be something I could believe in too. Can you understand that?"

"Yes."

She stiffened at the sound of his voice, for he had gotten up from the table also and was standing right behind her. Was he about to touch her? Did she want him to?

"What are you doing?" she asked.

Dusty laughed softly. "Research."

"Dammit!"

Laura spun around to slap him, but he caught her

hand before it touched his cheek. He was very strong. There was, however, no force in the way he gripped her wrist. As a matter of fact, his touch was curiously gentle. So was the expression on his face as he gazed into her eyes.

"Not that kind of research," Dusty said, the hint of a smile lifting one corner of his mouth. "Those pants are too baggy." He released her wrist and tapped her forehead lightly with his fingertip. "That's the part of you I'm researching, Laura. You're not the only one who has to believe in things before making a commitment."

"And you still don't believe in *me*, is that it?"

"I'm getting there," he replied. "I read your work today while you were getting the car fixed."

Her eyes widened and her arm dropped to her side. "I assumed you already had. Isn't that why—"

"Why I've been so tough on you?" Dusty interjected. "No. I told you I find it hard to keep up with the present sometimes. It was the media uproar I finally remembered, and I'm afraid I fell prey to a knee-jerk reaction."

"And came down on me without even knowing what you were talking about," she said angrily, "just like everybody else."

"Guilty. And I'm sorry." He held up his hand before she could open her mouth again. "It doesn't change anything, mind you. You still have the troublesome reputation, and I still have doubts about your motives. But I no longer doubt your abilities. It was a good paper, Laura. Damned good. A bit on the wild side, naturally, otherwise it wouldn't have attracted all that attention."

"I said I was good at attracting attention, didn't I?" Laura asked with a half-hearted smile.

He laughed. "A little too good, I'd say."

"It just got away from me. But this time I won't be so stupid," she informed him. "Or so naive."

"I'll make sure of that."

"I don't need a keeper!"

"That remains to be seen." Dusty put his hands on her shoulders. "You're doubly obsessed: committed to both the project and clearing your name. And you know what they say about the dog who chases two rabbits at the same time."

Laura shook her head. "I'm not going to lose either of these rabbits, Dusty. You'll see."

"Not by adding a third one, you won't. You don't have to prove anything to me."

"No?" she asked.

"Well . . ." Dusty took his right hand off her shoulder and held it in front of her nose, with the thumb and forefinger about an inch apart. "Maybe a little. For instance, I'm going to do something right now, and the way you react will tell me a lot about how easy—or how difficult—you'll be to work with."

Laura took a step back from him. "Try to kiss me and you're dead meat, Cantrell. Sex doesn't fall under the job description of a research partner."

"Darn! You mean I've been reading the wrong guidebook?" Dusty smiled and reached out for her. Expecting him to caress her cheek, Laura shied away. The hair on his arm tickled her neck. Although it actually felt rather pleasant, she didn't want to give him one iota of encouragement. He was doing fine all on his own.

"Don't!" she exclaimed. "I'm warning you!"

"Thanks. But it's not necessary." He chuckled throatily and murmured, "Not yet anyway. Look behind you."

He hadn't been reaching. He was pointing over her shoulder. She turned around and saw an eerie glow dancing in the deep shadows of a canyon a mile or so in the distance.

"Hot damn!" She shrugged his other hand off her shoulder and ran a few steps away from the RV for a better look. Then she came back. "Let's go!" she exclaimed.

"Bad news, Dr. Newton," Dusty said. "You failed the test. That was precisely the reaction I thought you'd have, and it is decidedly the wrong one."

"Assuming that I give a damn—which I don't— would you mind telling me why?"

"Because it's stupid. And you think you don't need a keeper? Ha!" Dusty went back to the table, took a seat, and poured himself another glass of wine. He sipped it and made a face. "Warm, dammit. I should have put the bottle on ice."

"Suit yourself," Laura said. "I'm going."

"No, you're not." He grabbed her arm as she passed him. This time he wasn't so gentle. "It would be full dark by the time you got there. You have no idea who it is, how many of them there are, or what they're doing."

"It's looters!"

"Maybe," he said. "Maybe not. Whoever it is didn't ask you to drop by for a visit. You might not be welcome. *Especially* if it's someone looting a grave."

Laura didn't bother trying to break free; he had a

grip like a vise. He wasn't hurting her, but neither was he about to let go unless she hit him over the head with the wine bottle, and she didn't bother trying that either.

She simply said, "Let go."

"No. Have a seat."

"No! I'm going to sneak up on them."

"Right."

Dusty gave her arm a yank to pull her closer, put a hand on her hip to turn her around and a knee behind her legs to knock her off her feet. It was a nice, smooth motion that made her sit down in his lap as if it had been her idea all along.

"Time for a tutorial," he said. "Comfy?"

"Goddammit! Let me go this instant!"

She wrigged around in his lap, trying to get away. Again, it was no use. In fact it was having the exact opposite effect. "Oh, my!" Dusty murmured. "Nice! But on with the lesson. Why do you suppose there are so many ruins in those canyons?"

"Eat dirt!"

"No, thank you. I just had dinner." She wouldn't face him, so he spoke softly into her ear. "The canyons are full of ruins and burial grounds because folks lived there. The Navajo; the people who came before the Navajo, whom they call the Anasazi; and probably others as well. Why?"

She wiggled. He hummed appreciatively. So she stopped fighting and answered, "Because they were protected from the elements! Now let—"

"Correct! But also because they were safe. And do you know why they were safe?" he asked. "No, obviously not, or you wouldn't have made that dumb remark about sneaking up on whoever it is out there. Canyons like those, with sandstone walls, are tricky to get in and out of. You have to know the way. And even if you do, every noise you make echoes off those walls, all along the canyon. They'd hear you an hour before you got to them, providing you didn't break your neck on the way over there in the dark before that."

Laura turned her face to his. "So?"

"So you assured me it was not your intention to jump out of the bushes and stop them. I replied that that was a relief, because it's going to be enough of a job just keeping you out of mischief. I have no desire to scrape what's left of your smart ass off a canyon wall. Got it?" he asked.

"I can take care of myself!" Laura objected.

"You are strong," Dusty admitted, "and possess a certain threatening demeanor that gives a man pause. But you ain't made of stone, sister. Quite the opposite." This time he wiggled *his* hips. "If you did come upon some looters, and they weren't the type who'd tie you up and leave you beside that convenient hole they'd been digging, they might be the sort who don't stop when a lady says no. If you get my drift."

Laura closed her eyes for a moment. When she opened them, she said, "Okay! So it was stupid."

"That's better. I'll up your grade to a B plus."

"But I still say we should go check it out first thing in the morning," Laura said. "I just got excited and jumped the gun. Can you blame me?"

Dusty smiled at her. "I suppose not."

"Will you please let me up, now?"

"Oh. Sorry." He released her. "I just got excited," he explained, grinning widely.

She stood up and moved away from him, feeling the hot circles of embarrassment over her cheekbones. Not for being stupid, or even his playful innuendo, but for the way her body had noticed every detail of his while she was sitting on his lap. The muscles of his chest pressing against her side; his breath soft upon her cheek; the definite hardness of him beneath her buttocks. He had indeed been excited.

And so was she.

"I . . . I think I'll go to bed now," Laura said.

"The sun isn't even all the way down yet!"

"I know. I'm . . . I'm suddenly very tired." She looked at him, her voice cross when she spoke. "I haven't had much sleep today, you know. Or last night either."

Dusty nodded. "I understand. And I suppose we will want to make an early start." He pointed toward the canyon where they'd seen the lights. They were still flickering, he noticed. "First there, to see what we can see, then on to some more looted sites. Agreed?"

"Yes." She put one foot on the iron step below the RV's door and stopped. "Thanks for the lesson, Dusty. Maybe I do need someone around to keep me from getting overzealous."

"My pleasure. I'll just make a quick drawing so we can find the right canyon tomorrow, then I think I'll call it a day too. Good night."

"'Night."

Dusty made his drawing, then sat in the gathering gloom, smiling to himself. This might turn out to be an enjoyable partnership after all.

10

It was a crude vessel by twentieth-century standards, a simple pot of coarse clay adorned with orange geometric designs. Any reasonably proficient modern-day potter could improve upon its symmetry, could, in fact, turn out several in the time it had taken a nameless, long-dead craftsman to make just this one. Of course, that artisan hadn't had an electric potter's wheel or a gas-fired kiln. But so what? Where was the value?

Nevertheless, the exhausted, sunburned man sank to his knees beside his rough, inexpert excavation, placing the fragile piece of pottery carefully into one of the padded pockets of his backpack. His heat-bewildered mind kept asking the same question over and over. What made the thing worth enough to fry like an egg for in this lonely, forsaken canyon, going against the laws of man and nature?

Mr. Pline had tried to explain it to him last week,

but Chester hadn't been able to grasp the concept, just as he'd never been able to understand how Pline's thirty-year-old English sports car could be worth twice as much as his own brand-new Cadillac.

Why did some things get worthless as they got older, while others became collector's items? At least the car looked good and went fast; this black and orange pot just sat there, sort of pretty but not half as nice as the crystal vase Chester had given his girlfriend for her birthday.

"There's more to it than beauty, or age, or even rarity," Pline had told him, pointing to a picture in the book on his polished teak desk. "Vessels such as this once held the elements of life for these people— kernels of carefully nurtured corn and precious water. It wasn't just a pot, Chester, it was a necessary item of survival in a harsh, arid land. It's an artifact from an ancient time, a memory of a different way of life."

Pline spoke with an intense energy that didn't quite fit his pale, somber face. His eyes gleamed feverishly. He wasn't all that old, late fifties perhaps, and yet his graying hair and sharp features made him seem older somehow.

But then, Chester Finch tended to think of anyone with as much money as Mr. Pline as being older. It made him feel better about being Pline's employee. Maybe he wasn't rich or particularly smart, but at least he still looked like the virile, vigorous man he was. Too much money and brains could age you.

"It's the history, the story behind a thing, that can make it valuable," Pline continued. "Do you understand?"

Chester blinked owlishly. "Sure."

"Even the pieces of a broken pot were important to them. What came from the earth was reverently returned to it in middens, which were considered sacred ground."

"What's a midden?" Chester asked.

"A refuse pile."

"Holy dumps?" Chester had to laugh. "I've heard of sacred burial grounds, but that's ridiculous."

Pline had smiled then, a chilling smile that meant he hadn't found Chester's joke one bit funny. He also smiled that way when he was about to assign him some particularly odious task. As Pline's smile broadened, Chester's vanished.

"You're being irreverent, Chester. Spitting in the face of the gods, so to speak."

"Sorry, Mr. Pline."

"Don't be. Your attitude will serve us both well," Pline informed him. "Whether you understand the value of Anasazi pottery or not is of no consequence. There are plenty who do, and plenty who will pay. While I appreciate the history behind the artifacts, it's the economics of the matter I'm interested in."

"But you don't have any to sell."

"That," Pline said, "is a situation I intend to rectify very soon, with your help. I have learned of a well-hidden pristine site where we can acquire some excellent specimens."

Chester's eyes popped open at that one. "You want me to go dig around in some old, abandoned Indian village?"

Pline nodded. "Of course, they returned more than pottery to the earth, you know. That's why I respect your bravery, Chester. Some men would be afraid to tread upon sacred ground with the intention of stealing from the dead."

Sitting in a plush Santa Fe gallery, Chester had been quite sure he didn't believe in ghosts. Out here in the dry, isolated canyon country, however, alone with the silence and swirling dust, he was starting to rethink his philosophy.

All day long the sun had beaten down like a living beast, baking him—an accusing, scorching eye in the cobalt-blue sky. Rivulets of sweat poured down his florid, dirt-streaked face. And every now and then, when he'd stopped for a moment to swig some of his precious supply of water, he could have sworn he'd heard someone—or something—calling to him, a hissing, sibilant moan upon the wind.

Now it was almost dark. He looked up at the cliffs, the empty doorways of the dwellings above him like mute, gaping mouths. The wind called again in its snakelike voice. It was a hot, parched wind, but Chester still shivered. He wanted to run, head for the nearest town, and have a stiff drink. Make that several.

Instead he sipped at his canteen, then grabbed his lantern and prepared to climb back into the hole. Pline wasn't paying him to be scared. He was paying him to dig, and there was a lot of work yet to be done.

11

Laura woke as the sun was just peeking over the horizon, feeling better than she had in months. She got out of bed and did ten minutes of gentle stretching, followed by enough sit-ups, push-ups, and leg lifts to raise her heart rate and a good sweat. Then she went to the door and poked her head out.

The RV was quiet. From where she stood she could see that Dusty had managed to make his own bed just fine without her, a point she would have to remind him of should he ask for help that evening. He was snoozing peacefully, sprawled out on his back with a pillow over his head, though the curtains were all drawn and the living room was actually quite dark.

Strange he'd still be in dreamland; since he'd found her at daybreak, she'd taken him for an early riser. Perhaps having her on his lap had so excited him that he hadn't been able to go to sleep right away. She grinned at the thought, surprised by her own wickedness. But she couldn't deny that she'd had a bit of trouble drifting off herself, and for the same reason.

Laura knew it wasn't wise to think of Dusty in such terms. He had praised her abilities and intelligence, appeared genuinely concerned for her safety as well as the success of the project. But he also still seemed to think she might freak out and do something to jeopardize not only his goals but her own too. His threat to stop her if she got out of line was very real, she was sure.

He didn't trust her to keep a cool head; Laura didn't trust him to let her do things her own, admittedly unorthodox way. Mistrust was not a good basis for a relationship of any kind, but especially not an intimate one.

Still, the attraction was there, and it was mutual. What would happen over the course of time was anybody's guess. In spite of her worries, Laura realized she was intrigued by the prospects. Unwise, certainly, perhaps even courting disaster, but those were the facts and there wasn't a damned thing she could do about them.

So she decided to put such thoughts aside and take a quick shower. After stripping off the oversize T-shirt she'd pressed into service as a nightgown, Laura grabbed some clean clothes, wrapped a towel around herself, and checked on Dusty again. Still out like a light. She crept down the corridor to the bathroom and shut the door behind her. The lock was a dinky thing, scarcely more than a psychological barrier, really, but she shot the little brass bolt anyway.

The hot water felt heavenly. If she hadn't been mindful of Dusty, Laura might have broken into song. Instead she hummed. For some reason the national anthem came to mind. Forty-eight hours ago she'd been dreading the coming of July, thinking only of how another month had passed without an idea for an image-mending project; now she had one and was actually looking forward to the future again.

With any luck, she'd be firmly settled into her research by the Fourth of July. The light at the end of the tunnel at long last, freedom from her brutalized reputation. How appropriate! Independence Day!

Laura stepped out of the shower and toweled off, taking special care with her feet. Hiking boots were notorious for causing problems, and she wanted to make sure she didn't have any raw patches where a blister could form. Gingerly, so as not to lose her balance, she put one foot up on the sink for a closer inspection.

There was a thump behind her. Then a hoarse, drowsy voice. "Shit! Damned door!"

"I'm—"

"Oof!"

The door flew open. Its tiny brass lock hit the floor with a *clink!* and Dusty stepped into the doorway, looking down at it and blinking sleepily. Then he saw a foot. Just one. And it was pink, pretty, and most definitely female.

In the instant it took him to realize there was a naked woman in his bathroom, standing on one foot with her back to him, Dusty's eyes went from almost closed to wide open. In another instant his gaze had traveled from her calf, up the back of an extremely well-formed thigh to one of the loveliest sights he'd ever awakened to.

"My God!" he exclaimed without thinking. Then he looked at her startled reflection in the mirror over the sink and added, "Oops! Sorry. I thought the door was stuck."

Laura was covering herself hurriedly with a towel. "Do you mind?" she asked, glaring at him over her shoulder.

"Excuse me. Terribly sorry," he muttered, backing out and closing the door as he went.

She heard him whistle softly in the corridor. For a moment she was mad, absolutely outraged. But after she had calmed down, finished checking her feet, and combed the tangles out of her hair, Laura's curiosity got the better of her. There was a full-length mirror on the back of the bathroom door. She stood in front of it for a moment, feeling silly, then abruptly turned around and studied her own backside.

Her buttocks were not a part of her anatomy she paid all that much attention to. In fact, as long as her jeans and dresses didn't suddenly get too tight, she never gave her rear end a second thought. But now she took a good look.

What could one say about one's own ass? It was nice, she supposed. Smooth and firm. She flexed her muscles. Yup. She had some. But she honestly couldn't see what all the uproar was about. Construction workers occasionally whistled; Carl had said it was every man's dream; and so far, Dusty's comments were all positive in the extreme.

Personally she thought it was a little too big. But who was she to question the opinion of an aficionado like Dusty? Laura smiled, gave herself a pat on the fanny, and went to put on her makeup.

Dusty's morning routine proved similar to her own. After he'd gone to the bathroom—ostensibly the reason he'd been in such a hurry earlier—he put on a pair of gym shorts, stretched out, and did some basic calisthenics. Whether it was his norm or for her benefit, he didn't wear a shirt. Laura pretended not to notice, even decided to cook breakfast this morning so he wouldn't think she was watching him.

But she was. Intently. As her first visual impression had foretold and subsequent physical experience verified, he was strongly built, with broad shoulders, well-defined chest muscles, and a hard, flat stomach. Like most men his age, which she put at or near forty, there was a trace of excess flesh over his hipbones. But not enough to mar his trim physique at all. His legs, covered with curly, light brown hair, looked quite powerful.

And when he turned his back to her, she discovered a pair of buns *she* could appreciate. She could also sympathize with his objections to baggy pants. The gym shorts, though fairly tight, didn't cling nearly close enough to suit her. But her imagination took over and gave his buttocks the masculine musculature she wished she could see.

Imagination had to suffice in another area too. But the indications were impressive.

All this she caught in covert bits and pieces from the kitchen, where she was whipping up a light breakfast of fruit, English muffins, and strong tea. Dusty nodded his approval of the prehike fare on his way to the bathroom.

He emerged showered, shaved, and smiling. "Sorry about barging in on you," he said as he slid into his seat at the table. "I'm not worth a damn until I've stretched out and had my shower."

"No harm done. It'll take a while for both of us to get used to sharing a bathroom, I guess. Tea?"

"Please."

Laura poured him some and sipped at her own while she nibbled on a muffin. "Sleep well?" she asked casually.

"Pretty good," he replied. "Once I got into bed."

"Oh? Something keep you *up?*"

How she'd managed to say that with such a totally innocent expression, Dusty would never know. There was, however, a definite spark of mischief in her eyes. So she wanted to play, did she?

"You know perfectly well how *hard* you made it for me to turn in right away."

She arched her eyebrows. "I made it hard?"

"Very. I had to do everything myself."

"Poor dear." Laura reached out and patted his hand. "I'm sorry if having me around is causing you to suffer unusual pressures."

"You were supposed to help me relieve them."

This game was getting out of hand. "I beg your pardon!" she exclaimed. "I distinctly remember telling you that sex was not in my job description."

"Sex? Who said anything about sex?" Dusty asked. "I was talking about how you left me to do the dishes. And our agreement that you would help me make my bed. That's what kept me up later than I had planned." He shook his head. "Honestly, Laura! Are we going to have to add sex to your list of obsessions?"

"Me? You're the sex maniac! Forcing me to sit on your lap like that. I had to leave before you lost control!"

"Before *I* lost control?" He chuckled. "You're the one who had to run and hide behind a locked door."

"I was not hiding!" she objected. "I was tired. I'll have you know I drifted right off and slept like a log."

"That's funny. You seemed . . . I don't know, agitated when you left me." She was wearing the teal-colored shirt today. Dusty looked pointedly at her cleavage. "Like maybe you wanted to get something off your chest."

Laura got up and cleared the table, then went to put their dishes in the sink. He was aware of how she'd felt last night, all right. And she didn't believe doing chores was what had kept him up either. The question was, what were they going to do about it?

She decided the best course of action was to change the subject. "Should we take a lunch with us?" she asked him from the relative safety of the kitchen.

"I don't think we'll be gone that long," Dusty said. "I'll put some candy bars or something in my pack. Do you have a camera?"

"In my duffel bag. I'll get it."

"I'll fill a couple of canteens. Then we'd better get going. Looks like it's going to be a hot one out there today, and I'd like to be back before noon."

It took them longer than Dusty had expected, to hike to the canyon pinpointed on his rough sketch; another half hour passed as they figured a good way down into it once they arrived. So by the time they were standing on its sandy floor, the sun was already high in the sky.

They paused to mop their brows and sip some water, then trudged on. Using an unusual rock formation on the canyon rim as a reference point, Dusty guided them toward their destination, picking out a solid trail while Laura followed close behind. The pinkish sand underfoot was pretty but treacherous; quicksand was not unknown in this area.

Compared with the desertlike environment of the mesa, which was some four hundred feet above them now, the canyon's vegetation was quite lush, with piñon pine, juniper, and many oddly gnarled live scrub oak. There was more animal life as well, skittering in the shadows cast by the canyon rim. Laura and Dusty followed that example, staying in the cool shade as much as possible.

The trail took a sharp bend up ahead of them, and Dusty called a halt just before they rounded it. "Now remember," he said quietly, "should we run into anybody—"

Laura held up her hand to cut him off. "I know. Just say hello and move along, without showing undue interest. We're just hikers, right?"

"Right." He smiled. "Actually, we probably won't run into anyone at all. If there were looters fiddling around down here last night, they'll have heard us by now. And since *we* haven't heard anything, they're either gone or in hiding. But if you suddenly get the feeling you're being watched," he added, "don't let on. Might spook 'em."

"You're spooking me." She poked him in the ribs with her finger. "Let's go."

They continued on around the bend, but were suddenly confronted with the end of their search—and the end of the canyon. They stopped dead in their tracks. Halfway up the wall facing them, nestled in a cavelike notch cut into the sandstone, sat what was left of the ancient equivalent of an apartment house.

"Cliff dwellings!" Laura gasped.

"Sure enough. Anasazi. A little the worse for wear, aren't they?"

Most of the walls had tumbled down. Here and there, an almost intact building stood among the rubble, windows and roughly T-shaped doors staring at them like black eyes. But most of what had once been a self-contained city of hewn timber and sandstone block had long since crumbled to dust.

"Vandalism?"

Dusty shook his head. "Time. And neglect."

"But why isn't it being worked?"

"Only so many of us to go around, and only so much money," he told her. "This is a small and relatively insignificant site. There are other, much larger places in better condition with more to tell. But it has been scouted out." He pointed to a ladder that gave access to the notch. "Without even a nod to detail, I might add. Someone's fixed up that ladder, but they didn't have nylon rope in A.D. eleven hundred."

"Looters?" she whispered.

"Or sightseers." Dusty made a slow scan of the

area around them. "Nobody here now though. No place to hide."

Laura took a step nearer to him. "How about one of those apartments?"

He squinted up at the dark windows. For a second he thought he saw a man's hand on one of the ledges. Then he realized what it was and said, "I doubt it. There're birds nesting up there. I don't think they'd be that peaceful if someone was sharing their roost." Dusty turned back to her and saw how close she was standing to him. "Want me to go take a look anyway?"

"No!"

"Don't want to be left alone, huh?"

"Don't be silly."

"Then you must be concerned about me." Dusty moved even closer to her, gazing into her eyes. "I'm touched."

She backed away. "I'd just rather not have to carry you back to the RV after you break your leg," she replied, eyeing the rickety wooden ladder. "Let's spread out and see if we can find anything of interest down here."

"Hmm?"

He'd already found something of great interest. A droplet of perspiration was trickling slowly down her throat. Dusty watched it, mesmerized, as it disappeared into the sweet valley between her breasts.

"What the hell do you think you're doing?"

"You look delicious when you sweat," he murmured.

"Would you cut it out?" She crossed her arms over her breasts, glaring at him. "Jeez-us! Talk about being a sexual obsessive! Are you going to help me look or not, Cantrell?"

"How about a kiss for luck?"

"I'll give you a fat lip if you don't stop diddling around," Laura promised. "Now spread out!"

"Yes'm."

They combed the canyon floor for any sign of recent activity. Laura found many pottery shards. There were also pieces of flaked chert, remnants of arrowheads worked by hand. She photographed it but didn't pick any of it up as a souvenir; even that seemingly innocent activity would be looting. The only thing she saw of any real interest were some footprints. They looked fresh.

"I've got some tracks!" she called out.

"Hell, that's nothing!" Dusty called back. "I've got an excavation!"

Laura joined him on the far side of the canyon floor. He was kneeling beside a patch of sand that looked just like all the rest to her. "Where?"

"Right there."

"I don't see anything."

"Are you telling an archaeologist he doesn't know his ass from a hole in the ground?"

"No, I'm telling him he's pointing at some dirt and saying it's an excavation," she replied. "What makes you think somebody was digging there?"

"The earth is damper here. See?" He squeezed some in his fist and it packed together loosely. When he got up and did the same thing a few feet away, it just trickled through his fingers. "Trust me. I know my holes, and there was a pretty big one right here last night. Deep enough to get down to the moisture beneath. If we'd waited till later in the day, the sun would have baked this top layer dry again and we'd never have found it."

Laura snapped a few pictures, then bent down to take a close-up as well. The place where she had her film developed would probably think she'd lost her mind.

"This isn't the rampant destruction I'd hoped for."

"Excuse me?" Dusty asked suspiciously.

Laura shot him a sidelong glance. "Don't look at me like that. I'm not getting flaky on you. It's just that if we want to show how careless and despicable these characters are, we'll need a bigger mess."

"Well, you can bet they didn't catalogue anything," Dusty said. "Or *he* didn't. I saw some footprints, too, big ones, and recent. Looks to me like this was one man, working alone. Must have been a real bitch of a job. But cheaper than hiring helpers, I guess."

"Could it have been a guy just adding to his own collection, do you think?" Laura asked. "I mean, this doesn't look like the sort of commercial operation we're after. And why be so careful to cover it all back up?"

Dusty nodded. "Odd, isn't it? The places I've seen that have been looted were totally ransacked. Holes all over the place, stuff that didn't interest them thrown everywhere," he said. "The kind of mess you were expecting. That's part of the problem; they usually leave a site so torn up you can't get one damned bit of useful information."

"While this looks like an attempt to return the site to its original condition—minus whatever he took, presumably. But if he got everything, why would he . . ." She trailed off, realizing she had just answered her own question. "He didn't get everything, did he? That's why he was so careful to hide the spot, so no one else would work his claim before he got back to loot it again."

"Good possibility," Dusty agreed.

"How soon do you suppose he'll be back?" she asked, looking around uneasily.

"Relax. I imagine it'll be a while, unless he's very greedy. If this is the same guy Flemming pointed out to you, he's worked this spot for two days in a row, long enough to risk getting caught." Dusty looked thoughtful. "We're dealing with an amateur here, I believe. The big commercial operations work with virtual impunity because they know they'll get away with it nine times out of ten. And even that tenth time all they'll get is their hands slapped; selling one intact artifact would cover the fine."

Laura put the lens cap back on her camera. "Then let's go find some big boys," she said. "We've agreed we don't want to waste time on amateurs."

"On the contrary, I think we might have stumbled on a prime opportunity here."

"How so?"

"The big boys are doing the most damage, but they're also the slickest operators. They know where and when to dig. We could knock around this area all summer and end up with nothing but photos of the aftermath to show for it," Dusty explained. "This guy may be an amateur, but that doesn't mean he's in it for the joy of ownership. And if he is selling the stuff, it might prove interesting to follow his trail and find out who's doing the buying."

"Are you suggesting we wait for him to come back and then tail him?" she asked, frowning. "That could take weeks!"

"True. However, it might be worth it. It'll be easier to follow an amateur than a well-seasoned pro, and tracking the course of an illegally obtained artifact would be an interesting addition to the project, even if nothing comes from it. Our main thrust is education, remember," Dusty pointed out. "But who can tell? We might luck out and he'll lead us to a big dealer or something. That would really get us some attention."

Her frown faded. "I knew I did the right thing by taking you on as a partner."

"As I recall, I didn't give you a choice," he said. But he was smiling. "I'll accept the compliment, however. It's a heck of a lot better than being called a sex maniac."

"I don't think we should just sit here twiddling our thumbs though," Laura told him. "I propose we go get some of the background documentation out of the way, then come back to wait for him."

Dusty put his arm around her shoulder. "Excellent idea, partner. It's hard to tell when he'll return. Not tonight, certainly, otherwise why bother filling in the hole? But we don't want to miss him either, so we should try to get back as soon as possible."

"Agreed."

She looked at him. His eyes were *so* green! The feel of his body pressing close to hers was doing delicious, indescribable things to her insides. And very disturbing things to her mind. What would it be like to kiss him, she wondered. Or to be beneath him, right here on the hot sand, his big, strong chest against her bare breasts? Laura felt a sweet ache as she thought of the powerful thrust of his buttocks as he took her, filled her again and again.

Dusty was watching another bead of perspiration roll down the gentle arch of her throat. This time he caught it on his fingertip just before it vanished into her cleavage. She inhaled sharply, but didn't say a word.

"Hot, isn't it?" Dusty murmured.

Laura took a step back from him, nodding. "We . . . We'd better be going," she said hesitantly, "before we bake."

"Uh-huh."

He took his arm from around her shoulder and reached for his pack. Laura turned and started walking, suddenly in a great hurry to get out of this quiet, deserted canyon. People had lived there once. Perhaps it was a lingering trace of emotion that had gripped her, the ghost of an ancient passion shared by two lovers who had stood in the same spot hundreds and hundreds of years ago.

Dusty fell in step beside her. "I still have those candy bars if you want one," he said. "Bit on the mush side though."

"No, thank you. You can have both of them."

"Nah. Too sweet." He grinned and brushed a damp tendril of her hair away from her cheek. "I do have a tremendous craving for something though."

"Fine," Laura said, pretending she hadn't caught his meaning. "But you'll have to cook it. I did breakfast."

He shook his head, chuckling, but decided to allow

her evasive tactic. "Okay. We'll have fish," Dusty agreed. "I guess I'll have to wait for the dish I really want. It obviously isn't quite ready for me yet."

After a lunch of halibut topped with hot-pepper cheese and chives that Dusty prepared in the microwave—proving he could do more than defrost or cook pancakes—they discussed where to go, then broke camp. In an RV, that was as simple as rolling up the awning, making sure there was nothing loose on the counters or tables, and then taking off. Like yesterday, it was slow going on the uneven terrain. The relative smoothness of two-lane blacktop was a welcome relief.

They had decided to make a roughly diamond-shaped tour of the major ruins of the Colorado Plateau, starting with the nearest of the Chaco Anasazi. From there they would head west into Arizona and Canyon de Chelly, north across the eastern tip of the Hopi reservation to Betatakin, then on up into Utah through Monument Valley. Mesa Verde National Park in Colorado would be their last stop. Then back south to wait for the return of their amateur looter.

Had they been tourists, with the intention of exploring the ruins in depth, such an ambitious tour would have taken them a week at the very least.

But Laura and Dusty weren't sightseeing. All of these areas had had trouble with looting and vandalism to some extent, usually in the remote sections seldom visited by law-abiding tourists. For the most part they would be skirting the edges of the ruins, doing more talking than looking, interviewing park rangers and Native American guides for background.

With luck, Laura would also be able to get the more spectacular sort of photos she needed of a recently looted site somewhere along the way.

So, while the RV would make the trip comfortable and convenient, Laura didn't imagine this would be anything even remotely resembling a vacation. They would be pushing hard, trying to gather as much information as they could and then get back as soon as possible. The project had begun in earnest now; the next few days would be filled not with fun but with hard work.

12

Laura groaned. "That's it. My brain is full," she said, leaning her head against the passenger side window. "Background research always drives me insane!"

"I'm not allowed to agree with you. Not about ruins," Dusty informed her. "They'd pull my archaeologist's license."

"They give you a license to dig?"

"I was speaking figuratively," he replied. "I'm supposed to be enthralled by every mound of dirt. A pile of ancient cooking utensils should send me into a paroxysm of rapture. But you want to know the truth?"

"Do tell."

He leaned over in the driver's seat and whispered, "I've seen these so many times that I'm bored out of my gourd." Then he pointed toward the distant horizon, barely visible in the darkness. "Still, we must press on. Betatakin awaits!"

"But it's dark," Laura complained. "I'm hungry, and my head is swimming with all the tales of theft and destruction I've heard in the past eight hours. Can't we press on in the morning?"

"We'll make better time at night without the tourists to dodge. And we'll be right there in the morning instead."

"Who cares?"

"But we agreed we should hurry."

She sat up straight and poked him in the arm. "Don't mess with a crazy woman, Dusty. Feed me and put me to bed, or so help me—"

Dusty applied the brakes so fast they were both pressed against their seat belts. He pulled over to the side of the road and looked at her, his eyebrows bobbing up and down.

"Put you to bed? Why didn't you say so?" When the road ahead and behind was clear, Dusty made a U-turn and headed back toward Canyon de Chelly. "There's a nice campground at the head of the canyon."

"I said *put* me to bed, not *take* me to bed," she told him. "And what I meant was I'm so beat I may fall asleep with my clothes on."

"I'd be more than happy to undress you too."

Laura sighed. "Just get us parked for the night, Romeo."

"Yes'm."

It was indeed a lovely campground. All the scenery they had viewed today had been absolutely breathtaking. There had just been so much of it in so short a period of time that Laura had reached her saturation point.

But she was overjoyed with one aspect of returning to this spectacular canyon. The campground had hookups, which meant she could use all the water she wanted for a shower.

They flipped a coin to determine who would cook dinner. Dusty lost. Muttering something about assessing her a penalty for delay of game, he went to the kitchen and started banging pots and pans. Laura headed for the bathroom. Her skin wouldn't like her for taking two showers in one day, so she decided on a nice, hot bath with plenty of baby oil, and proceeded to soak off what felt like several layers of ancient soil.

It had been an interesting day. Depressing too. A ranger at the Chaco Canyon ruins gave her some photographs he had taken of a looted site; a Navajo guide at Canyon de Chelly showed her some others of an area that had been vandalized; and both men had told her of the frustration they felt. There wasn't enough manpower to police even the parking lots, let alone every square mile of either park.

One thing had intrigued her more than any other, however. Carl Flemming had said the looting had recently gotten worse, and everyone she talked to today agreed.

Obviously the demand for ancient pottery and other artifacts—especially those of the Anasazi—had increased. But why? It was such an underground, black-market trade that finding out would be difficult. Perhaps the collectors smelled trouble in the wind in the form of recent efforts to stop the thievery.

Though largely ineffective—a batting average Laura hoped to change soon—those efforts might have brought about a grab-all-you-can philosophy and this sudden flurry of activity.

Whatever the cause, Laura wanted to get to the bottom of it. Tomorrow she would have to ask more specific questions. But for now, all she wanted to do was wolf down some of Dusty's excellent cooking and go to bed.

As she was climbing out of the bath, he knocked on the door and said, "Do you require mouth-to-mouth resuscitation?"

"No, thank you. Be out in a sec." Laura covered herself with a towel. As little good as the lock had been while on the door, it was even less effective sitting on the back of the toilet. "What's for dinner?"

"Split-pea soup and ham sandwiches."

"Gangway!"

She opened the door and brushed past him on her way to the bedroom. Dusty eyed her towel-draped form. "Glad you approve. Um, there's no reason to dress for dinner on my account."

"Go stir your soup," she told him, closing the bedroom door on his hopeful gaze.

"I'd like to stir *your* soup," he muttered.

Much to Dusty's surprise—and hearty approval—Laura came to the table dressed in a white blouse he had yet to see on her and the khaki shorts he liked so much. Her skin was pink and fresh after her bath. The blouse was fairly sheer; he could see the lacy white outline of her bra through its button-front.

"I love buttons," he said.

"Dusty . . ."

"Zippers are nice too."

Laura wagged a finger at him. "Look but don't touch."

"You little tease!"

"I beg your pardon!" she cried. "I didn't dress like this for your benefit." In fact, she supposed she had. Now that she had seen the effect it was having on him, though, Laura was pretty sure she'd made an error. "I was just hot after my bath."

Dusty put her soup in front of her, bending close to smell the herbal fragrance of her freshly washed hair. "You're hot all right," he said, the back of his hand caressing her arm.

"Calm down! Do you want me to go change?"

He straightened and sat down with his own bowl of soup. "No, no. I'll behave myself. Promise."

"Good."

"At least until we've finished eating."

In spite of what had sounded like an ominous warning, Laura didn't waste any time finishing her soup and sandwich. It was a nice, light meal, perfect for this time of night. The long day they had put in was starting to make itself felt upon her eyelids; she yawned and stretched her arms above her head.

"That was great, Dusty," she said. "But I almost fell asleep in my soup. Time for—"

"Dishes," he interrupted. "It's time for you to do the dishes. And then you get to help me make up my bed."

"Oh, for the . . . I'll wash the dishes. But you did just fine on your own with the bed last night."

"Be that as it may, you agreed to help me, partner. And help me you shall. It's easy," he said. "All you do is fold it out and straighten up the covers. And make sure the sheets are tucked in. I like 'em nice and tight at the bottom so my toesies don't fall out."

Laura sighed. "Oh, please! Take care of your own toesies!"

"You'd rather I take my bedroom back?" Dusty asked.

"All right! But first the dishes."

"Fine. I'm going to wash off some of this grit."

He got up and went down the hall, whistling. Laura ran some water in the sink, added soap, then put their plates and bowls in. She filled the pot with hot water and left it to soak while she washed the rest. Just as she put her hands into the sudsy water, however, Dusty let out a yell.

"Holy shit!"

She heard a heavy thud, than a groan of anguish. Her eyes went wide. "Christ! I forgot about the baby oil!"

Laura found him sitting on the edge of the tub, a towel wrapped around his waist. He was rubbing his forehead and cursing a blue streak. When he saw her, Dusty bellowed, "You left slime in my bathtub!"

"It's baby oil . . . my skin was dry . . . I . . . ." Her words tumbled over themselves in her concern. She bent to look at his head. "I'm so sorry! Are you hurt?"

"I don't know," he replied irritably. "I had one foot in and was cleaning your hair out of the drain." He paused to glare at her. "Slipped and hit my head on the faucet. Good thing I didn't jump right in. I might've broken my back!"

Laura had her hands to her mouth. "Don't say

that!" she exclaimed miserably. "God! Are you sure you're okay?"

"Peachy. Get me a couple of aspirin, will you?"

She got them from the medicine cabinet, along with a paper cup full of water. He took the painkiller, then stood up and looked at himself in the mirror. There was a bump just above his right eyebrow about the size of a quarter.

"Keen," he muttered. "Put one on the other side to match and I'd look like *Australopithecus.*"

"It's not *that* bad!"

Dusty turned from the mirror. He was smiling a bit now. "No, it's not. I'm fine. Sorry I yelled at you."

Laura shook her head. "No, you had the right," she said. "That was a stupid thing to do. I could've killed you! I'm so sorry and—"

He cut her off by putting a finger to her lips. "And you'll never do it again, right?" She nodded. "That's all I want to know. Put up a sign or something."

"Slippery when wet." Laura chuckled. "Okay."

"Now, unless you want to join me in the tub . . ."

She was out the door like a shot, followed closely by Dusty's laughter. He'd really given her quite a scare with the fall, so she went to the refrigerator and took out the remainder of the wine from last night. While she finished the dishes, she sipped it straight from the bottle. Her nerves were pretty calm by the time she was done.

But she still had a guilty conscience. So she decided to do penance by making Dusty's bed. As he had said, it was an easy task, once she figured out the mechanism. She fluffed the pillows and smoothed out the covers, then bent to tuck the bottom of the sheets in nice and tight.

"There. That should keep his toesies safe."

Dusty came up behind her. "Thanks! But you missed a spot," he told her.

"Where?" she asked without turning around.

"Right there," Dusty replied. He pointed over her shoulder to the covers on the far side of the bed.

Laura leaned over to tuck them in. Dusty reached across her back to help. Then he slipped—or pretended to. One way or the other, the result was the same: Laura went facedown on the bed and Dusty came down on top of her. When she tried to roll out from under him, she reached a hand back to push him off at the same time—and felt nothing but smooth, bare skin.

"You're naked!"

"This would be a lot more fun if you were too," he whispered in her ear.

"Try and do a guy a favor," she muttered. "Get off me, you social misfit! This is *not* comfortable."

Dusty nibbled on her earlobe. "Then just move your left leg a little . . ." He wiggled his hips. "Mmm. Much better, don't you think?"

Laura clutched at the blanket as his manhood slipped between her bare thighs. "Oh! What are you doing?"

"What's the matter? Never heard of safe sex?"

"That's disgusting!" She reached behind her and grabbed a handful of his hair. "Get off!"

"Ouch! Easy on the hair. If you want to grab something, grab that." Dusty pried loose her fingers, then maneuvered her arm around until her hand was atop his right buttock, keeping it there with his own. "That feels nice. Now, you don't really think I'm disgusting, do you?"

"Yes!"

Laura struggled, but it wasn't any use. Nor was she winning the battle going on inside her. The feel of him between the soft, sensitive skin of her upper thighs was driving her crazy. Dusty moaned, obviously seeking even more sensitive ground.

And heaven help her, she really didn't want him to stop.

"Dusty, please—"

"You feel so good," he murmured. "Go ahead and hate me if you want. But when I saw you there, bending over like that . . . your beautiful legs . . . I couldn't help myself, Laura. Haven't you ever wanted somebody so much you threw caution to the wind?"

No, she hadn't. Her relationships with men had not been the best—mildly interesting on occasion, sometimes little more than convenient carnal rest stops along the road of her busy life and career. Or like Carl Flemming, flings that had seemed like a good idea at the time but were instantly regretted the morning after.

But there was something happening to her right now. She didn't bother trying to define it. Dusty had awakened a need within her, one that fit his description exactly. Uncontrollable.

Laura turned her head so she could see his face and admitted, "You feel good too. But I don't like being held down, Dusty. Please?"

Eyes wide, he rolled to his side. His eyes grew even wider when she unzipped her shorts and took his hand, guiding his fingers past the elastic of her panties. She stiffened at his first touch, then sighed.

Dusty kissed her, softly, but her mouth opened and she met his tongue with her own. She arched her neck back to deepen the kiss, greedy for the taste of him.

He started to pull off her shorts, but she shook her head, urgently returning his hand to its former position. Then her fingers sought out his throbbing manhood. Dusty gasped.

"Just this for now," she murmured against his lips. "I want you. But I'm not that . . . comfortable with you yet. Do you understand?"

Dusty nodded, smiling at her. "Of course."

With his chest against her back, they lay on their sides and pressed tightly together, pleasuring each other. It was powerfully erotic, yet somehow innocent. What had happened to those younger days? What law had been passed during the sexual revolution that dictated a person should go straight to intercourse without stopping to discover sexuality along the way? All Laura knew was that she enjoyed this simple, mutual act more than she had believed possible.

Dusty seemed to read her thoughts, his green eyes agleam with discovery. She unbuttoned her blouse, teasing him, but refusing to let him unhook her bra. "Later," she promised, turning to face him.

"How *much* later?"

"I'm not worth the time?"

Kissing her on the forehead, he replied, "Of course you are. Take as long as you want." Then he plunged his tongue into her willing mouth.

To make up for any disappointment, she held him tightly between her legs and increased the tempo of her stroking thumb, enjoying his groan of approval. In turn, Dusty's light, deft touch became more insistent, urging her on toward release.

She climaxed fast and hard, shaking in his arms, smothering her moaning cries against his chest. Then it was Dusty's turn. She moved against him, rubbing her thighs together and concentrating her stimulation on his most sensitive spot while flicking his nipples with her tongue.

He came with a ferocity that surprised her, burying his face between her breasts. For a moment they collapsed beside each other, panting. Then Laura rolled off the bed and stood up.

"That was nice," she told him, bending to give him a quick kiss. "Thank you."

"Thank you?" Dusty chuckled. "I knew you were a puzzle the moment I first laid eyes on you, Laura. You haven't disappointed me." He sat up and pulled her closer, running his tongue along the gentle swell of her belly, making her shiver with delight. Then he looked up into her eyes. "Thank *you*. I can hardly wait to see what you'll do next," he said, slipping one fingertip beneath the lacy edge of her bra. "And to see more of you."

"You will." Grinning, she pulled away from him. "In time. Good night, Dusty."

His mouth dropped open. "You're going to bed?"

"I am. And so are you."

"That's more like it!"

"In separate beds," she informed him.

"But—"

"If I'm not comfortable enough with you to make love yet, I'm sure not ready to sleep next to you." She turned and headed for the back of the RV. "Sweet dreams."

Dusty felt one hell of a lot more relaxed than he had last night, but it was still going to be quite a while before he could fall asleep. He turned out the lights, then leaned back against his pillows and lay there, thinking.

Laura Newton was without a doubt the most unusual woman he'd ever dealt with. One minute a come-on, the next a physical threat. Some sensational foreplay, then an abrupt departure. All with the promise of more to come, but without the sort of first-date, second-date timetable he had grown accustomed to in his admittedly sparse experience.

He'd met some pretty exotic women, a side benefit of an occupation that had taken him around the globe. But an awful lot of the places he had visited were very much off the beaten path, and almost all of them took a dim view of an American running around trying to score off the local talent. So he had also spent a lot of time alone, without the opportunity to polish up on the social graces. Somehow, though, he didn't think any man had enough experience to deal with Laura. She was one of a kind.

Ready for his touch, but only on her own terms. Ready to share pleasure with him, but not a bed. For a woman who had gotten into so much hot water for advancing avant-garde ideas, Laura certainly was going back in time with her approach to human sexuality. Dusty felt rather like a teenager, wondering how far his girlfriend would let him go next time.

It was such an old-fashioned feeling, he had to laugh. But it was a *good* feeling too. Very exciting. He hadn't looked forward to being with a woman this much in a long time. Then again, what did he expect from a brilliant student of mankind?

"This is weird!" he exclaimed softly to himself. "But I like it!"

13

The Pline Gallery was so ritzy it even had a patio, where all the fat-cat clientele could sit beneath fringed turquoise umbrellas, nibbling on little squares of toast topped with caviar and sipping French champagne.

Chester Finch preferred cheese crackers and beer. But if an expensive snack was what it took to convince some rich jerk to drop a few grand into Pline's lap, thus assuring Chester's salary, he was all for it. Another round of fish eggs and bubbly for the man with the bulging wallet.

At this hour of the morning, however, the patio was empty. Afternoons were best for sales appointments; this was the time of day Pline reserved for gloating over recent acquisitions. And he was gloating plenty over the stuff Chester had brought him. While he sat there peering at the pots and chuckling,

Chester leaned back in his padded redwood chair and enjoyed the pleasantly scented Santa Fe breeze.

"Marvelous," Pline said. "Simply wonderful." He glanced at his employee and smiled. "You did very well, Chester. Very well indeed. Any problems?"

"Nah. Hotter'n blue blazes during the day and damned cold at night. And all that freakin' digging." Chester stretched, easing his tight back muscles. "A weaker man would've died, I'm tellin' ya. But I ain't weak."

Pline's eyes narrowed. "I wasn't inquiring as to the rigors of the task, you moron. I mean did you see anyone, or more importantly, did anyone see you?"

"No, sir. Nobody came snooping. I kept it quiet during the day and at night only used the lantern an hour at a time when I had to."

"Good. And you covered everything up like I told you?"

Chester nodded solemnly. "Yeah. She's all buttoned up. Seems like a waste of energy though."

"It's not. When I first heard about the site from our friend Flemming, he was in charge of that dig and we didn't have anything to worry about. But the damn fool got greedy and sold some things to another, less discreet dealer. It got back to his funding institution somehow and they sent a team to replace him. So now we must take every precaution."

"Poor old Carl."

"Compassion, Chester? From you?" Pline uttered a short, curt laugh. "It's his fault you had to fill in that hole, remember. How sympathetic are you going to feel when you're digging it back out again?"

"Still . . . It's kinda creepy, you know?"

Pline sighed. "Creepy? The man was hit by a car, Chester. It happens every day. Mexico is not the safest place in the world for pedestrians."

"I know. But with him carrying those trinkets he took from his dig? And he's not the only one who's been hurt either." Chester waved a hand at the pottery on the table. "Maybe the papers are right; this stuff is cursed or something."

"Garbage!" Pline shouted. "Artifacts are a commodity. If a person trips on a Navajo rug and breaks his neck, it simply means that person was clumsy, not that the rug is evil. These pots were no more cursed by an ancient Anasazi medicine man than my loafers were cursed by Gucci! It's a story cooked up by some harebrained reporter to sell papers, Chester."

Chester looked away from Pline's florid face. "Yeah. Sure." Pline hadn't been in that canyon at midnight, listening to the wind calling his name. "Whatever you say, Mr. Pline."

"Look at me when I'm talking to you!" Pline ordered. Chester did so. "Don't go getting superstitious on me now, you idiot. The samples you brought me are superb, thus proving it's worth the risk to cut out our usual middlemen. Now I want you to go back and clean out that site."

"All right! Jeez!" Sometimes Chester wanted to bust his employer a good one, right in the pompous kisser. He clenched his ham-sized fist beneath the table and tried to calm down. "I figured I'd take a week off and—"

Pline held up his hand. "You'll leave tomorrow morning."

"But I was hoping to go to Phoenix!"

"Save your energy for digging, Chester. Your girlfriend will appreciate you all the more when you show her the bonus."

"Bonus?" Chester asked, a greedy gleam in his eyes.

"I want you to leave tomorrow morning and be back by nightfall the following day. Do that and I'll double your usual rate."

Chester would be the first to admit he wasn't a genius, but he sure knew avarice when he saw it. Mr. Pline wouldn't offer that kind of moola unless he was going to make one hell of a profit off this booty.

"Boy, oh, boy," Chester said, shaking his head uncertainly. "I'll have to haul ass down and back. Dig for twenty-four hours straight in between. Money's nice, but it ain't worth my health, Mr. Pline. And if I'm working that fast, I won't be able to tippytoe around like last time either. More chance of getting caught in the act."

"Bullshit! I know you, Chester. You *like* physical labor. And you'll watch your backside, all right. Besides, this time around you can tear the damned place apart and leave it that way." Pline glared at him for a moment. Then he smiled. "Tell you what. Double time, *plus* an extra two hundred for every reasonably intact artifact you bring back. That should make you forget this superstitious nonsense as well as satisfy your rapacious soul. And I'll have some assurance that you won't get in so much of a hurry you'll break things. Deal?"

"Deal!" Chester held out his hand. Pline just looked at it disdainfully, so he dropped it back onto the table. "Mind my asking why you're in such a hurry all of a sudden?"

Pline shrugged. "A combination of factors. I have an important client coming the day after tomorrow and need something special. Then there's the new team at Flemming's dig. I don't want to lose our cache to some underpaid, overly righteous scientist. It also takes time to forge certificates of legal ownership and authenticity; we're coming into the prime season for sales and I want a good inventory. But ironically enough, it's that story making the rounds about looted artifacts bearing an Indian curse that necessitates this haste."

"I thought you said it was garbage," Chester reminded him uneasily.

"It is. And old garbage at that. Flemming's accident just brought it to the surface." He steepled his fingers and touched them to his lips, gazing thoughtfully at the specimens of ancient pottery in front of him. They were already sold, sight unseen. "But gossip fans the flames of commerce, Chester, and a good businessman must strike while the iron is hot."

14

Laura was even livelier than she had been yesterday. Dusty understood; he was feeling pretty bouncy himself. She did not, however, seem inclined to talk about what had happened last night. Though he certainly didn't understand *that* effect of their delightful encounter, Dusty went along with her unspoken request not to discuss it.

They had gotten up at dawn again, this time without any bathroom surprises. After a quick meal, they got right back out on the road. Betatakin was beautiful in the morning light. But in Dusty's opinion its rugged, desolate beauty didn't hold a candle to Laura's. The way her brown curls moved gently in the breeze, highlighted with golden sunlight; her eyes, doelike but so serious, as she listened to the Native American guide they talked to; the easy, sensual grace of her walk. It was a real test of his control not to carry her off to a corner of the practically deserted ruins and make love to her.

But Dusty was content to watch her, be close to her, and let her set the pace of their relationship. What she was doing, he realized, was showing him that she wanted a definite separation between work and play. Today, they were partners, serious scientists conducting research. Tonight, if all went well, they would again experiment with their new-found role of increasingly serious lovers.

Unfortunately all did not go well.

They first heard the news of the far-fetched rumor at Betatakin. Then they stopped down the road in Kayenta to buy a paper and found it splashed all over the front page. Evidently, people who had recently come into contact with looted artifacts were getting hurt. The police were calling this sudden rash of unexplained accidents bad luck. Indians long angered by the desecration of their ancestral burial grounds were calling it just deserts. Predictably enough, the press was calling it a curse.

But when Laura finished reading the article and called it the angle she'd been looking for, all hell broke loose.

"Ridiculous!" Dusty cried. "We both know Flemming is an asshole. He was just in a hurry to sell his swag before he got caught with it, and stepped in front of a taxi. But a curse? That's a load of horse manure, Laura!"

Laura was sitting there, drinking iced tea and trying to stay calm. The RV's air conditioner was humming. So were her nerve endings.

"I'm not defending Carl. A month or two lying helpless in a body cast might do him good. With any luck he'll get a sadistic nurse," she said. It made her feel guilty, but she grinned anyway. "And I am most certainly not giving credence to this . . . this junk in the paper. Personally, I think Carl pissed somebody off and they squashed him. All I said was that he finally did something right. By causing all this fuss, he's given us the key we've needed to unlock the full potential of our project, Dusty. Don't you see?"

"All I see is you, Laura," he replied, "going off the deep end. Again."

"How dare you!"

"I dare because I'm your partner. And as such, I'm telling you it's over." He slammed the newspaper down on the table. "We have to call the project off, but quick. All this superstitious nonsense . . . Jeez-us, Laura! Getting involved in this crapola is just begging for a replay of your ultraviolet debacle!"

"It is not. It'll just require more delicate handling, that's all." She scowled at him. "Besides, partner or not, this is *my* project and it's not over until I say it is!"

"Care to bet on that?"

"Meaning?"

Dusty stood up, stuffing his hands in his pockets and giving the swivel chair a vicious spin with his foot. "Do I have to spell it out for you? If the media can take one fool who gets run over by a car and turn it into a curse just because he happens to have looted Anasazi artifacts, what do you suppose they'd do if they found out the Ultraviolet Wacko is researching that very subject?"

"And just how are they going to find out?"

"May I remind you of why I forced my way into this project?" Dusty was standing in front of her. He bent over and put his hands on the arms of the chair, trapping her in her seat. "I'm the control, the rational part of the team. Maybe you can't see how easily this could become a three-ring circus, but I sure as hell can. And I'm not about to let you turn us both into clowns. It's over, Laura."

Laura just sat there for a moment. With each second that passed her anger grew, until it was a rage as uncontrollable as the passion she had felt last night.

She threw the rest of her iced tea in his face. "You bastard! To think I was actually starting to like you!"

"Dammit!" Dusty straightened, tea dripping off the end of his nose. "I was starting to like you too! But I have no desire to go down in public flames with you! Somebody has to stop you for your own good, Laura."

"Try it!"

"I will! All I have to do is alert the press to Dr. Laura Newton's latest weird adventure, then get out of the way and watch the fur fly."

Laura jumped to her feet and started to slap him. But she remembered what had happened the last time and changed her mind. "Go right ahead, you coward!"

"I am not a coward!"

"No?" she asked. "I've come up with a way to make this project a success, and you're too afraid to even listen to me, aren't you?"

"Absolutely not. The point is that it doesn't matter

what you've come up with. This was a delicate situation to begin with and now it's getting out of hand," he said. "And I am not going to be involved in it."

"That's *my* point. If you want to cut and run, that's fine. But you can't stop me. The only way you're going to prevent me from doing what I have to is to hog-tie me."

"Don't tempt me."

"Damn!" Laura put both hands on his chest and shoved. It didn't move him much. "You would! Probably try and get me from behind while I was tied up too. Right?"

Dusty clenched his teeth, so mad he could barely speak. He grabbed her by the shoulders and gave her a shake. "Don't you dare turn this into a sexual issue!" he roared. "If you want to fight, by all means let's fight, but leave our feelings for each other out of it!"

"Feelings? Ha!"

"All right, dammit!" He put his arms around her and pulled her roughly against his chest. "I enjoyed myself last night," he told her, staring directly into her eyes. "I know you enjoyed it too. All day long I've been watching you, wishing I could at least talk about it. But I didn't! And do you know why? Because it was obvious you wanted to keep it separate from the project. So keep it separate now, Laura. If you want me to listen to you, fight like a scientist and not a petulant schoolgirl!"

He pushed her away and went to get a towel to wipe off his face, needing the distance from her.

Laura stood there, teeth clenched, wanting to scream at him.

Instead, she sat back down and tried to get a grip on her temper. She was fully prepared to go on alone, but she didn't want to. Maybe her feelings for Dusty were tied up in it somehow; Laura was too confused about them to tell. But she did know she needed him more now than ever.

The theory she was working on could take her research in a dangerous direction, not only for the risk of getting caught up in the sensationalism surrounding the curse but because of who she felt might be behind it. Laura smelled a rat—and an opportunity to show her peers, especially Dusty, that she was truly a person to be reckoned with.

Dusty came back into the living room and sat down. "Are you ready to listen to reason yet?" he asked.

"Are you?" Laura returned defiantly.

He shrugged. "For all the good it will do. Whether you can convince me you're onto something or not, the project is probably over anyway," Dusty replied. "You were famous, or rather infamous, a short while ago. Right now the curse is only a local-interest piece. But one of the wire services might pick it up and send a reporter who remembers you."

Laura shook her head. "That's not going to happen."

"And why not?"

"Because they're too stupid to see what's going on, that's why!" she exclaimed. "You read the article; these rumors aren't new. The circumstances of Carl's accident just started them circulating again.

Suddenly everybody who ever came into contact with a pottery shard claims to have been possessed by spirits. Car wrecks, hunting accidents, you name it, whatever misfortune befell them, it was all the fault of Uncle Harold's Indian-art collection. That's not major news, Dusty; it's an anecdote, something they'll tag on after the sports to leave people laughing."

"All right. That makes sense." He crossed his arms over his chest. "So why aren't *you* laughing?"

"Because I'm smarter than they are. I do see what's really going on," Laura informed him. "I'd been wondering why looting was on the rise. Now I think I know. These rumors just hit the papers, but they've been around. And nothing stimulates a collector's imagination like a mystery. Rather than scaring them off, it has actually increased demand for ancient Indian pottery, bringing more looters out of the woodwork to fill that demand."

Dusty groaned. "That theory is as flaky as the rumors themselves!"

"Maybe," she agreed. "I will admit it's one I'll never be able to prove. But I can prove my second hypothesis. I'll bet if we check around, we'll find that all this hoopla is causing prices to skyrocket."

"So?"

"So what if even a fraction of the rumors are true?"

"True? You have gone nuts!"

She glowered at him. "Just hear me out, okay? I'm not talking about the curse; that's obviously a hoax. But what if it's a hoax perpetrated by a group of looters—or more likely, a group of unscrupulous art dealers—to stir up business and drive prices through the roof?"

"Surely you're not suggesting they've been injuring a client here and there to keep rumors of the curse alive?"

"That's exactly what I'm suggesting. If my theory is correct, and if I can prove it, the police will have the legal tools to stop at least this one group. Hopefully, the furor will help the education efforts, and public concern will curtail the rest." Laura paused to smile at him. It was, however, a smug, vindictive smile. "My project will be a success; my nemeses the media will look like dim-witted pawns in the looters' scheme; and you, partner, will have to eat crow for doubting me. How's that grab you?"

Dusty was aware that true genius often manifested itself in bizarre leaps of logic, taking what seemed like two totally unconnected things and finding a link between them. He was also aware that Laura was very bright and had shown just that sort of ability in her paper on ultraviolet light and crime.

But that theoretical work had gotten her laughed at and scorned by her peers. So could this idea.

He took a deep breath, then blew it out slowly, looking at her with a mix of grudging respect and exasperation. "It grabs me as a potential disaster!"

"You think I'm wrong?"

"I'm not going to argue with you about it either way, Laura," Dusty replied. "All I'm going to say is that you could be too damned smart for your own good."

Laura grinned triumphantly. "Then you *do* think I'm on to something, don't you?"

"Don't rush me! I'm the rational one, remember?

If you want me to believe this . . . this theory, you're going to have to prove it to me just like you'll have to prove it to the public. And that's the part that has me worried," he said. "Just how do you propose going about it? Your Dr. Violet alias isn't going to get you past a roving reporter should we come across one."

"I don't think we will, but I don't intend to tempt fate in any case. The first thing we're going to do is stop messing around the ruins—too high profile. I think we should go back right now and wait for our looter."

Dusty shook his head doubtfully. "*If* there's anything going on, he seems too small-time to be involved in it."

"Probably," she agreed. "But he might lead us to a dealer or somebody else who is. If not, we'll still get an opportunity to trace the artifacts' route, and maybe find out if demand and prices are skyrocketing like I think they are. Besides, it's the only trail we have to follow into this mess."

"True."

"So let's go!"

Laura stood up and started toward the kitchen to secure everything for the road. Dusty got to his feet and blocked her path. "Just a second. I'm not saying I buy all this yet, mind you," he told her, "but I do owe you an apology."

"I accept. Now—"

"And you owe me one too," he interrupted.

"I do not!"

This time his touch was gentle as he pulled her into his embrace. "You do. I would never tie you up and take advantage of you, Laura. Never."

"Oh." She looked away. "That. I . . . I am sorry

about that remark. You were right. I was letting my feelings get in the way. It won't happen again."

"Of course it will. You won't be able to help it. Just like I won't be able to play the total professional all the time."

He dipped his head and kissed her, parting her lips with the tip of his tongue. At first Laura resisted, then slowly gave in, their mouths melting together as one. When he finally released her from his tender clutches, her face was flushed and she was having trouble catching her breath.

"I think you'd better get up there and drive," Laura said. "Or we won't make it before dark."

"What a tease you are! I've half a mind to find out exactly what you meant by that."

"Drive," she said sternly, then stepped around him and continued on to the kitchen.

Dusty watched the sensual motion of her hips as she walked and suppressed a groan of frustration. Then he turned and went to the driver's compartment.

This was insane! What had made him agree to forge on beside this alluring but cantankerous female? Had he listened to reason? Or his libido? Whichever, at least he'd be there to stop her if she started to make wacky waves. Right then and there he made a vow to himself. No matter how terrific she looked in shorts, he'd bail out on her and shoot her down if things got too strange.

Maybe. One thing was for sure. If he didn't stop spending so much time looking at *her* ass, he could very well end up without a way to cover his own.

15

They arrived with enough time before nightfall to scout out the canyon. The looter hadn't returned. So they hiked back to the RV to get a bite of dinner. It was dark when they finished; with the darkness came the knowledge they might soon be in each other's arms.

But it was a quiet sort of thing, full of uncertainty, sneaking up on them in gradual, tantalizing steps. Although there would be intimacy of some kind between them—they were too aware of each other to simply say good night—neither of them knew what form it would take. Dusty wondered if they would make love. Laura wondered if she could possibly prevent it. For now, they sat beneath the awning, watching the stars and trying to have a strategy meeting while the tension between them built to fever pitch.

"How long are you planning to wait?" Dusty asked.

Laura cleared her throat. "Excuse me?"

"For the looter. How long?"

"Oh." She was glad it was so dark now he couldn't see her face very well. "As long as it takes, I suppose."

Had she thought he was talking about something else? Lord, he hoped the answer wasn't the same for that too. Dusty wasn't sure himself what he'd do if push came to shove; she could undoubtedly detect that uncertainty whenever he talked about blowing the whistle on her. If Laura was going to wait indefinitely before she allowed him the full pleasure of her delectable body, he'd go crazy.

"That could take quite some time."

"I know," Laura said. "But we don't have much choice. Why? You have somewhere else you want to be?"

"No. I'm exactly where I want to be." Or with any luck at all he soon would be. The thought made him ache. "How about you?"

"Oh, I'm having a wonderful time."

Dusty moved uneasily in the darkness at her elbow. "Are you being sarcastic?"

She smiled. Touchy! Would he be one of those men who were so concerned with their performance that he made the act of love seem like a contest? "Not at all. This is the most important project of my life to date. And I enjoy a challenge. Don't you?"

"Within reason," he replied. "Sometimes the challenge is greater than the reward. That takes the fun out of it."

"Meaning you have to be assured of great success before you even try?"

"Not assured. But reasonably certain that the pot at the end of the rainbow is at least filled with honey."

"Gold," Laura corrected. "Pots at the end of rainbows are reputed to be filled with gold, I believe."

He chuckled throatily. "You go after your reward, I'll go after mine. I happen to like honey pots."

"That has a very sexual connotation."

"Hell, Laura." Dusty moved his chair closer to hers. "So does this whole damned conversation."

"Oh, really? I hadn't noticed," she lied. "But I am curious about this honey-pot thing. I'm aware of its usage and to what it refers, but I'm not sure I understand the correlation. Does it have something to do with sweetness?"

Dusty put his hand on her thigh. "Most definitely."

"So it's . . ." Laura paused, feeling a shiver though the night air was still warm. So was Dusty's hand. The skin of her leg was tingling beneath his touch. Good thing she'd decided to wear her jeans this evening. "So it's an oral term, then?"

"Very. To some men anyway."

His hand was moving up her thigh, closer and closer to her femininity. Now she was *very* glad she'd worn jeans. A twitch would have put his fingertip inside shorts. Her rate of breathing had increased, and her voice was growing hoarse.

Laura had to clear her throat several times before she could ask, "And to you, Dusty? Are you thinking oral thoughts when you talk about honey pots?" She laughed nervously. "Hey! That rhymes!"

"I'll show you exactly what I'm thinking."

Dusty pressed his hand between her thighs. When she put her hand atop his and shuddered, Dusty shuddered with her.

He stood up abruptly. "Let's go inside."

"No."

"No?" Dusty groaned. "Don't do this to me!"

Laura reached up to touch his face. "I meant I don't want to go inside. I . . . I need the darkness. Okay?"

There wasn't much of a moon, and they hadn't bothered with a lantern. The only illumination came from the stars and the pale glow of lights through the curtains covering the RV windows. Dusty could barely see her; she was just a warm, very feminine shape moving near him in the dark.

His eyes widened when he heard the snap of her jeans. Then came the sound of her zipper being pulled down. A softer noise followed, that of denim slipping off smooth legs. Laura sat down in the chair and reached for his hand. Dusty sank to his knees between her bare thighs.

Although her sweatshirt was still on, she hadn't worn a bra. So even if he was denied the sight of her breasts, he could feel them at last. They were full and round, heavy in his hands, with large, sensitive nipples. She moaned as he massaged her, gripping him with her knees. His hands wandered down her ribs to her stomach, then fleetingly brushed her, making her jump. Laura wove her fingers into his hair, feeling a thrill of excitement as he replaced his fingers with his tongue. His head dipped lower.

She inhaled sharply at the first delicate touch of his tongue. "Yes! Oh, yes!"

Dusty nipped lightly at the skin of her inner thighs. "Sweet," he murmured. "Sweeter than honey. Laura, you are the most amazing, beautiful . . ."

Laura didn't wonder why he stopped talking. She knew. His tongue was busy doing the most beautiful, amazing things to her. She slipped down in the chair and pressed herself against him, toes pointed straight out in response to a pleasure almost too intense to bear. Her head rolled from side to side and she gasped for breath.

"Oh! Oh! Stop!"

But Dusty didn't stop, knowing somehow that she didn't really want him to. He kept on, teasing her with the artful motion of his tongue. Laura went wild, the sweet spasms of her orgasm shaking him too. She was so strong!

Afterward, he raised up and wrapped his arms around her waist, savoring her panting and rapid heartbeat. "So help me, Laura," he said softly, "if you say that was nice and go to bed, I'll strangle you."

"You damned near did me in already!" she exclaimed. "And it was nice! So very nice!" Laura kissed him. "Now I'm going to do something very nice for you too."

"Mmm! Now we can go inside. I don't need the dark."

"Maybe not. But I still do."

Laura pushed him down in the chair behind him and stood up, pulling on her panties and jeans while Dusty sat there, going quietly insane with anticipation. Then she got down on her knees.

Again the sound of a zipper broke the intense silence around them. She pulled down his briefs to free his manhood and held him in her hand, chuckling wickedly at the way he thrust his hips forward.

"Impatient?" Laura asked.

"You're an evil woman, Laura Newton."

"When the need arises. And it certainly has!"

As Laura's lips and tongue worked their magic, Dusty moaned, jerking and clutching at her shoulders, letting her know in every way how much he was enjoying himself. Laura loved it; men were usually so afraid of losing control of their emotions that they were quiet and reserved even in sex. This was a real man, one who knew the difference between strength and coldness, who had backbone but was not ramrod stiff.

Or at least not stiff of personality. He was very hard where a man should be, throbbing in her hand, powerful yet deliciously sensitive. Laura enjoyed herself too, just as vocally, her every moan driving him to a climax that made her gasp with surprise. Still, he was ready for more afterward, reaching for her when she stood up.

Laura bent to kiss him, then took his hands from her hips and put them to her face. She shook her head. "Not yet," she said softly.

"You're worth the wait," Dusty told her. "As long as you realize there's a limit to my endurance."

"Not from what I can see."

"Tease!"

"Sex maniac!"

Dusty nodded. "As far as you're concerned, I plead guilty. When?"

"Wouldn't you like to know?" she asked haughtily.

"Desperately. In fact, you might say that question has become the focal point of my existence," Dusty replied. He got to his feet and zipped up his pants. Then he put his arms around her, gliding his hands over the firm, rounded curves of her buttocks. "When?"

"Men of integrity don't ask such things. Besides, I'd rather surprise you." Smiling, Laura kissed him softly, then pulled away from him and started to clear the dishes from the table. "Now, are you going to help me? Or would you like to tuck in your toesies all by yourself tonight?"

"I've got a better idea," Dusty said, running his fingertips down the gentle arch of her spine. "Why don't you offer to keep them warm for me?"

Laura shivered. "It's not your feet I'm worried about. It's your hands. Here." She gave him the dinner plates. "That should keep them busy for a while."

Since Laura had lost the coin toss, she had done the cooking, so Dusty washed the dishes. True to her word, she helped him make his bed—careful to keep him where she could see him this time—then kissed him good night and strolled toward the bedroom. Dusty watched her longingly.

"I guess it's time I admitted something to you," he said. "I gave you the only key, but that door is easy to open without one."

Laura glanced back at him. "I trust you."

"I was afraid you'd say that."

"At least as far as opening doors without an invitation is concerned," she amended. "The rest of my trust isn't as easy to win. Good night, Dusty."

"Sleep well."

She went into the bedroom and closed the door. For Dusty, it represented both a frustrating barrier and a challenge he was determined to meet. "Damn," he muttered as he turned out the lights. "It's hell being a man of integrity."

16

It had been Mr. Pline's idea to paint the four-wheel-drive truck in camouflage colors. Chester thought it was overly cautious, considering that there were plenty of arroyos dotting the area where you could park a truck this size and have trouble finding it again yourself. Since tooling along in it made him feel like a desert rat about to take on Rommel, however, he put up with the strange coloration.

But caution could be overdone. Chester wasn't about to park as far away as he had last time. One knapsack with a few pots hadn't caused him any trouble at all; several of them packed full of artifacts was a different matter entirely, even for a bull of a man such as himself.

So he found a dry wash only a few hundred yards from the canyon and slipped the truck into it. There was a sandstone ridge between him and the dig that poor sap Flemming had been operating. Figuring that

if he couldn't see them, they couldn't see him,
Chester grabbed his gear and took off.

It was eleven thirty on the first of July. The heat
was already a bear and would get worse. Then there
was the thought of facing that eerie, whispering wind
again tonight. But he'd be too busy digging his ass off
to notice heat, cold, or even ghosts. All he was seeing
were dollar signs.

Laura had gone to work on the outline for her
paper immediately after breakfast. Again, she wasn't
talking about last night. Though this frustrating
behavior was getting on Dusty's nerves, he decided to
put up with it for one more day. Tonight, he vowed,
would be the night. Let her try to pretend nothing
happened when she woke up in bed beside him!

For now, though, he was doing his best to be the
perfect research partner, bringing reference books to
her and even making lunch. She ate, then went back
to work. Her capacity for concentration was enor-
mous. Dusty kept busy fixing things around the RV;
a rolling home had as much if not more maintenance
than a stationary one.

But when the afternoon stretched into early evening, he called a halt to his repairs and went to tell
Laura he would not allow her to work all night. He
had other plans.

After the worst heat of the day had passed, Laura
had moved outside under the awning. She was sitting
at the table, hunched over her notebook. Dusty came
up behind her and put his hand on her shoulder.

"How's it going?"

She looked up at him and smiled. "Good. I've got

the background all laid out, and I fleshed out the interviews we conducted. We need more than hearsay on the rest, though, more personal experience."

"I'm sure we'll get it," he said. "If we're not whistling in the wind, that is."

"We're not."

"You're something else, Laura." Dusty pulled out a chair and sat down beside her. The shadows around them were getting longer, signaling the approach of sunset. "How can you be so positive when all you have is a thin theory and a few suppositions?"

"One must have the courage of one's convictions."

"Uh-huh. Especially when that's all one has to go on."

"We'll get more. I wish our friend would hurry back though. I'm all caught up with the paperwork." Laura stood up and stretched. "What'll I do tomorrow?"

With her arms stretched over her head like that, the hem of her T-shirt rode up high on her midriff, displaying a lovely crescent of honey-colored skin. He had to fight the urge to grab her and nibble on her tummy.

"I could think of several things," Dusty replied.

Laura saw the hunger in his gaze and looked down at herself. She immediately dropped her arms. "I'll just bet you can."

"It'll be dark soon."

"Yes."

"And you know what that means."

She nodded, feeling the sensuality in his voice washing over her like the warm breeze blowing across the mesa. Tonight? Tomorrow? Laura knew she couldn't put him off much longer. In fact, she didn't want to.

Still, there were so many question marks between them, especially concerning matters of trust. Would he really go through with his threat to discredit her further if he decided he didn't like the way the project was going? Was it not the worst kind of folly to give in to arousal when the man who was the object of your desire could bring your world crashing down around your ears?

Definitely. She knew she should put her foot down and break off this unwise liaison. Maybe he was just playing along with her until he got what he wanted. Once they made love, perhaps he would decide the risk he was taking by associating with her was no longer worth it.

Except for the added stakes of the project and her bid to clear her name, however, such fears were always present when a man and a woman got together. Some men were only after sex; some women too. Laura couldn't honestly say she expected or even wanted anything more from this relationship herself. All she knew was that she had never needed a man this much before.

Caution had already been thrown to the wind. It was far too late to try to grab it back.

"Gosh!" Laura exclaimed suddenly. "I've been working so hard I hadn't really noticed the time. I suppose I should cook dinner, since you've done double duty in the kitchen today. Thanks."

He shrugged. "No problem. I'm the same way when I get involved with something. I just submerge myself and stay that way for hours. Even days, on occasion."

"Me too," she admitted. "I've been that way all my life."

"Yeah. Probably why we're both still single."

Laura turned her face away, feeling embarrassed for some reason she couldn't fathom. When she glanced at Dusty out of the corner of her eye, she saw that he, too, seemed embarrassed and was gazing at the sunset. She joined him.

It was very still. Overhead, a bird of prey screeched, possibly an exclamation of triumph at having spotted a potential meal somewhere below. Then Laura heard another sound, a faint metallic clank that echoed for an instant and then was gone.

"Did you hear that?" she asked.

"What?"

"Just listen." They were both silent for a moment, but the sound didn't repeat. "I don't hear it anymore."

Dusty stood up. "What was it like?"

"I don't know. Metal bumping on metal, I guess."

"Or a shovel hitting stone?"

Laura looked at him, her eyes growing wide. Dusty spun on his heel and dashed into the RV, emerging a few seconds later with a powerful pair of binoculars. When he had parked the RV upon their return, he had done so in an indentation in the ridge that concealed them not only from the Flemming dig but the canyon as well. Now he stepped out of that indentation and took a look around.

"Could've come from the dig, I suppose. Can't even see it from here though. I don't know if the sound would have carried that far." He swiveled to scan the canyon rim. "Uh-oh," he muttered. "There goes the neighborhood."

"He's here?" Laura jumped up and ran to his side.

Dusty handed her the binoculars. "Tell me what you see on the opposite rim," he said, pointing. "Right there on that rock formation above where we found the ruins."

"Whoa! These things have got quite a range. Still, it's hard to tell . . . Looks to me like a rope dangling down into the canyon."

"That's what I see too. Must've climbed down. Then he'll use the rope to pull up the booty afterward."

She lowered the binoculars. "Pillaging made easy."

"And fast," Dusty said. "I'll bet he's got a truck or something close by this time. Everything it takes to make a quck getaway with all he can grab."

"What should we do?" she asked.

"He'll probably work all night. But I doubt he has a two-day dig in mind this time around. Good thing we know the way so well now. I suggest we eat a hearty meal, then work our way over there under cover of darkness."

"And do what?"

"Find a place to hide and await his departure," Dusty replied. "I don't know. Maybe we'll come across his vehicle and can see if there's anything in it that'll tell us where he's going to take the stuff."

Laura left his side and went back under the awning. Dusty followed. She was frowning, obviously deep in thought, and just as obviously mad at herself.

"Dammit! I didn't even stop to think about how we

were going to do this. What if we can't find his vehicle? What if it doesn't have any clues in it? What if—"

"Hey!" Dusty exclaimed gently. "Calm down. While you've been working, I've been thinking about what we would do when he got here. First, we have to be closer than we are right now; he arrived without us knowing it and he could leave the same way. Second, we have to be ready to follow him the instant he does take off. The terrain is rougher once you leave the mesa, and it'd be easy to lose him in the hills."

She was far from convinced. In fact, she was highly agitated. "That's what I mean! I've seen you do a lot of amazing stuff with that thing," she said, pointing at the RV, "but it's not exactly made for that kind of cross-country travel, now is it? And even if it was, don't you think we'd be a wee bit conspicuous?"

"Yes. But that's no reason to malign my Scheherazade. Like the original, she has a trick or two up her sleeve."

"What? Wings?"

"Dinarzade."

Laura blinked. "Scheherazade's little sister?"

"Very good! Glad to see you didn't spend all your time reading anthropological tomes."

Dusty led her to the back of the RV where a bulky shape beneath a tarp was attached to the rear bumper. He unsnapped an edge of the covering and lifted it so she could see what was beneath.

"A motorcycle!"

"Equipped with a CB. We motor over there as far as we dare, which will be quite a ways: Dinarzade is very quiet. Then we stash her. When our looter leaves, I take off after him while you come back to the RV and wait until I give you a shout on the radio."

"Why can't I go with you?" Laura asked, frowning.

"Because I can move faster alone, that's why. Don't worry. I'll be in constant contact," Dusty assured her. "All you have to do is head for the main road and follow my directions until we can meet up again. If something happens, stay where you are and I'll follow the guy—not too closely, of course—to his destination and then retrace the highway route until I find you." He grinned. "Now, is that a plan, or is that a plan?"

Laura gave him a grudging nod of approval. "Okay. But that doesn't cover what I should do if you break your fool neck on that thing."

"Relax. I grew up in California."

"So?"

"The three B's of a good California education, of course," he replied. "Blondes, beaches, and bikes. I spent my youth on them."

"On the blondes, for the most part, I'll bet."

Dusty put his arm around her shoulder. "Jealous?"

"You wish." She pushed him away. "All right. I'll go along with this scheme. But I still don't like it."

"If you're that worried about me," he said, "maybe we should share a hearty send-off as well as a meal."

There was no mistaking the send-off he had in mind. "We're working again, Dusty," Laura told him sternly.

"I work better with proper motivation."

She gave him a sly little smile. "Then do a good

job, come back in one piece, and maybe we'll share a homecoming. Now, let's eat. We've got a long night ahead of us."

It was long. It was also chilly; their hiding spot was a perfect receptacle for the wind. They had found the looter's truck and in it a box of matches with PLINE GALLERY printed in fancy pink lettering. But there wasn't an address, nor did it necessarily mean that's who he was doing business with. So there they sat, waiting for something to happen.

Laura reached out and punched Dusty on the arm. "So much for doing things your way. I'm bored and I'm cold."

"The sun will be up in a couple of hours."

"Then I'll be bored and hot."

"Jeez-us! Bitch, bitch, bitch. Come over here next to me and I'll keep you busy while we wait."

"You have got to be kidding," she said. "How can you even think about sex at a time like this?"

He grabbed the foot of the sleeping bag she was wrapped up in and dragged her over to him. "Shh! Just help me get these zipped together. Shared body warmth, you see. Just the ticket to take the chill off."

"Well, okay. But no funny stuff," Laura warned.

They wrestled with the bags for a while, trying to be as quiet as possible. They were in a hollow not far from where the looter had parked his truck, fairly well hidden behind some scruffy-looking piñon pines. Still, they had gotten close enough to hear the looter digging for all he was worth down in the bottom of the canyon. He had to wear out soon. Any moment now he might climb back up that rope.

At last they got the bags joined and they nestled together like spoons, his front to her back. The position was not without its memories for Laura.

"Don't try anything, buster. I'm not in the mood."

Dusty nibbled on her neck. "Not even a little?"

"No."

"Suit yourself." He fumbled around at her waist for a moment, managing to work his hands beneath her windbreaker. Then he got under her sweatshirt. "Mmm. That's better."

"Says who? Didn't I tell you . . ." Laura trailed off in a moan as he cupped his hands over her breasts. "Stop that!"

"Object with a bit more conviction and I might."

She couldn't. The light touch of his fingertips on her nipples made her tingle all over. With the tingle came a delicious warmth that spread through her. Laura relaxed against him with a sigh. He held her tight.

"I've spent so much time complimenting your derriere that I've neglected to tell you how absolutely beautiful your breasts are," he murmured, his lips close to her ear. "At least you feel wonderful. I wish I could see you."

"You will."

"Promise?"

"Just shut up and hold me, will you? You're so warm!"

"So are you." He yawned. "We may as well take a nap."

"I'm too wound up to sleep," Laura mumbled.

Dusty closed his eyes. "Me too."

The sun was shining when they woke up. The looter was loading his truck. And Dusty found that the circulation to his arms had been cut off, virtually trapping him inside Laura's sweatshirt. He wiggled around, trying to get some feeling back into his hands.

"What the . . ." Laura mumbled.

Stuck, unable to use his arms yet, Dusty did the only thing he could. He pushed her face around to his with his shoulder and tried to cover her mouth with his own. It wasn't the best idea he'd ever had.

Laura protested. Loudly. "Mmph!"

Luckily, the looter was making too much noise of his own to hear her muffled exclamation. Dusty shook his head urgently, his lips still pressed to hers. Her eyes opened wide with understanding.

He drew back his head. "Shh!" he hissed softly.

She nodded. Then she realized the predicament they were in and glared at him. Mouthing the words, she told him, "Get your hands off me!"

"I'm trying!" Dusty mouthed back.

Finally, silently, they managed to get enough slack in the sleeping bags for Dusty to disentangle himself. Then they both turned over on their stomachs and peered out of their hiding spot at the looter.

He was built like a fireplug, practically a cylinder of muscle from thick neck to big feet, with two beefy protrusions for arms. But as strong as he obviously was, he was quite literally dragging his feet. It must have been a new and irritating experience for him, because he was raging at himself with every faltering step.

"Shit! Come on, dammit! Move your fat ass!"

Filthy, bleary-eyed, and, from all signs, close to total exhaustion, the man went back and forth from the canyon rim to the truck, loading his booty. When he finally had it all securely stashed, Dusty and Laura thought, for sure, he would fall on his face. In fact, he did stand there for a full minute, gazing at the truck and teetering uncertainly.

Then he climbed laboriously behind the wheel and started the engine. It seemed to take him several tries before he remembered how to shift gears. But at last the truck jumped forward with a growl and a jerk, and he was under way. For a horrible moment Laura thought he might lose control and crash into their hiding spot. But the side of the truck just brushed the trees and rolled by, gaining speed on the sandy, uneven ground. In a few seconds he was out of the arroyo and speeding away.

Dusty started to jump up, forgetting that he was still in a sleeping bag—and that Laura was in it with him. He made it only halfway to his feet before her weight pulled him back down. He landed on his side and started rolling, Laura naturally coming along for the ride. They rolled out from behind the trees, flopping over each other as they went, to land in a heap in the middle of the arroyo.

"The zipper!" Dusty cried. "Get the zipper!"

"You're lying on it!"

They flopped over again, struggling for all they were worth. Laura still couldn't reach the zipper, so she tried to climb out of the bag. Unfortunately,

Dusty was trying to do the same thing. As she lifted her knee to get a foothold she hit him squarely between the legs.

"Oof! Oh, God!"

He pitched forward on his face. Laura scrambled over his back and at last extricated herself from the sleeping bag. But Dusty just lay there, groaning.

"Stop fooling around!" she yelled, pulling on his arms. "You're letting him get away!"

"I . . . can't . . . breathe!"

"Shit!" Laura pulled him to his knees, then made him sit on his heels and forced his head down, pushing on his back to force air into his lungs. "Come on, damn you! Honestly! How did we ever survive as a species when you guys have such vulnerable parts just hanging there?"

Much to Laura's relief, Dusty was one of those who recovered quickly. He pushed her away and got to his feet, glaring at her.

"Thanks ever so much, Laura. That's one of my favorite ways to wake up in the morning."

"Move!"

Dusty flipped her off, then turned and ran up the sandy embankment of the dry wash to where he'd stashed the motorcycle. Laura listened expectantly for the quiet *putt-putt* of its engine. Nothing. She dashed up the bank after him.

"Well?" she demanded.

"Won't start," Dusty replied. He jammed his foot down on the kick starter. The engine gave a coughing gasp, but that was all. "Damn! Come here and push."

Laura did as he asked, getting behind him and pushing as fast as she could. He steered for the embankment and went over the edge, letting out the clutch as he did so. For a moment the engine caught, then quickly died. Dusty hopped off and pushed the cycle himself for a shot distance, with the same results. Then he let it fall over and gave it a kick.

"Bitch!"

Standing at the top of the embankment, Laura looked down at him, hands on her hips. "This is great. Come on, Mr. California Biker. Do something!"

"What would you have me do?" he yelled back. "I think the plug's fouled. By the time I pull it, clean it, and put it back in, the guy'll be long gone." He stomped to the mouth of the arroyo and looked around. "Hell, he's already disappeared into the hills. Can't even see his dust. We lost him."

"We?" She scrambled down the bank and joined him at the end of the wash, cursing all the way. "*You* lost him! You and your bright ideas. Dinarzade, my ass!"

Dusty turned to her. "Oh, yeah? If you hadn't kicked me in the balls I might've been able to fix it in time."

"It was an accident! And it wouldn't have happened if you hadn't been feeling me up!"

"You sure didn't object last night," he pointed out.

Laura crossed her arms over her breasts and looked away. "I fell asleep."

"So did I." He sighed heavily. "It was nice too."

"Yes," she admitted, glancing at him. "It was."

They glared at one another for a moment, then slowly started to smile. Dusty stepped over to her and kissed her lightly on the forehead.

"Sorry," he said.

"Me too. What are we going to do now?"

"We still have this," Dusty replied, pulling from his jacket pocket the box of matches they'd found in the looter's truck. "No address, but we should be able to dig one up easily enough."

Laura looked doubtful. "He could've gotten those anywhere, Dusty. Somebody might have given them to him."

"True. But it's all we've got to go on." He put his arm around her and started walking back to their hiding spot. "So we'll just have to hope for the best. Let's grab your camera and take some shots of the damage he undoubtedly did, then fix our ride and get the show on the road."

"Brother!" Laura muttered. "It's a good thing we don't follow people for a living, huh? We'd starve to death. Are you sure you're okay?"

"Nothing a little ice won't fix. Care to apply it for me when we get back to the RV?"

She grinned. "I don't think that'll be necessary. I have the feeling you're going to be just fine."

17

Santa Fe was beautiful. There was an intense, ethereal quality to the sunlight that dazzled the eye and a unique blend of fragrant vegetation that delighted the nose. Sitting high on a plateau overlooking the vast southwestern desert, with mountains close behind and in the distance on every horizon as well, it was little wonder the town attracted artists of every description.

And where there were artists, there were art galleries. Hundreds of them. But Laura and Dusty were interested only in one. The Pline Gallery was an excellent example of what modern craftsmen could do with up-to-date building practices and ancient ideas. Laura imagined there was a code of some kind that required such distinctively New Mexican architecture in this part of town, but still it was a nice touch.

Aided by a listing of galleries Dusty unearthed in

his bedroom, they had discovered that Santa Fe was their destination and had headed there posthaste, arriving in the late afternoon. After settling in at an RV park they had walked to the gallery, formulating their plans along the way.

Having learned from their earlier botched attempt at playing private eye, they had decided to approach this situation in a fairly straightforward manner. They would go into the gallery and pretend to browse, with the intention of looking for any sign of suspicious behavior.

Since the sort of artifacts they were looking for were of the under-the-counter variety, it was doubtful they would see any. Nor were they likely to see the looter. It wasn't any wonder he'd looked dead on his feet; he had done a lot of damage at the canyon, even dismantling the remaining walls of the dwellings. Such vigorous destruction would undoubtedly call for a long nap. If he'd even made it this far. And if this was where he sold his goods in the first place.

But it was the only lead they had, and neither of them was willing to admit to the possibility that this could be a wild-goose chase. There was, however, one small problem with their plans. A sign on the front door informed them that the Pline Gallery took visitors by appointment only.

"Now what?" Laura asked.

"Leave it to me."

Dusty stepped up to the door and lifted his hand to knock. She stopped him, not at all sure they were dressed well enough to gain admittance to such a plush establishment. Laura was wearing her desert pants and the teal top, while he had on baggy gray cotton trousers and a yellow knit shirt. Both were in their hiking boots.

Santa Fe took on a sophisticated sheen in the summer. But until the season started, usually with the opening of the opera a bit later this month, such casual attire was very common. This gallery, however, appeared to have an air about it that went against the customary informality.

"I'll bet there isn't a price tag in this place under four figures," Laura said. "We don't look very well-to-do."

"That's why I brought my credentials." He reached into his back pocket for his wallet, taking out a credit card. Its platinum-colored plastic flashed in the sunlight. "I told you to leave it to me, didn't I?"

Dusty knocked on the door. It opened and an older man stood there, looking at them coolly. "May I help you?"

"Do you sell pottery?"

"We do," the man replied. Even in his impeccably tailored gray flannel suit, Laura thought he looked like a gray-haired weasel. He glanced pointedly at the sign on the door, then back at them. "Do you have an appointment?"

"No, but—"

"I'm sorry. You'll have to call and make one." He started to shut the door. "This is not a curio shop."

Putting his foot in the doorway, Dusty thrust his credit card in front of the man's face and said, "We're not after curios. Perhaps you could bend the rules just this once and make an appointment on the spot."

The man's eyelids flickered as he looked at the

card. Nor did he fail to notice the ring on the little finger of Dusty's right hand, fashioned from a polished gold nugget. He smiled, suddenly the picture of genteel hospitality.

"But of course we can! I'm Mr. Pline, the owner. Won't you come in?" He opened the door wide, waving them inside with a gesture of his carefully manicured hand. "Sorry for the hesitation. We try to screen our clientele, you see."

"Of course," Dust said sympathetically as he and Laura entered the gallery. It was, in a word, spectacular. "I understand. With this many fine things, you can't afford to let just any riffraff barge in."

"Quite," Pline agreed.

On the white walls hung beautiful Navajo rugs as well as original oils depicting typical desert scenes; display cases contained turquoise-and-silver jewelry and other small handmade items of wood, stone, and clay. Everywhere Laura looked, in every nook and alcove, excellent examples of Native American artistry beckoned for her attention.

She stepped across the red tile floor to a display of Pueblo pottery of every type and size imaginable. Polished black and polychrome, smooth, carved, or incised, they represented the full range of the Indian potter's craft. Many pieces were of museum quality, some quite old.

But none were of the age she and Dusty were looking for. "Don't you have anything . . . special?" she asked.

"My wife," Dusty said, shooting her a warning glance, "is an obsessive collector, Mr. Pline. When she says special, I think she means something no one else has."

Pline's eyes narrowed slightly. "I assure you those pieces are unique, madam. And extremely expensive. I had to outbid a museum for that Acoma polychrome olla by your left hand there."

"Still . . ." Laura turned her back on the display with studied disdain. "Simply everyone has things like these."

"I beg to differ, madam. That polished black serving bowl, for instance, is from the eighteen hundreds. It—"

She held up her hand. "Too recent."

He stared at her for a moment. Then he turned and looked at Dusty, who was doing his best to act the part of a doting but embarrassed husband. In fact, he was so mad at her he could have spit nails. The plan was to browse, not arouse suspicion. Dusty held his breath and waited for the gallery owner to throw them out.

Instead Pline stepped behind one of the display cases and asked quietly, "What are your price constraints?"

"Oh, money is no object," Laura assured him. She smiled at Dusty. "Right, dear?"

"Within reason, *dear*," Dusty returned, teeth clenched.

"Just as I thought." Pline sighed and gazed at each of them in turn. "I wish you people would leave me alone," he said. "It's such a waste of my time, and my time is extremely valuable. I deal in art, not information."

"Excuse me?" Dusty asked.

Pline sighed again. "What are you? Reporters? Magazine writers, perhaps?" He pointed at Laura. "I know I've seen your face somewhere before. Television? Yes. Let me think . . ."

That was the last thing Laura wanted to let him do. "All right," she said sheepishly. "You've got us. My name's Laura Violet and this is my producer, Doug Hiney. We're trying to put together a piece for the networks on this Anasazi curse thing."

"Why resort to this imbecile subterfuge?"

She shrugged. "Sorry. But would you have let us in if we'd told you what we were up to?" Pline shook his head. "Neither would the other places we've been today. That's why we tried to trick you. What tipped you off?"

"For one thing, young woman, if you're going to pretend to be a married couple, you should have the intelligence to wear rings," Pline replied smugly. "And the absolute last thing a serious collector would say is that price is no object. What they're really hoping to find is a dealer who doesn't know what he's got. The sort of ancient pottery I assume you're looking for is often mistaken for junk by the uninitiated."

Dusty raised his eyebrow. "You do handle it, then?"

"From time to time I come into possession of a piece, yes. Legitimate objects, mind you, with full documentation and in compliance with all federal, state, and local laws. While you two . . . reporters," he said disdainfully, "are interested in those items obtained illegally by looters. I don't deal in stolen goods, Mr. Hiney. And the curse is poppycock."

"But it has increased business, hasn't it?" Laura asked him. "You get more requests for appointments than you did a few days ago, don't you?"

"There has been a resurgence of interest. I tell people the same thing I'm telling you right now. Go find a black-market trader and ask him." Pline came out from behind the display case, holding his arms out as if herding sheep. "Now, if you don't mind, I have a very important client to prepare for this evening. A *paying* client."

They allowed themselves to be escorted to the door. "We can pay too, Mr. Pline," Laura told him. "For the right item. Such as a lead on where to find one of those black marketers."

"Try a dark alley somewhere. I'm sure the two of you have a better acquaintance with such things than I." He opened the door and glared at them. "Please leave."

They did so, wincing as Pline slammed the door behind them. Dusty turned to her. "Well, you certainly screwed that up. We were supposed to look around, not confront the man, Laura."

"He knows something," she said. "I can feel it. All I wanted to do was get him to talk. You're the one who came up with the sudden marriage and put him onto us."

"Bull. He had us pegged as something other than collectors the moment you opened your mouth. Didn't I tell you to let me handle it?"

"Oh . . . screw you!"

Laura turned and stalked off down the street. Dusty followed and put his hand on her arm to slow her down.

"Wait."

"Don't touch me!"

"Come on, Laura. I'm sorry. We won't get anywhere by picking on each other," he said. "That was pretty quick thinking on your part. At least he didn't figure out what we're really up to. Nice work."

She smiled reluctantly. "Thanks. I suppose you did get us in the door. I didn't have a clue on that."

"But Hiney?" Dusty asked.

"I thought you'd like that."

"I did. Almost cracked me up though."

"Then he would've thought we were crazy as well as the scum of the earth." She frowned. "Seems as if Mr. Pline has had a few curious visitors lately, doesn't it?"

Dusty nodded. "Yeah. I don't like that. The curse must have hit the news wires. I didn't much like the way he was looking at you either. I think he almost made you."

"Well, he didn't. That's what counts. But what do we do now?" Laura wanted to know. "We pulled that one off, but just barely. I don't see us skulking around dark alleys."

"Detectives we ain't," Dusty agreed. "Still, I think there is an alley we should look into. The one behind the Pline Gallery. You're right; he knows something."

"You felt it too?"

"You bet," he replied. "The guy dressed nice, but a three-piece suit can't disguise a rodent. What say we go grab a bit to eat, maybe see the sights, and then finish up with a moonlight stroll back this way?"

Laura put her arm through his and grinned. "And

if we just happen to stop to check out the exterior architecture of the Pline Gallery, who's to notice?"

"Now you're talking."

"Lead on, Hiney."

It rained a little while they ate. But the sky had cleared by the time they were through, so they took a walk through the historic neighborhoods along the Santa Fe River. Afterward they simply went wherever their noses took them, until it was dark enough to head back to the gallery.

The streets were fairly quiet, and most of the shops closed by the time they got there. Following Dusty's lead, Laura ducked down a passageway that led in behind the building. Being as nonchalant as possible under the circumstances, trying to look like tourists who had lost their way, the pair strolled hand in hand alongside the six-foot adobe-block wall that separated Pline's patio from the alley and the foothills to their right.

In some spots the top of the wall was uneven, dipping slightly in true rustic style, so Dusty had to duck every now and again. They thought the gallery was closed and deserted, but there were lights in the windows and they weren't about to take a chance. Up ahead, the wall curved away from them in a gentle arc, marking the end of the alley. But before they reached that point they came upon an opening in the wall; there was a private driveway leading up to the back of the gallery.

And in that drive was parked a truck painted in desert camouflage colors. "Look!" Laura exclaimed softly. "It's—"

Dusty clamped his hand over her mouth. She was about to protest when she realized he was pointing past the truck at the gallery's rear entrance, where a sliver of light spilled out into the darkness. Someone hadn't closed the door fully, most likely a looter still sleepy from his labors.

She nodded her understanding, and Dusty released her. Together they crept up the driveway to the door and peeked through the crack. This time it was Dusty who muttered a soft exclamation. In tearing out the walls of the cliff dwellings, their lucky looter must have come across a hidden cache of household items.

It was a treasure trove of Anasazi artifacts. Pots, bowls, and water jugs were spread out all over the red tile floor of what looked to be some sort of workshop. There were also implements of bone, wood, and stone, and a few scraps of coarsely woven cloth. Some of the things were completely intact, while others were cracked or had pieces missing. All were filthy with dirt, dust, and age.

All except for one particularly nice pot sitting on a workbench against the far wall of the little back room. It had been painstakingly cleaned—by an expert, Dusty's trained eyes told him, probably Pline himself. But there was no one in the room now.

Laura took her camera out of her purse, nudging the door farther ajar with her foot at the same time. Dusty grabbed her arm and squeezed a warning, but she just smiled and showed him the film-speed indicator. He nodded. There would be no flash, and her camera was of the old, manual-advance design that didn't have a motor drive.

Still, he jumped at the tiny click of the shutter. Laura took a few shots of the items on the floor, then tiptoed as far into the room as she dared, to take a few of the pot on the workbench. She almost had a heart attack when Dusty tapped her urgently on the shoulder.

He pressed his lips to her ear and said in a barely audible voice, "There's someone out on the patio."

Eyes wide, she followed him back out of the workroom, gingerly returning the door to its original position with trembling hands as she went. They moved to the truck and squatted on their haunches in the deep shadow behind it, listening intently. The sound of voices reached their ears, drifting over the patio wall. Two people were talking. One was Mr. Pline, the other a woman.

"I'm so glad you could accommodate me on such short notice," she said. "But I needed something . . . fresh."

"My dear lady, I would move heaven and earth for you."

"You should, considering the amount of money I've spent in your gallery over the years."

Pline cleared his throat. "Quite. In truth, it was a near thing, involving a considerable amount of hard work and expense on my part. Mr. Flemming ran into some trouble, you see."

"Don't sandbag me, Pline," the woman snapped. "We've already come to terms. Ridiculous too. I agreed to such an outlandish price only because I am well aware of the market pressures—and the cause of those pressures. Flemming ran into trouble? Ha! I'd say trouble ran into him."

"Excuse me?"

"Poop! You told me yourself that Flemming had been one of your prime sources for artifacts in recent months. You know about pottery, I specialize in people. His accident was quite a windfall for you, wasn't it?"

"Preposterous!"

"Oh?" She laughed. "Demand is up. Prices are up. And you just so happen to have discovered a fresh supply."

"What are you suggesting?"

"Nothing! There's no reason to be angry, Pline. I'm only saying I'm well aware of why the check I'm about to write you is so large, that's all. But it's as large as it's going to get, so let's move along. I'm in a hurry."

"Very well. Shall we go view the object? It's really quite extraordinary."

"That won't be necessary."

"But I always give you some background, explain the finer points of the construction and—"

"I'm buying this one as a gift," the woman interrupted.

"A gift? Most generous! May I ask for whom?"

"Can you keep a secret?"

Laura and Dusty couldn't see them, but evidently it was either a rhetorical question or Pline indicated that he could. They strained to hear, but the woman was whispering.

"Good heavens!" Pline exclaimed breathlessly.

"Am I a shameless name-dropper or what?" the woman said, the tone of her voice indicating she didn't feel the least bit ashamed. "I'm presenting it to him at a private soiree I'm having on the Fourth of July. Afterward, he's going to make a speech before a throng of admirers and the media, while I light up the sky behind him with fireworks." She laughed gaily. "It's going to be quite an event!"

"But surely . . . Do you think this is an appropriate gift?"

"He'll adore it."

Pline had a coughing fit. "He collects Anasazi pottery? Isn't that a bit, um, risky for a man in his delicate position?"

"Silly! I mean he'll adore it because I gave it to him. The only thing he collects is favors, just like any other politician. He won't even know what he's looking at."

"Then why bother with something so rare and expensive? Let me show you some excellent Navajo rugs, or perhaps—"

"A gift reflects the taste of the giver, Mr. Pline. Price and rarity didn't even enter into my decision. I'm one of the richest, most influential women in this country. By making a gift of this pot, I'll be thumbing my nose at all those bleeding-heart liberals and stuffed-shirt academics who've been giving me grief over my collection of ancient Indian artifacts. They say it's history, I say it's nothing more than a wise investment. And I'm not going to let anyone tell me where I can or can't put my money."

"You read the article on Flemming. Aren't you the least bit concerned about the rumors?"

She laughed again. "The curse? That's another reason I was willing to pay so much. Such a delicious mystery! It is, I believe, one of your biggest selling points these days. But of course, after I present my gift, you'll have an even bigger one, won't you? The market will go crazy!"

"But consider the possibilities!"

Her voice turned stone-cold. "Here is your check. Now wrap that thing up. And make sure it's secure! I'm not paying for a box full of shards, Pline."

"I know my business." Pline's voice was just as cold. "Rest assured you'll get everything you've paid for. Chester!"

They heard a door open, then heavy steps coming across the patio. Someone, another man, yawned loudly. "Yeah?" he asked in a gruff voice.

"Box the olla for transport, please."

"The what?"

"The pot on the workbench, Chester. Move!"

The man grunted and they heard him shuffle off. Laura looked at Dusty and whispered, "Sounds big."

Dusty nodded. "And tired," he whispered back.

On the patio, Pline was saying, "The papers aren't ready yet. Shall I mail them to your Colorado Springs address?"

"Do whatever you want," the woman told him brusquely. "I don't care. It'll probably just end up in a bathroom, holding toothbrushes anyway."

Pline gasped. "But that's an outrage!"

"Quit being so high-and-mighty and pour me some more of that champagne. And can we please go inside? The air stinks out here."

"Stinks! I'll have you know that Santa Fe . . ."

Their voices faded. Dusty risked a peek over the wall and found they had gone inside through the sliding glass doors that let out onto the patio; he could see them talking. Pline was gesticulating wildly and showing the woman the display of modern pottery that had caught Laura's eye earlier.

Dusty squatted back down behind the truck. "Let's get the hell out of here," he whispered in Laura's ear.

"You betcha," she whispered back.

They tiptoed down the driveway and into the alley, then walked back the way they had come as quickly as possible, keeping their heads low. Only when they were well away from the gallery did they speak again.

Dusty whistled. "We certainly got our nickel's worth tonight, didn't we?"

"I'll say," Laura agreed. "All we need is to identify the big guy and we've got a solid, verifiable trail of looted artifacts from that canyon through Pline's gallery and right into the hands of a buyer."

"Interesting transaction, wasn't it? There at the end I got the distinct impression Pline was trying to get her to choose another gift."

"So did I. He was even talking about the curse as if he believed it, when he told us it was poppycock. But why?"

He shrugged. "Righteous indignation, maybe. She didn't sound very appreciative of the pot and indicted whoever she's giving it to wouldn't be either. Or maybe he's worried about the quality of his documentation; he was going full speed ahead with the deal until she whispered that name to him, as if he suddenly realized the pot would get a lot more scrutiny."

"Either way, I don't think Pline likes her. In fact, I do believe he hates her," Laura said quietly. "If there is skulduggery connected with the curse, and he's involved in it somehow, I'll bet you dollars to doughnuts she might become the next victim."

Dusty considered that for a moment. "I think you may be right. Remember what Pline said? Something about how she would get everything she paid for?"

"It wasn't just what he said, it was the *way* he said it. Sure sounded like a veiled threat to me."

"What do you want to do?" Dusty asked.

"I don't think we have much choice," Laura replied. "We've got enough evidence to charge Pline with dealing looted artifacts, and that's a good start, but I want more. We've got to see my theory through, Dusty; we follow her and see if Pline or someone we can connect to him tries to hurt her."

He gave a sigh of relief. "*Tries.* I'm glad you put it that way. For a moment I was afraid you wanted to document one of the so-called accidents too."

"No! Of course, if I'm right—and I'll admit I still have a lot of proving to do on that score—we may not be able to prevent something from happening to her. But we've got a better chance of tipping the cops off to what we think is going on if we're there, right?"

"Stands to reason. There's only one problem," Dusty pointed out. "We don't know who she is."

Laura smiled at him. "*Au contraire.* She is a rich, influential woman who holds private soirees for political bigwigs, and she has an address in Colorado Springs, Colorado. As I happen to live there too, I know exactly who she is. And I must say I wouldn't mind muddying her name a bit. Drucilla Farnsworth is a real bitch."

She started laughing. Dusty looked at her curiously and asked, "What's so funny?"

"I was just thinking. She practically accused Pline of having something to do with Carl Flemming's accident. As much as I dislike the woman, I am a bit flattered she agrees with my theory. The Farnsworths didn't make their money by being stupid."

"How did they make it?"

"Oil," Laura replied. "At least initially. Unlike a lot of her father's friends, they were quick enough to diversify before the market went sour."

They stopped at an intersection and Dusty bent down to loosen the laces on his hiking boots. "Man, I'm walked out."

"We'll have plenty of time off our feet."

"What?"

"I said we'll have plenty of time to rest our feet." Laura had to raise her voice to be heard. Some idiot at the far end of the street was revving a car engine. "I propose we go to the RV, get a good night's sleep, and take off for Colorado first thing in the morning."

Dusty straightened from attending to his boots. "I hope that doesn't mean we have to go right to bed."

"Well—" The idiot who had been racing his motor was now squealing his tires. "What the hell is going on back there?" She turned and looked over her shoulder.

Just in time to see a black sedan jump the curb not more than a hundred feet from them.

"Look out!" Dusty yelled.

He grabbed her around the waist and dragged her into a nearby doorway. They could have reached out and touched the car as it went by. It squashed a trash can flat on the sidewalk where they had been seconds earlier, then glanced off the wall of the building, sparks flying and its engine screaming like a wounded beast. Then it lurched back onto the street and sped away into the darkness.

The closest Laura had ever come to fainting was that day on the talk-show stage. But she came even closer now. Her eyelids fluttered and she slumped against the door behind her. If Dusty hadn't still been holding her, she would have crumpled to the ground.

"Crazy bastard!" Dusty yelled, shaking his fist at the disappearing sedan. Then he looked at Laura. "Are you okay?"

She nodded. "Yeah. Just shaken," she replied in a weak voice. "Did you get a license number?"

"Hell, no! I was too busy trying to keep it from being tattooed on our butts! Shit!"

"Dusty?" Laura asked.

"Yes?"

"Am I nuts, or did somebody just try to kill us?"

He put his arms around her. "Don't be silly. For what? They aren't in possession of stolen artifacts."

"Well, there have been some so-called accidents," she reminded him.

"That *is* nuts. Nobody even knows who we are or what we're doing. It was just an idiot, Laura. Probably drunk or stoned out of his gourd."

Laura leaned against him. "You're right. I just don't deal well with coincidences, I guess. Do me a favor?"

"Anything."

"Take me home, give me a stiff drink, and then take me to bed."

He started to open his mouth, but she stopped him with a kiss. Then she told him, "Yes, you heard me right. I said take me to bed. Coincidence or not, I don't want to sleep alone tonight."

18

The strong drink was rich, dark Jamaican rum that Dusty had picked up in his travels. It brought tears to Laura's eyes and a warm, languid feeling to her soul. By the time she'd consumed two fingers' worth of the potent stuff, her hands no longer trembled and she was quite certain Dusty was right. They had almost been victims, but of a drunk, not an arranged accident.

Laura put her empty glass down on the table, then stood up and took Dusty's hand. "I've changed my mind," she said.

His mouth dropped open. "What?"

"I've changed my mind about letting you take me to bed," Laura repeated with a sly smile. She tugged on his hand, urging him to his feet. "I'm going to take *you* to bed instead."

"Why, you . . ." Dusty stood up and reached for

her. She slipped away. "Didn't anybody ever tell you what can happen to a tease?"

"Oh, my! That sounds promising. Care to follow me and fill in the details?"

She turned and walked toward the bedroom, exaggerating the sway of her hips with every step.

Dusty groaned. "Woman, I'd follow you anywhere."

In the bedroom, Dusty started to turn on the lights, but she put her hand on his and shook her head. He gave her such a pleading look that she had to laugh.

"I'd rather have candlelight," she told him.

"But . . ."

Laura's fingertips whispered across his lips, down his chest, then lightly brushed his masculinity through his pants, feeling him stir beneath her touch. "Come on. Surely a renowned archaeologist can dig up some candles."

"Hell," he growled. "I'll make some if I have to."

Dusty left the bedroom. She could hear him rummaging through drawers, tossing things aside and cursing. A few moments later he returned, holding three large candles. He quickly found places for them, then lit them, filling the room with a soft, cozy glow.

"See? Isn't this nice?" she asked.

"Yes. You're so beautiful."

He reached to unbutton her blouse, but again she slipped away. She sat on the edge of the bed and beckoned to him, holding her arms out. "You first," she said. "If I'm going to pay for my teasing, I want to be able to see how good a job I'm doing. That way I'll know the price is right."

"It's growing by the moment," he warned.

Dusty stepped over to her, pulling his knit shirt over his head and tossing it aside. Laura ran her hands over the hard planes of his chest, down his taut stomach muscles to the waistline of his slacks. There she paused.

"Boots, please," she requested. "Mine too."

He hurriedly took off his boots and socks, then hers, holding her tiny feet in his big hands for a moment before standing up again. Laura unbuckled his belt, then slowly lowered his zipper, grinning up at him. His pants fell to the floor, and he kicked them aside. She put her thumbs into the elastic of his briefs.

Inch by inch, Laura pulled them down over his powerful buttocks and thighs, revealing him to her hungry gaze. The sight of his throbbing and erect manhood made her shiver with anticipation. She touched him with the tip of her tongue, chuckling throatily at the way he jumped.

Moaning, Dusty said, "Laura . . ."

"Shh! I want the grand tour."

Laura got up and stepped around him, her hands roving over his arms, across his broad shoulders, delighting in the heat of his skin. His back was wide and well-muscled, and lower she found the strong, smooth buttocks she'd imagined that day she'd seen him in his gym shorts. So strong!

She turned him and put her hands on his chest, pushing him toward the bed. He sat down, leaning back on his elbows, watching her. Laura ran the tip of her tongue over her lips.

"Your turn," she said softly.

Unbuttoning her blouse, she shrugged it off her shoulders and let it flutter to the floor. Then she leaned forward, teasing him with a delicious view of her full, soft breasts trapped in their lacy prison. She raised her eyebrows, her smile an invitation.

Dusty lifted a trembling hand and unhooked the front closure of her bra. Sweet, milky white with luscious, dusky-pink tips, her breasts tumbled free. He sat up and held them in his open palms, cherishing them.

Laura gasped, then kissed him, plunging her tongue into his mouth before she straightened to continue undressing for him.

Her smile was devilish, her deep brown eyes full of promise that the best was yet to come. She unbuttoned her pants, pulled down the zipper, then turned around so her back was to him and let them fall.

"Oh, Laura!"

She laughed wickedly. "You like?"

"One fifty-two?"

"Hmm. You're getting warmer." Laura put her hands on her hips and bent over in a smooth, graceful movement, removing her panties as she did so. Bending down, she looked at him from between her knees. "You're upside down," she murmured.

"And in awe of your beauty!" Dusty ran his hands up her legs, following every curve. "Many cultures worship the female form," he whispered, his own voice reverent. "Especially the buttocks, which are a sign of fertility and sexuality at its most elemental. Laura, you are a goddess. One fifty-six."

It wasn't a guess. She unfolded herself without turning around and stood before him, legs slightly spread, feeling more appreciated than she ever had in her life. Excitement was at a fever pitch within her, the soft touch of his fingertips upon her inner thighs making her weak in the knees.

"My highest score, right on the button," she told him, her voice shaky with desire. "I'm sorry for doubting you."

"You're forgiven."

Laura shuddered as Dusty pressed his lips to each plump buttock in turn, nipping playfully with his teeth. Then he wrapped his arms around her waist and pulled her into his lap. Laughing, they sprawled on the bed, eager mouths melting together. And then, as quickly as it had come upon them, their laughter went away.

She had teased him to the point of madness, and now it was time to pay. Her body was ready for him, willing to accept every ounce of his strength. Gladly. Laura was at the point of madness too.

"I want you, Dusty." Laura rolled to her back, her hands clutching urgently at his hips. "I *need* you inside me."

Dusty spoke her name in a hoarse sigh. "Laura."

As desperate to feel her warmth around him as he was, he still took her slowly, filling her a tender centimeter at a time until she had all of him. Eyes wide, panting for breath, Laura dug her fingers into his buttocks and held him there for a moment. Then she relaxed and moaned, encouraging him with a tiny nod of her head. Dusty began to move within her, his throaty, masculine groan of enjoyment driving her wild. She writhed beneath him, meeting his every thrust.

His orgasm came quickly, too quickly for Laura to join him, but his love cries so delighted her that she tumbled soon after him. Still hard and throbbing inside her, Dusty dipped his head to leave a trail of kisses down her throat to her swollen breasts. He took each erect nipple into his mouth in turn, sucking gently, using his teeth to delicately arouse and tease.

Laura felt a great sense of emptiness when he withdrew from her. But then she realized he was only beginning again and cried out in joy. So soon! Dusty's thrusts were not so gentle now, and she met them in kind, wrapping her arms around him and forcing him even deeper.

"Yes! I want you, Dusty! Please!"

"You're driving me crazy!"

"Good!"

In a frenzy they searched for and found another mutually pleasurable position, and then another and another, until Laura was moaning in ecstasy again. On her hands and knees in front of him, feeling completely shameless, she moved her hips in circles and became the aggressor, taking him on a breathless ride. Surprised at her own need, she guided his hand until he understood. It excited him beyond reason, coaxing him to an unsurpassed virility. This time they climaxed not in turns but together, a shuddering peak that left them totally spent.

Clinging to each other, they kissed, their tongues

communicating what soft sighs and tender words could not. Utter satisfaction. They had had a shaky beginning and would undoubtedly encounter that bumpy road again. But here, now, they fit together as if destined for each other all along. It was a powerful thought, one that accompanied them into the warm, welcome blanket of sleep.

19

"**D**usty," Laura muttered. "I'm hot."

His eyelids fluttered open. "Again?"

"Not that kind of hot." She grinned sleepily. "Did you turn off the air conditioner last night or something?"

Dusty noticed it then. The air around him seemed thick and heavy; it even smelled hot. Suddenly he came completely awake. "Holy shit!" he cried, jumping out of bed. "Smoke!"

His first thought was of the candles, but he remembered getting up during the night to blow them out. The room was dark. He jabbed at the light switch. Nothing. Then he heard a noise, like dry, crackling leaves, coming from the opposite end of the bedroom. Doing his best not to trip over their hastily discarded clothing, Dusty picked his way over there, noticing that the smoke increased with each step.

Peering through the haze at the base of the far

wall, he saw that the paneling was blistering and starting to char in some spots. On the other side of that wall was the RV's generator. Something must have shorted out. Right before his eyes, one of the charred spots began to glow cherry-red.

Dusty moved quickly to the bed, hauled Laura to her feet, then wrapped the quilt around her and shoved her toward the bedroom door. He joined her there, pulling his robe from its hook and shrugging into it. They were both coughing from the smoke now. Checking the door and finding it cool to the touch, he opened it, grabbed Laura's arm, and pulled her down the corridor toward the RV's side exit.

They burst outside into the gray light of dawn, almost colliding with a man who was running past with a large fire extinguisher cradled in his arms.

"You're on fire, pal!" he yelled.

"No kidding."

Dusty half dragged Laura to a nearby picnic table and sat her down, then ran to the back of the RV, where the man with the extinguisher was liberally hosing down the generator compartment. Another man arrived, clad only in his underwear. But he had an extinguisher, too, and joined the fire-fighting effort. Seeing that they had the exterior under control, Dusty dashed forward and went back inside, covering his mouth and nose with the sleeve of his robe.

There was still a lot of smoke. It stung his eyes and tore at his throat as he made his way toward the bedroom, pausing to snatch his own fire extinguisher from its place in the kitchen. Seconds later he was painting the rear wall white with a fire-smothering blast of dry chemicals. That done, Dusty tossed the empty cylinder aside and left the smoke-filled RV, opening windows along the way.

A small crowd of fellow mobile travelers had gathered. In the distance, Dusty could hear the sound of a siren, then the guttural growl of a rapidly approaching fire truck. He went and sat down beside Laura. Wrapped in her quilt, she was sipping at a glass of water a woman standing nearby had given her. She handed it to him, and he gulped it gratefully.

The man who had been first on the scene came by on his way back to his trailer. "That was a close one, pal."

Dusty nodded. "Yeah. Thanks for your help."

"Sure thing."

"Where's the other guy?"

"Went to put on his pants," he replied. He grinned and pointed at the fire truck that had pulled up behind Dusty's RV. "A couple of those fire fighters are women."

"Thank him for me if you see him."

"Will do." The man waved and continued on his way.

Dusty put his arm around Laura and held her tight. "You okay?" he asked. She nodded. He kissed her on the cheek. "I'm getting the feeling somebody doesn't like us."

"Two accidents in one night is a bit much, isn't it?"

"I don't know about the near miss with the car. But this wasn't an accident, Laura," Dusty informed her. "I had an automatic extinguisher system installed that watches over everything, including the propane tank, all fuel lines, and the generator. It should have gone off long before the fire started to burn through the bedroom wall."

"It could have failed," she said.

"Not likely. They've been using the same kind of system on race cars for years with excellent records. I'll buy one coincidence, but not two." Dusty held her even tighter. Until now, I was just going along with this theory of yours. It made a screwy kind of sense, but I didn't believe it. Now I do. We've stumbled into the middle of something with this line of research, and it sure as hell isn't an Anasazi curse."

The fire department stayed on the scene long enough to make sure there weren't any smoldering embers that could rekindle the blaze. They also informed Dusty that his wiring had shorted out, and that part of the extinguisher system that metered temperatures in the generator compartment had failed, both possibly due to tampering. Dusty made light of it, assuring them he'd have his insurance company look into the possibility. In fact he was quite certain it was arson. But there were already enough people wandering around asking questions; for Laura's sake—and his own—he didn't want to add any nosy reporters to their ranks.

With that in mind, he also arranged to have the RV towed to the nearest repair facility as quickly as possible. While waiting for an estimate on the time it would take to fix poor, badly singed Scheherazade, they had breakfast in a café nearby and talked things over.

"Why we've become the object of all this attention is obvious," Dusty said. "If caught, the most a looter or dealer faces is a fine, and even that is far from assured. We've got some fairly convincing evidence on Pline and the big guy, maybe enough to make the charges stick, but they wouldn't be out to murder us because of that."

"Besides, the big guy never saw us and I'm pretty sure we managed to convince Pline we were television reporters trying to dig up something interesting on the curse," Laura pointed out. "There's no way they could know we're onto them. At best Pline might be worried we'll stick our noses where they don't belong."

"Exactly. And since he'd be crazy to try and do us in to save himself a fine, that means we're onto something else. Something that makes it worth the risk to attack us just for snooping around. In that light, your theory about the curse stops looking screwy and starts making sense."

"Gee, thanks."

Dusty patted her hand. "No offense. So, that's the *why*. For whatever reason, it looks as if some person or group is selectively harming those who come into contact with Anasazi artifacts. We stumbled into the midst of it and started asking questions, for which we've almost been made victims ourselves." He paused to sip at his tea. "It's the *how* that bothers me," he continued. "We don't know for sure if any of this is Pline's doing. We've been cagey, but out of necessity we've also talked to a lot of people about looting and looted sites. Any one of them could either be involved or be an informant. They may not know who we are, but they know what we look like, and my RV is very distinctive."

"Crap," Laura muttered. "You're right. I had the courage of my convictions; I knew my theory was correct. But who's behind it? It could be looters or dealers, even an outraged group of Indians, for all we know. How am I going to prove it if I can't be sure of where the threat is coming from?"

"You can't." Dusty took her hand and held it. "I'm sorry, Laura. But this really does put an end to the project."

She pulled her hand away. "It does not!"

"It does!" The other diners in the café turned to stare at them. Dusty lowered his voice. "In the first place it's gotten too dangerous. Or have you forgotten we've almost been squashed flat and burned to a crisp?"

"No, but—"

"In the second place we're stuck," he interrupted. "Without any proof to back up what we believe is happening, the police would think we're loony. They might even laugh so hard they'd let the media in on the joke. That'd be fun, wouldn't it? How can we continue this crusade of yours when we don't even know which windmill to tilt at anymore?"

Laura leaned forward and scowled at him. "Your stripe is showing again, Dusty."

"Stripe?"

"The yellow one down your back!"

"Dammit! It's common sense, not cowardice!"

"Then apply a little more of it," she told him. "We still have a lead to follow. Last night you agreed with me that Pline issued a veiled threat to Drucilla Farnsworth."

"Veiled? It was damn well wrapped in cotton!" Dusty exclaimed. Again all eyes focused on the battling pair. He threw some money down on top of the bill and stood up, offering her his hand. "Come on!"

Laura ignored his hand, but she got to her feet as well and followed him out of the café. When they were back to the relative privacy of the street, she resumed her argument.

"Are you trying to deny you have a hunch about Pline?"

"No," Dusty replied. "I'm trying to convince you of the dangers of leaping into things head first. Leap one brought us to the edge of this mess and almost got us killed. What's the second one going to do? Put us smack-dab in the middle, without a clue as to who we might piss off next?"

"So you're just going to quit?" she asked incredulously.

"*We're* going to quit," Dusty corrected. "Maybe Pline's in on it, maybe he isn't. Whoever it is plays rough. You've got enough to raise a fair stink, Laura. Take it and run."

"You run. I'm going for the rest of it."

He grabbed her arm. "Like hell you are!"

Laura took a swing at him. By now she should have learned not to mess with Dusty. He caught her fist inches from his left eye and held it, forcing it down to her side.

So she kicked him in the shin.

"Goddammit!" he bellowed, letting her go and grabbing her ankle. Laura took off like a rabbit.

Dusty hopped around like one for a moment, breathing through his teeth. Then he went after her. "Come back here!"

When she reached the RV repair shop, she stopped, her back to the wall of the building. He circled in on her warily, keeping an eye on her feet. "I'm sorry," she said.

"You're going to be even sorrier."

"What are you going to do, Dusty?"

"I'll think of something when I get my hands on you."

Laura held her arms up in a gesture of submission. "All right! Do your worst! I'm really, really sorry. I just get so damned mad when you order me around!"

He grabbed her and pushed her against the wall, holding her there with his body. "And I get mad when you won't listen to me." But the feel of her breasts pressing into his chest slowly drained the anger out of him. Taking her face in his hands so she couldn't turn away, Dusty kissed her. "Dammit, Laura," he whispered in her ear. "What am I going to do with you?"

"Let me go," she replied. "Or come with me. Those are your only choices. This lead will take us to Colorado, Dusty. That's my home. You can rant and rave, even talk to the press if you feel you must, but you can't stop me from going home."

"Shit!"

Laura took his hand. "Come here," she said, leading him to the service bay where his RV sat, blackened and forlorn. "Look at that. How can you quit now, Dusty? Don't you want to stop whoever did this? Maybe we don't know who's behind all this or why, but we do know they're despicable, maybe even deadly."

"It's just a bus, Laura. It can be fixed. Human beings aren't that easily repaired. And no one's been killed," he reminded her. "Yet. If we keep poking, we might be first."

"Any of the accidents reported so far *could* have been fatal. That's why we can't quit. Drucilla Farnsworth is a human being too," Laura said. She gave him a lopsided grin. "Just barely, mind you. But worth saving, I guess. If there's a chance we can put a stop to this . . ."

She let the statement hang there. Somehow, Dusty was quite sure it would come back to haunt him; if not Pline, then whoever she dug up next; if not the Farnsworth woman, then the next potential victim of the so-called curse. There was no stopping the Ultraviolet Wacko.

He nodded. "Yeah. I suppose you're right."

"You know I am."

Dusty sighed and shook his head, exasperated. Then he went to find the repairman. It was bad news. The fire had destroyed the RV's generator, air-conditioning compressor, various relays and wiring, as well as the back wall of his bedroom. Parts would have to be replaced, a new wall custom-built, and the whole RV cleaned from stem to stern of smoke residue. Insurance would cover the expense. It was the thought of leaving Scheherazade behind that bothered him.

Laura sympathized, but the necessity was obvious. "Two weeks! Tomorrow is Independence Day, Dusty. She'll give the pot away at that private soiree of hers, and if we haven't dug up any more information by then, you know what that means."

"We can stop?" he asked hopefully.

"No. We'll have to follow that pot wherever it goes, for the sake of continuing the documentation of its route, if nothing else."

Dusty ran his hands over his face. He needed a shave, and between last night's frolic and the fire that morning, he hadn't gotten very much sleep. "Laura," he said, "I am not going to let you drag me all over the country, chasing some damned pot."

"Then we'd better pack our bags and get going, hadn't we?" She gave him a big smile. "Who knows? Drucilla might decide to give it to her friend a day early."

"Hey, fella!" Dusty called out to the mechanic. "What's the quickest way to get to the Albuquerque airport from here? We have to catch a plane. And fast!"

20

Laura's house was in the foothills on the west side of Colorado Springs, surrounded by lilac bushes and situated beneath the spreading branches of blue spruce, elm, and silver-leaf maple trees. It was what real estate agents referred to as a bungalow, which meant it was almost as small as Dusty's RV. She liked it well enough, and after living in Scheherazade the place did seem bigger to her. There was, however, a sense of immobility to it now that gave her an odd feeling of claustrophobia.

But it did have a shower, washing machine, and a big hot-water tank, which were the first things she availed herself of after they stepped through the front door. She left Dusty to fend for himself in the small kitchen; neither of them could stand airline food, so they had both forgone lunch. Some of the passengers around them had too, perhaps because the pair smelled rather like they'd been trapped in a smoke-house.

Though she hadn't thought the odor that bad earlier, when she emerged from the shower some while later feeling clean and fresh, she took one whiff of Dusty and pushed him into the bathroom with a half-eaten tuna fish sandwich still clutched in his hand. Smoke-drenched or not, he made good tuna salad. While he showered, she had hers on a bed of lettuce with carrot and celery sticks.

Laura was sitting at her tiny kitchen table, opening mail when he came out. He put his arms around her from behind and hugged her.

"Better?" Dusty asked.

She sniffed. "Much." Laura turned to look at him, half expecting him to be naked. But he had a towel wrapped around his waist. "Pink is not your color."

"It was the only towel I could find."

"That's because it's one of the few I own."

Dusty looked around him. Except for the bedroom, he could practically see the whole house at a glance from where he stood. "I noticed you have a rather Spartan life-style."

"I don't like clutter," Laura informed him. "No room for it even if I did." She watched as he went to the kitchen window and looked out, then moved into the living room and gazed out the windows there as well. "Something wrong?"

"Hmm?"

"You seem . . . ill at ease."

"Oh." Dusty strolled back into the kitchen and sat down in the chair opposite her. "It's just that I haven't been in a house for a while, I guess. Before I got the RV I had an apartment in Sausalito." He chuckled. "A modern cliff dweller, if you will. I wasn't there much. Most of the time I was traveling, doing research, living in tents or whatever rudimentary shelter was available."

"Then you found the gold mine?"

He nodded. "It gave me the wherewithal to sort of retire. I say *sort of* because I still work, only now I don't have to hustle so hard for grant money or even prove the viability of my projects if I don't want to."

"Did you ever teach?" Laura asked.

"Don't we all? You have to have some connections. I still sub on occasion and do a few lectures when I feel I have something to say. I was always footloose; these days I can follow my wanderlust without starving."

Laura put her elbows on the table and propped her chin in her hands, gazing at him thoughtfully. "Now you've got me feeling ill at ease."

Dusty flexed his chest muscles. "My manly charms getting to you?" he asked.

"No." She grinned. "Yes. But don't change the subject. I envy you. Riding around with your home on your back like some nomadic snail. It's a very attractive life-style to someone like me, who has always prided herself on breaking new ground, trying the offbeat."

"We're not so different," Dusty told her. "You channel your wanderlust into your work, that's all."

"To the point where I'm no longer sure where the hell I'm going, unfortunately," Laura said with a deep sigh. "Before everything got shoved out of kilter,

I led what I thought was a nice, stable existence. Lately I've come to the realization it was nothing more than an illusion. Traveling with you these last few days has brought me to a rather terrifying conclusion, Dusty: I don't *want* to go back to the life I used to lead."

His eyebrows arched. "The respect of your peers has lost its golden gleam?"

"No. I still want that. I *need* a certain amount of it if I hope to continue my career," she replied. "But I don't want to spend that career waiting for the day when my predilection for the bizarre makes me a crackpot again. Freedom, that's what I want. The freedom to tell them to go screw themselves. And for that I have to have a shining triumph. Raising a ruckus with this project isn't enough anymore. I'm going to have to bring down the house."

Dusty groaned. "I don't like the sound of that."

"The key to it is right in front of me. I can feel it. There's something we're missing, Dusty. But what?"

"Here we go," he muttered. "I'm going to get dressed now, if that's okay with you."

It must have been, because Laura continued as if she hadn't heard him. "You know what bothers me? Who ran over Carl Flemming? Any number of people might have had reason to hurt him. He's greedy, mean, and would double-cross his own mother. But since his accident started this whole uproar with the curse, I don't think it was a simple payback. Whoever did it knew he was under suspicion for stealing artifacts, making him the perfect vehicle for their publicity stunt. Hurt Carl, tip off a hungry, imaginative reporter to the looting angle—and bang! Instant curse."

In a house this small, Dusty had no choice but to listen to her. "That doesn't narrow the field any, Laura," he told her from the bedroom.

"On the contrary, I think it does," she objected. "We have every reason to believe that what happened to Carl was anything but an accident. Therefore, the object was to grab publicity and start the ball rolling on the curse rumor. But since Flemming was supplying artifacts to Pline, I doubt Pline would risk using him toward that end. What if he put two and two together like I did and started pointing a finger?"

Dusty came out of the bedroom tucking a white cotton short-sleeved shirt into his jeans. He was frowning. "I think you're onto something there. For that matter, you could even take it a step farther. Why would anyone involved in the looting risk it?"

She stared at him, eyes wide. "They wouldn't, would they? Carl was the perfect vehicle, but he was also plugged into the black market. They'd be more likely to use a high-profile collector as their sacrificial lamb, and not one who could or would name names. Damn! Who does that leave?"

"And why are they doing it?"

"Lord!" Laura put her head down on the table and moaned. "You're right about me being too smart for my own good. I've just talked myself out of the only theory that made any sense."

Dusty patted her on the back. "I think it's time you faced up to something, Laura. You're so obsessed with clearing your name that you've forgotten the most basic rule of research: Never force the facts to fit your suppositions."

"You're right." She sighed and lifted her head off the table. "Would you rub my neck, please? It helps me think."

"Sure thing, partner."

His strong hands worked wonders on her tight muscles. Laura relaxed and let her mind drift. "What the hell is going on, Dusty?" she mumbled.

"I assume that's a rhetorical question."

"Uh-huh."

"You realize, of course, that we may never know?"

"I won't accept that."

Dusty blew out a deep breath. "I didn't think so." Something banged against Laura's front door. The noise made him jump. "What was that?"

"Ouch! Easy on the neck. It's just the newspaper."

"Oh. Sorry." He let go of her and went to get it, then plopped it on the table in front of her. "At least we'll have something to read while we think."

Laura glanced at the newspaper without much interest. Dusty had returned to massaging her, now concentrating on working his way down her back. She moaned softly and closed her eyes.

Suddenly, they popped open. She grabbed the paper and read the headlines again. "Oh, my God!"

"What?" Dusty asked, peering over her shoulder.

"The President is coming to Colorado Springs!"

"Gee, that's nice." Dusty had slipped his hands into the waistband of her jeans and was massaging the base of her spine. "Let's go to the bedroom so I can do a thorough job."

"That's it!" Laura spun around in the chair to look

at him. "That's who Drucilla Farnsworth was talking about. She's going to give the pot to the President on Independence Day!"

"So?"

"Don't you see? We knew we had stumbled onto something big, otherwise why would anyone bother with us? But we've managed to build a pretty good argument that whoever is behind it isn't involved in the black market. Right?"

"Probably," Dusty replied. "Because Carl's so-called accident played a major role in all this, and he was too close to them to be a wise choice of victim. What are you getting at?"

"That whoever hurt Carl and started rumors of the curse wasn't interested in pottery at all!"

He frowned. "Then what were they interested in?"

"Making the news! Their only goal was to create a wave of national publicity. The curse is a smoke screen, Dusty! Someone has carefully fabricated this entire thing as a cover for their plan to harm the President of the United States!"

Dusty sat down in the other chair. "Laura," he said softly, "it's finally happened. You've burned out your brain."

"Would you just think about it for a moment?"

"No."

"But—"

"What did I just tell you about forcing the facts?" he interrupted vehemently. "It's a fact that Flemming was in a suspicious accident. It's a fact that we almost had a couple of our own, equally suspicious, while researching the path of stolen artifacts. But to conclude that those facts and an admittedly illegal but otherwise innocent gift from Drucilla Farnsworth to the President adds up to an assassination plot is nothing short of total insanity!"

Laura stood up, glowering at him. "What if it isn't?"

"It is!"

"Dammit! Open that narrow, rust-encrusted lockbox you call a mind for a moment and listen to me! It's wild, maybe even crazy, and I'll grant you I don't have a leg to stand on as far as proof. But it is at least theoretically possible, isn't it?" Dusty turned away from her. She moved in front of him again and yelled, "Isn't it?"

"You've flipped."

"It is and you know it. So how can you sit there and argue with me? Are you willing to gamble the President's safety on your stubborn insistence that you have all the answers?" Laura asked. "What if you're wrong, Dusty?"

Dusty got up and went to look out the window. He was silent for a long time. Finally, he said, "All right. We do know there is some kind of menace connected to owning looted Anasazi pottery at the moment. And the President is about to come into possession of just such an artifact. We'll have to at least try to warn somebody about the possibility, I suppose." He turned from the window to look at her. "But I'll tell you something, Laura Newton. I've had about as much as I can stand of these flashes of idiosyncratic logic. I'm beginning to wonder why I helped you that day. I should have taken one look at you and kept on walking."

21

After his arrival at Peterson Air Force Base on the east side of Colorado Springs, the President of the United States would be transported via motorcade to a hotel a short distance away. There he would attend an intimate party being given in his honor by Drucilla Farnsworth and a small group of her friends, including several local and state officials. Immediately following this soiree the President would be bustled off to a nearby public park, where he would speak before the populace—or rather the whole country, for the media, naturally, would also be there in force. He would then enjoy a fireworks display arranged and funded by Drucilla Farnsworth, return to Air Force One by motorcade, and depart.

At least that was the itinerary made available to the public. When, where, or how the President would actually arrive, travel, and leave was anybody's guess, which was exactly the way the White House advance team wanted it.

The command headquarters for this group of security and publicity management personnel was located in a conference room of the hotel where Drucilla's party would take place. Even at six o'clock in the evening, it was a well-organized madhouse. In the corridor outside that room, however, chaos prevailed. It was easy to see why the news of an impending Presidential visit had been kept secret until now; Laura and Dusty were just two more bodies in a sea of others who had flocked to the hotel the moment the announcement had hit the afternoon paper.

As an aid in keeping the boisterious crowd down to a manageable size, one member of the team stood at the end of the corridor nearest the hotel lobby, handing out forms and droning orders in a flat, emotionless voice:

". . . take a form. Phrase your request in ten words or less or we won't read it. The President is not visiting any lodges, churches, or schools. He will not deviate from his agenda to eat at your restaurant or pose for a picture in front of your place of business. There will be no further additions to the Farnsworth party guest list, period. If your request falls outside these restrictions, take a form. Phrase your request . . ."

Passing that point, form in hand, Laura and Dusty took their place in a queue of other hopefuls. At the end of that line was the team's public liaison officer.

His desk was situated at the very front of the conference room, all but blocking the doorway, so that every person, phone call, and scrap of paper had to go past him before being channeled to the appropriate member of the advance team. Not many did.

"Next!" he yelled.

They watched as one of their ranks was shown to the nearest exit. The man in front of Laura muttered, "Another one bites the dust."

Laura had put their names—their real ones—in the appropriate places on the form, along with all the other information requested. Now she was pondering how to phrase her request. "What should I say?"

"Next!"

"Better make it short and to the point," Dusty replied.

"Next!"

She grimaced. "I'll say! And attention-grabbing."

"Next!"

Laura scribbled two words on the form, then held it up for Dusty to read. He nodded. "Yeah. That'll either get us inside to talk to somebody or arrested. Probably both."

"Next!"

Every now and then, rather than his curt bark they would hear a thump, and someone would be allowed into the conference room. When they got close enough to the door they could see that the liaison officer held a rubber stamp. If he read a form he liked, he would literally give it his stamp of approval. But the three people in front of Dusty and Laura were all denied admittance and sent away.

"Next!"

Laura swallowed thickly, grabbed Dusty's hand, and stepped up to the desk. The liaison officer took her form and read it over. His eyes widened. Then he looked up at the pair standing in front of him.

He didn't stamp their form, nor did he yell for the next person in line. Instead he turned and waved to someone in the conference room. Almost instantly a man appeared in the doorway. His suit was dark blue, his white shirt crisp, and his expression no-nonsense. The liaison officer stood up, handed him the form, and whispered the two words Laura had written on it in his ear.

"Step into the room, please," the man in the blue suit told them. His voice was polite, but it was not a request.

They did as he asked. Dusty looked above his head as he went through the doorway. Just as he thought, a metal detector had been set up to screen everyone who walked into the room. He also thought the detector would scream bloody murder if the man in the blue suit were to pass under it. Dusty was suddenly glad he never carried much change.

Unfortunately, Laura wasn't as lucky.

Beep!

"Give me your purse," the man ordered quietly, "then step back and come through the doorway again."

She did so. No beep. Keeping his eyes on her, he handed the purse to a man at a nearby desk who could have been his carbon copy, right down to his polished black shoes. That man looked through Laura's bag, found her heavy metal key ring, and nodded.

"It's clean."

"Come with me, please," the first man said.

Laura returned to Dusty's side. "May I have my purse?"

"Of course."

She collected it, then followed Dusty and the man in the dark blue suit to the back of the conference room, where portable office dividers had been placed so as to create a private cubicle. Mercifully, the man who was sitting behind the desk in that cubicle was in his shirtsleeves, which he wore cuffed up on his forearms. His lack of a blue suit, however, didn't detract from his equally no-nonsense manner.

He took Laura's form and waved the other man back to his duties. "Assassination attempt," he said. "Two words guaranteed to get our attention."

"That's why I wrote them," Laura told him.

"Ambiguous though. Are you threatening us with one, alerting us to one, or making some kind of sick joke?"

From the look on his face, Laura imagined it wasn't the sort of joke he'd laugh at. Quite the opposite. "We're scientists," she replied. "In the course of a research project we've been conducting, we came across what we believe could be a plot to harm the President."

Dusty wished she'd go easy with the *we*, but he supposed it was too late to disown her now. "We don't have any proof," he interjected. "Just a theory. But we felt it was our duty to come here and warn you."

He nodded. "I see." Sighing, he swiveled his chair and scooted it closer to a computer terminal that sat on a table next to his desk. Glancing at the form she had filled out, he said, "Well, let's see who I'm talking to here. It takes a bit. Why don't you tell me the whole story while I'm calling up your files."

"Files?" Laura asked. "What files?"

The man chuckled. "*Everybody* has a file, Dr. Newton, even me. Especially me. It's just a record of who you are and what you've done, maybe any trouble you've gotten into."

Dusty cleared his throat. "Is this really necessary?"

"I have to know you're not a couple of crackpots who make a habit out of reporting assassination attempts. We do run into those occasionally." He smiled. "Don't worry. I'm not looking for unpaid parking tickets or anything."

"Shit!" Laura muttered under her breath. "You've got to believe us. We're not . . . I'm not a crank!"

He kept smiling, but he kept typing too. "Of course not. Go ahead, I'm listening. But please, no men from Mars, okay?"

Trying to beat the information scrolling across his video terminal, Laura told him everything they had found or thought they'd found. Dusty emphasized the things she said with descriptions of the two attempts on their own lives. The man nodded, occasionally glancing at them with raised eyebrows. But he never stopped reading for long.

Finally, both their story and their files came to an end. The official leaned back in his chair for a moment, hands behind his head, evidently finding something very interesting about the conference-room ceiling. Then he put his hands on the desk in front of him and looked directly at Laura.

"That's the biggest load of crap I've ever heard in my life," he said quietly.

Laura jumped to her feet. "It's true!"

"What's the matter, Dr. Newton? I notice you haven't been in the public eye for quite some time. Getting lonely out there on the lunatic fringe, is it?"

"Now just a minute," Dusty objected sternly. "There is no reason to—"

"*You* I'm interested in," he interrupted, pointing a finger at Dusty. "You've been a lot of places, Dr. Cantrell. Some mighty hot places, if you get my drift. Central and South America. The Middle East." He tapped his video terminal. "I see you've even been to Russia on one of your so-called archaeological expeditions. Dig up anything interesting, comrade?"

Laura banged the desk with her fist. "That's enough! We came here to warn you, dammit! The President may be in danger!"

"The President is *always* in danger, missy. He arrives in less than twenty-four hours; we have enough to do protecting him from real threats, without adding this bullshit to the list."

"Will you at least increase security?" she asked. "We can describe Pline and his man so you can keep an eye out for them. And this pot Drucilla Farnsworth is giving him is an illegally obtained artifact. Don't you want to tell him—"

"Enough!" the man bellowed. "I have wasted enough time on you two. It's our job to see that the President comes to no harm while he's in town, and we'll damn well do that job without your help! As for the rest of this nonsense—"

"It is not nonsense!" Dusty exclaimed. He stood

up, wondering what he was doing there arguing
Laura's case for her. This was insane! "Is this the
treatment we get for doing our duty to flag and
country?"

"Just what this event needs," the other man muttered. "A couple more flaky patriots." He got to his
feet as well, leaning across the desk with his hands
on his hips. "Listen up, you two! If the President
wants to accept an invitation to speak at a friend's
private party while he's in town, that's his business.
If that friend wants to give him a gift of a rare objet
d'art, that's her business. Do you know who you're
maligning? Drucilla Farnsworth! Christ! If I were
you, I'd keep your ludicrous theories and allegations
of stolen pots to yourselves. Find some other way to
make the papers. Otherwise, you could easily find
yourselves with your heads on the academic chopping
block instead."

"Is that a threat?" Laura asked quietly.

"You're goddamned right it's a threat! And here's
another: Stay out of our way. If I find you two wackos
peddling this shit anywhere near the President, I
will personally lock you up for hindering the Secret
Service!" He stepped to the opening in the cubicle
and yelled, "Henderson! Show these civic-minded
citizens to the door. Hell, take 'em outside and put
'em in their car. I want 'em out of here now!"

One of the men in the dark blue suits appeared.
Laura couldn't tell which one. They looked like
identical twins.

"Jeez-us! What do they do, stamp you guys out
with a cookie cutter or something?"

"Remember that face, Henderson. His too. If you

see them hanging around here again, nab their butts!"

"Yes, sir."

"And you, Cantrell," he said, his nose almost touching Dusty's. "I'm going to do a little more digging on you. There's something about you I don't like. I'm *real* interested in finding out what you did on your travels."

Dusty smiled at him. "I'm interested in you too. Especially the size and shape of your cranium. Sloping frontal bone with protruding brow; narrow-set orbits; wide mandible. I have a colleague who would give anything to have a skull like yours," Dusty informed him. "For his collection. I imagine he'd put it right next to the Neanderthal section."

"Get these flakes out of my sight!"

They were escorted, none too politely, all the way out to the hotel parking lot. The man in the blue suit stood there, watching them, until they got in their rented car and drove away.

"I don't think he liked us very much," Dusty observed.

Laura was furious. "Asshole! How dare he accuse us of making this up?"

"Come on, Laura. You said it yourself: It's a wild, crazy-sounding theory, and we don't have a shred of proof. I didn't much care for his attack on our characters, mind you, but he was within his rights to tell us to butt out."

"Within his rights?" She glared at him. "It's his job to protect the President. He should act on every threat no matter how crazy-sounding or who does the telling, Dusty. Hell, the stupid bastard wasn't even concerned about the leader of our country receiving stolen goods!"

Dusty took his eyes off the road for a moment to glance at her. "Calm down! Give the man some credit. He did hear us out, didn't he? I'm sure that we at least managed to put some small part of his security-conscious brain on alert. But you can hardly expect him to risk pissing off his boss and a powerful woman like Drucilla Farnsworth just on our say-so. In my opinion, we've been handed some pretty sound advice, Laura; stay out of this and let him do his job."

"Like hell I will!"

"Are you nuts? If we don't we'll end up in jail! You've stepped over the line now, and I'm warning you . . ."

"Warn away," Laura told him, folding her arms over her breasts. She gazed at him, a smug smile lifting the corners of her mouth. "Your threats don't mean a thing. You, Dr. Douglas Cantrell, are now on record as supporting the latest cause of the Ultra-violet Wacko. Go ahead and explain that to the press. I dare you!"

"Shit!" Dusty exclaimed.

She was right. He was guilty—or rather, flaky— by association. The sweet temptation of Laura's body had lulled him into a false sense of security. He'd been certain he could control her, or at least hold her in check with the threat of more bad publicity. Now he'd procrastinated himself out of options.

"Welcome to the wonderful world of disreputable scientists," Laura said. "How does it feel to emerge from anonymity, Dusty? Are you enjoying the attention? Do you like it so much you feel driven to get any reaction you can out of people, even if it's laughter and scorn?"

"Dammit! What's driving *you* now? Patriotism? Or have you become so blinded by this quest to clear your name that the thought of risking what's left of your reputation no longer scares you? That guy is serious, Laura. We'll be grabbing attention from jail if we don't stop."

"I'm serious too, Dusty. If I'm right, something awful could happen tomorrow. Since we're apparently the only ones who give a damn, we have little choice but to blunder onward, come what may," she informed him. "I've never been terribly patriotic; I readily admit that I sense an opportunity to get the triumph I need out of this. But I would sure as hell rather prove myself by exposing this scheme rather than documenting what my gut is telling me will be its horrible outcome. We have to get somebody to listen to us!"

"How?" he demanded. "We're short on time and even shorter on credibility. If we go to the local police, they'll just consult with the feds and we'll end up in the hoosegow. The media would find the whole thing fascinating, I'm sure. But that, too, would get back to our friends at the hotel. Then we'd not only get locked up but be the feature story on the evening news as well. What do you suggest we do?"

"Just shut up and let me think, will you?"

Dusty was thinking too. This was what it had been like for Laura. Accused of being a crank. Desperately trying to find a way to make people take her seriously again. It was a frustrating, even frightening experience for a man who had always taken it for granted that his reputation was secure.

But what really scared him was that it didn't make any difference where her bright mind led them next. He'd rather forget the whole thing, keep her safe, and celebrate the Fourth by making some fireworks of a different sort—in bed. Laura, however, had become more to him than a delightful sleeping partner. Whatever happened, Dusty would have to be a participant in it; her damnable persistence gave him no choice.

"I've got it," Laura announced suddenly. "Take a right up here and head west."

Dusty sighed. "I just know I'm going to hate myself for asking this question. But where are we going?"

"Drucilla Farnsworth's, naturally."

"Naturally," he said through clenched teeth. "She's the one person who can destroy us the fastest if we make her mad, so of course she's the first one you want to see. As long as we're going to get our heads chopped off, we might as well get it over with quick, right?"

"Think about it. Why is she giving the President this particular gift?"

"I believe she told Pline it was a statement, a way of thumbing her nose at people who raise a ruckus over artifacts of that age coming into private hands. People like us, in other words," he pointed out. "She's also well aware the pot was looted and doesn't give a shit, Laura. What on earth makes you think she'll even listen to us?"

"Because she's aware of the curse too."

"So? She called it a delicious mystery, remember?"

"Yes, but what she doesn't know is that it could be part of a plot to hurt her friend the President. If we can convince her of what we believe her gift could bring about, she might be willing to call off the ceremony, thereby throwing a monkey wrench into the plot as well."

He shook his head. "Drucilla Farnsworth did not strike me as a very reasonable person, Laura. Providing we can even get to see her, which I doubt, she's more likely to laugh in our faces and kick us out—if we're lucky. Besides, how are you going to convince her there's a plot when you haven't even managed to convince your own research partner?"

"Wait a minute," Laura said, eyeing him suspiciously. "You make it sound as if you're just along for the ride."

"Somebody has to keep you out of trouble."

"I'm getting a little tired of hearing that, Dusty."

"Then stop looking for it!" he exclaimed. "When this project began, all I had to worry about was making sure you didn't trivialize the subject. Then you changed the rules on me by bringing the curse angle into it. Suddenly, I had to make sure you weren't headed for the same kind of disaster you had before. Now you've managed to parlay a simple research project into an assassination plot. God! I don't even know what the hell I'm doing here anymore!"

Laura studied his face intently. "That's a very good question. You say I haven't convinced you, and yet you backed me up with that guy at the hotel. You say you're worried about me getting into trouble, and yet you seem willing to get in trouble yourself just to keep an eye on me. What exactly do you hope to get out of all this, Dusty?"

The answer was quite simple. Somehow, at some point along this crazy path she'd led him down, he'd come to care for her. Whether it was love, lust, or a mixture of the two, Dusty liked the feeling. He didn't want it to go away, ever.

But he replied, "Judging from the suspicion in your voice, I imagine it doesn't matter what I tell you. You'd think I was only lying so I could continue to 'go along for the ride,' as you put it. So let's just say I'm confused and leave it at that for now, shall we?"

"If you're that confused, maybe *you* should leave."

"I would if I could," he told her. "But I can't." They were coming to an intersection. "Which way?"

"Left. Then follow the signs that point to the zoo. She lives near there, in a great big house on the mountainside."

"Perfect," Dusty muttered. "That way, after we've confronted the lioness, they can feed what's left of us to the bears."

22

They had gotten in to see the White House advance team by writing two words on a form. Gaining an audience with Drucilla Farnsworth was going to be a lot tougher.

There was an iron gate across the driveway leading onto her property. At that gate was a very unfriendly-looking guard. And clutched in that guard's hand was a leash attached to the collar of a German shepherd with an even meaner appearance.

Laura didn't know if this was normal security for Drucilla or a special measure to keep away anyone hoping to gain a last-minute invitation to her party. She didn't have a clue how they were going to get by it. In spite of his confusion about why he was going along with her—a rather sudden and suspicious development, in Laura's opinion—Dusty was apparently confident he did have a way.

He pulled right up to the gate. Neither the guard

nor his German shepherd seemed particularly glad to see them. They both approached the car. Both were snarling.

"What do you want?" the guard asked.

"We wish to see Drucilla Farnsworth, please," Dusty replied in his most ingratiating voice. "About a very urgent matter."

"I'll bet. Name?"

"Douglas Cantrell."

The guard pulled a small notebook out of his pocket and consulted it. "You're not on the list. Take off."

"Please, sir," Laura chimed in politely. "Isn't there someone we can talk to about making an appointment?"

"And who are you?"

"My name is Laura Newton."

Again he consulted his book. "You're not on here either."

"Of course I'm not, dammit! I just told you I needed to make an appointment, didn't I?"

His dog started growling. "Listen, lady, if this is about the party, you can forget it. I've been turning people away all afternoon and evening. Famous ones too. *You* I don't know from squat. Take off."

"Are you an off-duty cop?" Dusty asked.

"Hell, no. I do this for a living."

"Good."

Dusty reached into his back pocket and pulled out his wallet, from which he removed a twenty-dollar bill. He held it out to the guard. The guard looked at it and started laughing.

"It'd take more than a twenty for me to let you

through that gate, pal. Like a guaranteed salary for life."

"All we need is the name of whoever makes Ms. Farnsworth's appointments. Twenty bucks is pretty good pay for a name."

"The last guy gave me twenty-five."

"I can probably call the Chamber of Commerce and get it for free. Going once . . . going twice . . ."

The guard snatched the bill out of Dusty's hand and stuffed it in an already bulging pants pocket. "The guy you need to talk to is William Lloyd, Farnsworth's public relations man. But it won't do you any good; she isn't here."

"Is Mr. Lloyd here?"

"Why should I tell you one way or the other?"

Smiling, Dusty took two more bills out of his wallet and held them in front of the guard's face. "Because if he is, you can earn yourself another forty for going to that intercom over there and telling him you have two people at the gate with some bad news about the pot for the party."

"The pot?" He scowled. "You mean drugs?"

"None of your business. Just tell him."

Apparently he decided that forty dollars would buy a lot of dog food. "What the hell," the guard said with a shrug. "Bad news about the pot for the party. At least it's original. I was getting bored with the stories of alien invaders."

He took the money and strolled over to the intercom. In a moment he returned, shaking his head and chuckling to himself. "Congratulations, pal. You got yourself a meeting with the man. Back up so I can open the gates."

Yet another guard met them at the front of Drucilla's house. Dusty hoped this one would let them in without much trouble; he was running short on cash.

"Step out of the car, please, and hold your arms away from your sides," the guard requested.

They did as they were told. The man ran a handheld metal detector over each of them, first Dusty, then Laura.

Beep!

"Key ring," Laura said quickly. "In my purse."

He verified it, then escorted them up a broad stone staircase to the front door, where still another guard was waiting. They were escorted into a grand, spacious foyer. Everywhere Laura looked there was something of great value. Sculpture, fine antique furnishings, lovely hand-painted vases—and all set against a decor that was as opulent as anything she'd ever seen. Even the hallway that the guard led them down was lined with oil paintings in ornate frames.

The guard knocked on one of the heavy oak doors.

"Yes?"

"I have the people from the gate, Mr. Lloyd."

"Bring them in."

He did so, then left, closing the door softly behind him. Laura and Dusty went to the middle of what they assumed was called a study, though library would have fit too, as well as in-home office. The room, every bit as opulent as what they'd seen so far, was as big as Laura's entire house. She looked at Dusty. Dusty looked back.

"You've gotten us into deep shit," he whispered.

"Yup," she whispered back. "But remember this, Mr. Reluctance. *You* got us through the gate."

William Lloyd was very handsome, with jet-black hair and a personable smile. His manner, however, was that of a man in a hurry. "You have five minutes to tell me how you know about a gift that only I, Ms. Farnsworth, and a small group of her closest friends are privy to."

Laura gave Dusty a taunting but appreciative wink, then moved closer to the big antique maple desk Lloyd was sitting behind. "It's quite simple, Mr. Lloyd. We know about it because we were there when she bought it, and overheard the whole thing."

"Overheard? You mean you were spying on her?"

"Not her. The man from whom she bought the pot."

Lloyd frowned. "And just why were you doing that?"

"Because he's a thief. A looter. Drucilla Farnsworth is going to give the President of the United States a stolen artifact, Mr. Lloyd. And it could conceivably get him killed."

He arched his eyebrows and cleared his throat, then waved at the leather-upholstered chairs in front of his desk. "I think you'd better have a seat and tell me the whole story from the beginning."

They did so. Five minutes on the dot after they had entered the study, Lloyd stood up and came around his desk, sitting on the corner closest to Dusty. He had a very odd gleam in his eyes.

"Dr. Cantrell. Dr. Newton. Thank you." Lloyd stretched out his arm and shook each of their hands in turn. "Thank you so very much indeed!"

"At last!" Laura exclaimed. "If you didn't believe us, I don't know where we would have turned next."

"But of course I believe you! You see, I've suspected for some time that the artifacts Drucilla was investing in were, shall we say, not on the up-and-up," Lloyd told them in a confidential tone. "But it was a private obsession, so I turned a blind eye to it. When she told me she was going to give one to the President, however, I really got worried. You're certain this pot was looted? I received some documents earlier this evening from the Pline Gallery that appear quite genuine."

"We know the site it came from, trailed the person who looted it to Pline's gallery, and have pictures of it in his workroom alongside other artifacts stolen from the same site," Laura assured him. "Those documents are obviously forgeries. Now, about the President—"

"Excellent!" Lloyd interrupted. "I said I turned a blind eye, but in fact, I was hoping to find a way to persuade Drucilla to get rid of her collection. This is it. And so much more! I really can't thank you enough!"

"All the thanks we need is to stop this plot against the President, Mr. Lloyd," she told him with a happy smile.

"Plot?" He laughed. "Oh, that. That's utter nonsense."

Laura's smile disappeared. "But—"

"And even if it isn't, the Secret Service will deal with it. I'm not surprised they laughed at you though. It really is quite a far-fetched tale!"

"Just what *are* you planning to do?" Dusty asked.

"Why, stage the biggest publicity coup of this decade, naturally! With proper handling, I can get rid of Drucilla's troublesome collection, save the President untold embarrassment in front of the Native American lobby, and make them both look like heroes at the same time!" He stood up and strutted around the room, gesturing with his arms to emphasize the grandeur of his idea. "First, I'll open the ceremony up to the public, especially the press. Then, with all of America watching, Drucilla can announce that she and the President have uncovered this crime against history, point fingers at the thieves, and donate all of the stolen artifacts to a prominent museum!"

"I beg your pardon!" Laura cried, her concern for the President temporarily forgotten. "That's *our* research you're talking about!"

"Naturally we'll give you credit for it, Dr. Newton," Lloyd assured her with a winning smile.

"You're damned right you will. But there's a price for allowing you to use it in this manner," she informed him. "Call off the ceremony. You can still have your publicity coup; but I insist that you abort the President's visit."

"Impossible."

"Then no deal."

Lloyd continued to smile. "I'm sure we can come to terms on this. It's a grand opportunity for us all. I'll look good, Drucilla and the President will look even better. But you, Dr. Newton, have the most to gain. With some extra work on my part, I believe I can help you clear your name."

Laura slumped in her chair and sighed. "Damn!"

"I recognized you right off the bat, of course. After

all, publicity is my job and I'm very good at it. With that in mind, I have a proposition for you."

She didn't say anything. So Dusty took the initiative. "We're listening," he told the grinning PR man.

"I must have the weight of your research to add credence to this affair—and to force my decision upon Drucilla. She's a grand woman, really, but a bit odd and stubborn as a mule."

Dusty nodded. "I know the type."

"In return," Lloyd continued, "I'll give you all the credit you deserve. After the fact, of course. I can't have the Ultraviolet Wacko onstage with my client and the President, now can I? No use confusing the press; they're confused enough as it is. But afterward I'll make your roles in all this public." He put his hand on Laura's shoulder and added, "I really am good at my job. Come what may, I'll make sure you come out of this a hero as well."

"Sounds good to me," Dusty said.

It sounded good to Laura too. With one exception. "Aren't you both forgetting something? There's a little matter of a possible plot to harm the President. None of us will look very good if he's hurt or killed during this publicity gimmick, now will we?"

"While I'm inclined to think you've simply jumped to a rash conclusion," Lloyd said, "one way or the other, it's not our job to protect the President. You informed the people who are responsible, and they told you to take a hike." He shrugged. "What more can you do?"

"Mr. Lloyd has a point, Laura."

He did indeed, and she knew it. What else could she do? Lloyd was clearly not going to cancel the party. And he was so hot on this idea of his that he could probably find some way to convince Drucilla to go along with it, as well as make everyone believe it, even if Laura refused to let him use their research as evidence.

"All right," she said at last. "But I still think it would be best to cancel the whole damned thing."

Lloyd shook his head. "As I said, that's impossible. It will be hard enough to persuade Drucilla to accept this change of plan. Nor does the President bow to my whim. And he certainly wouldn't listen to a theory his own Secret Service has already heard and rejected. If it's any consolation," he added, "by making this a public rather than a private affair, there will be increased security and less chance of anything dire happening."

Dusty agreed. "Another good point."

"I suppose," Laura said.

"Then it's settled." Lloyd clapped his hands and rubbed them together. "Now, I must get to work! There's so much to be done and so little time!"

"We'll get out of your way and let you get to it, then," Dusty said, getting to his feet.

Laura got up as well. "Thank you, Mr. Lloyd," she said. "I think. We won't really know until after the President is safely away, will we?"

"Think positive, Dr. Newton! It's going to be a glorious Fourth! I believe I'll move the whole thing to the park," he said, stepping behind his desk again. "Oh, dear! The caterers! Well, they'll just have to change the menu to beans and wienies. For a crowd of several hundred thousand. My God! This day will go down in history!"

Dusty took her hand and pulled her toward the door. William Lloyd was already on the phone, giving orders and looking thoroughly at ease in spite of the task before him.

"Relax, Laura," Dusty told her. "Lloyd obviously knows what he's doing. It's not every day you get a chance to be part of history."

"Right," she muttered. "I just hope we don't live on in infamy as well."

Back in the car, Dusty wound his way down the side of the mountain away from the Farnsworth estate. He was whistling. "Why the long face, Laura?" he asked her. "I thought you'd be jumping for joy."

"Didn't you once tell me that a good scientist reserves judgment until the final results are in? Lloyd's plan sounds fine in theory; if it works out we'll be sitting pretty. But if it doesn't . . ."

"You worry too much."

"I'm a firm believer in Murphy's Law, Dusty," she told him. "The whole town is already getting dippy. That park will be a human zoo tomorrow night. Extra security or not, something could go wrong—with tragic results."

Dusty frowned. "Why do I get the feeling you're not done poking your nose into this yet?"

"Maybe because I'm not," she replied.

"Shit! Lloyd was right, Laura. We've done all we can. Why don't you sit back and let everyone do their jobs?"

"I'll let them do their jobs, but I refuse to just sit

back and watch it happen. I'm going to that wingding."

"Don't be stupid!" Dusty exclaimed. "What good would that do? They told us to stay clear, remember? Even if you did see something out of the ordinary, no one would listen to you. In fact, they'd nab you for interfering and you'd end up the center of attention—in front of whirring television cameras, no doubt. That would spoil the whole thing."

Laura gazed at him, her brow furrowed in thought. It was dark now, and in this neighborhood there were few street lamps. But occasionally the headlights of an oncoming car would illuminate Dusty's face. His expression, however, was unreadable, Anger, perhaps, with a touch of frustration.

"Spoil what, Dusty?" Laura asked.

"Lloyd's publicity coup, of course. What did you think I meant?"

"I'm not sure. Just having another of my idiosyncratic flashes, I suppose," she replied.

He groaned. "Heaven help us!"

She was having a flash, all right. A big one. Laura had realized the night they'd made love that Dusty was getting closer than any man ever had to winning her heart. They had shared so much, especially pleasure, and he'd stuck to her like glue throughout all the twists and turns she'd thrown at him. He hadn't always been pleasant about it, but he'd stayed.

Why?

She would have liked to believe he was smitten with her too. But she'd been banged up enough by life to be leery. Maybe she had fallen for him, but she still didn't trust him. He had, after all, threatened his way into this project. It was a good thing he had, because Laura wasn't at all sure she could have gotten this far without him. Now that it was nearing its culmination, however, her mind was full of questions about the central role Dusty had played.

If there was a plot against the President, it hadn't sprung up overnight. It was probably in the works long before she had gone to Carl's dig. Whoever was behind all this had known enough to use Carl as a pawn in their game, which meant they were probably keeping tabs on him, waiting for the right moment to put their plans in motion. That, in turn, meant they might have known about her arrival on the scene— and her midnight departure.

Did Dusty stumble over her that morning in the desert by innocent coincidence? Or had he been looking for her? His concern about a person with her reputation taking on such a delicate research project had seemed genuine, but it could have been an act, a means by which he could force her to accept him as a partner. Did he care for her, desire her, remain so close to her to keep her out of trouble, as he said? Or had he been holding her hand all this time to keep her from getting in the way?

"Why was that Secret Service man so interested in you?"

Dusty laughed. "Like you said, he's an asshole. I have been to a lot of unusual places. You know the intelligence community—always seeing something in the shadows."

"No, Dusty. I *don't* know the intelligence community," Laura said. "Do you?"

He glanced at her but was unable to see her face clearly in the darkness. "What's gotten into you?"

"You knew they'd laugh at us, didn't you?"

"Of course I did! With your reputation, did you really expect them to take you seriously?"

"I thought there was a chance," she replied. "Showing my naïveté again, I guess. But you knew we didn't have a prayer. That's why you were willing to let me try. You knew they'd only laugh and throw us out, thereby defusing any threat I might represent to the plan."

"Laura," Dusty said with a sigh, "I don't have the slightest idea what you're talking about."

She had pressed her back against the passenger door, trying to get as far away from him as she could. A dawning horror had gripped her, forming an icy ball in the pit of her stomach. There were too many serendipitous coincidences.

"How did you know Lloyd would let us in?"

"Jeez-us!" he cried. "I didn't *know.* There wasn't any mention of the pot or a gift of any kind in the paper. I put two and two together and figured it might rattle him enough to get us an appointment. It worked pretty well too," Dusty added proudly. "We walked out of there with a solution to your problems, didn't we?"

She nodded. "Oh, yes. A nice, juicy steak to throw the nosy bloodhound off the trail. Lloyd's in on it, isn't he? Is Drucilla? Or are you and your spy friends going to make her a victim of the curse, too, just like Carl and the others?"

"For heaven's sake!"

Dusty pulled off onto the shoulder of the gravel

road. Looking around wildly, Laura saw that while she had been busy talking, he had made a wrong turn.

Then panic washed over her in a chilling wave. He knew precisely what he was doing. They were on a section of the mountain road where there were no houses and no lights except those of the city twinkling far below. Behind her, a scant foot or two from the side of the road, a yawning precipice waited to receive her into its rocky depths. All he had to do was open the passenger door and push her out.

Dusty put his hand out to her. "Laura . . ."

"Stay away!"

She pressed herself even tighter against the door. That way he would have to fight her to reach the handle; right now there was so much adrenaline rushing through her veins she felt she could fend off ten men his size.

"Who do you work for?" she asked, trying to distract him. "The Russians?"

"Are you nuts? Laura, I am not a spy! Nor am I in on this plot. Hell, I don't even believe there is a plot, except in your obviously addled imagination! I've been on your side through all of this."

"Sure." She sneered at him bitterly. "Helping me every step of the way. I show up at Carl's dig, then leave in the dead of night; you're sent to find out who I am and what I'm doing. I tell you about my interest in the looting; you figure I might cause trouble, so you force your way onto the project. I figure out the curse angle; you help me assume it's Pline who's behind it."

"If you'll recall, I was also nearly killed with you.

Twice. And later I agreed with you when you came to the conclusion that neither Pline nor anyone else connected with the looting was a very likely suspect. Explain that!"

"Easy. The run-in with the black sedan and the fire were just attempts to scare me off. They looked close, but you were right there, ready to save me. And they happened *before* I figured out there was an assassination plot in the works. That's when you saw an opportunity to use me as part of the plan, right?" Laura asked. "When the President gets it, the feds will remember my warning. But their first reaction will be the same as mine was: Go after Pline. And while they're chasing down that blind alley, you, Lloyd, and whoever else, will be using the hubbub caused by the curse to make a getaway. I played right into your hands, didn't I?"

"If you say so," Dusty replied. "This is your fairy tale, not mine. Let me ask you a simple question, Laura. If I'm who you think and have made you part of the plan like you say, aren't you now too big a threat to keep around? You've got me pegged. I'm already about to do in the President. What's a crazy little scientist compared with that?"

"That's why we're here, isn't it?" she asked quietly, trying to keep her voice from shaking. "But let me tell you, it's not going to be easy. If I can, I'm going to take you with me over this cliff!"

Suddenly, the headlights of an approaching car washed over them. Taking advantage of Dusty's surprise, Laura turned quickly, yanked on the door handle, and swung herself out before he could stop her. He had parked so close to the edge of the road that for a horrible moment she thought she might slip on the gravel and do his job for him. But she regained her balance and dashed around the back of the car into the road, waving her arms madly.

The other car was making its way though a winding series of curves up ahead of her. As it entered the last switchback, it passed through the headlight beams of their rental. For an instant, Laura saw it clearly.

Then the black sedan with a large, battered swatch of bare metal on its side rounded the curve and headed straight for her. Transfixed by its lights, all but blinded, Laura opened her mouth to scream, knowing that her voice wouldn't even be heard over the roar of the sedan's powerful engine. But she didn't have time to do anything else.

Dusty didn't have time to be gentle. He grabbed her arm and pulled, practically dislocating it, then put his hand in the middle of her back and sent her sprawling onto the hood of their rental car. Jumping onto the hood himself, he wrapped his arms around her and held on tight.

The black sedan glanced off the side of their car in much the same way it had off that brick wall last night in Santa Fe, putting another deep gouge in its side. Metal screeched against metal, and pellets of safety glass rained down on Dusty's back as the side windows shattered. They were almost thrown off the hood by the impact, but Dusty grabbed the windshield-wiper gutter with one hand and held on to Laura with the other.

Roaring, the sedan sped on past. Seconds later

they heard it skid to a stop on the gravel. This time, the driver was going to come back for another try.

"Get in!" Dusty yelled, slipping off the hood and pulling Laura with him.

The driver's door would be a total loss, so he opened the passenger side. He jumped into the car, dragging her right behind. Glass was strewn everywhere and there was a spider web of cracks in the windshield, but the engine was still running. Dusty put the mangled rental car in gear and stomped on the gas.

They took off like a shot. By the time the sedan had turned around, Dusty was already through the switchbacks and onto a section of straight road beyond.

"Take the next right," Laura told him, amazed she was able to speak at all.

"You sure?"

"Trust me."

Dusty did what she said, spraying gravel in an arc as he took the turn at high speed. Immediately, the dirt road gave way to pavement. Their economy rental was no match for the black sedan, but they had the advantage of the distance they'd gained before it had been able to follow them and the fact that they were heading back into an area of lights and houses.

It was enough. Barely. Dusty turned down one particularly well-lighted street and pulled over to the curb. The black sedan stopped at the end of the block, hesitated for a moment, then squealed off. They were safe. For now.

Laura was staring at him. "You saved my life."

"And damned near got myself killed doing it, I

might add," Dusty said. He sounded a little surprised. "I guess that's the sort of damned-fool thing a man does when he loves someone as much as I love you."

She blinked. "But all I am is a liability now. A stubborn liability that won't give up. Even if you do love me, you couldn't afford to . . . Unless you're not . . . Oh, God!" Laura threw her arms around him and started to cry. "I love you too, Dusty! I'm so sorry for what I said. I just—"

"Went flaky on me?" Dusty supplied. "That's okay. In a way, I'm kind of starting to enjoy it."

Laura sobbed, pressing her face against his shoulder. Dusty let her get it out of her system. Finally, she wiped the tears from her eyes and pulled back so she could see him. He was grinning.

"What's so funny?"

"You," Dusty replied. "I mean, really. Me, a spy?"

"Well, you're certainly my hero. And you know what that means, don't you?"

"What?"

Laura kissed him, then whispered in his ear, "The hero always gets the girl in the end."

"In the end, huh?" Dusty's eyes gleamed. "Now that's a theory I'll stand behind one hundred percent."

"Take us home, Dusty. Before anything else happens, I have some making up to do."

23

It was their most passionate night ever. They left no erotic stone unturned in their search for pleasure and fulfillment. Flushed with the excitement of their new love, they made a profound ritual of touching, tasting, and learning every square inch of each other's skin. Again and again Dusty came to a throbbing climax deep within her; over and over Laura cried out in joy at possessing him so completely.

When their bodies could take no more, they fell asleep in each other's arms, only to awaken an hour or two later with sly, hungry smiles on their faces. And then, slowly, they would start all over.

Sunrise came, golden and bright, to rouse them by mutual habit from exhausted sleep. They took a shower together, lingering beneath the hot, stinging spray for much longer than it took to wash each other from head to toe. Then they shared a breakfast consisting of everything they could find in Laura's refrigerator, from eggs to sliced tomatoes, and went back to bed.

By noon, however, with both their need for sleep and their sexual hunger temporarily sated, the pair at last climbed out of bed to face what was left of the day. This would be, they knew, either the best or the worst July Fourth of their lives.

Laura's meager stock of food was depleted, so they ordered a pizza delivered and ate it at the kitchen table, discussing what they would do. Their options were limited, as was their knowledge of what was really going on.

"That black car didn't come upon us by accident last night," Dusty said. "It had to have followed us, just like it did the night we left the gallery in Santa Fe. But how and when did he pick us up yesterday?"

"He?"

"I got a glimpse. It was a man," Dusty explained. "Not that big ape of Pline's either. Somebody knows an awful lot about us, Laura. They know we're in town and that we represent enough of a threat to want us dead. The trouble is, it could be anyone. I think you're right; they've been keeping an eye on you from the time you first contacted Carl."

Laura put down the piece of pizza she was nibbling on, her appetite gone. "I was too . . . preoccupied to think about this last night. But they probably know where I live as well, don't they?"

"I'm not saying I wasn't just as carried away as you were, mind you, but I did consider the possibility. I'd say it's a fair bet they know where we are. It's an even better bet that as long as we stay here, we're safe. At least until after they've accomplished their aims."

She arched her eyebrows. "So you believe me now?"

"I don't have much choice. Coincidences can lead one to jump to conclusions, like they led you to accuse me of being a spy," he pointed out with a smile, "but you've finally won me over. We're here with our theory about a plot, the President will be here in less than six hours, and somebody made another attempt on our lives last night. It wasn't a coincidence; no pissed-off looter or dealer was driving that car, trying to squish us because we poked our noses into their business. There's something more nasty afoot than a curse. They're out to get the President, all right."

"And you think if we stay put, we'll be safe?"

"Last night the guy in the black sedan just saw a prime opportunity to knock us off where we wouldn't be found for a while, and he went for it. They have more important things to do today, I'm sure," Dusty replied. "As long as we stick to public places and don't get in their way, they'll wait until afterward to tie off the loose ends."

Laura lifted her chin defiantly. "I'm not running away with my tail tucked between my legs, Dusty."

"If you wanted to do that, you wouldn't be the same woman I fell in love with," he informed her, leaning across the kitchen table to give her a kiss. "I don't know what we can do, other than go to that celebration and keep our eyes open. There's a chance we've already stirred things up enough to stop them. If we haven't, the Secret Service will probably handle it. But whatever happens, it's bound to be a spectacular finish to our project, and we've earned the right to be there front row center."

Should anyone from the White House advance team spot them, Laura and Dusty wanted a good reason for defying the order to stay away. So the first thing they did was gather together and update all their documentation. If they were caught, maybe they could use it as an excuse for their presence, explaining that William Lloyd needed it for his publicity coup.

As Laura hadn't had time to develop the film she'd shot during the course of their project, that was the next order of business. While waiting for the one-hour service at a nearby mall, they also went shopping for hats. Laura got a big straw one with a floppy brim, Dusty, a canvas model that pulled down over his ears. Both would keep the hot July sun at bay, but the real purpose of the headgear was to hide their faces as much as possible.

The mall was only a few miles from the airport, so their next stop was at the rental agency to turn in their car for one in better condition. Although the agency attendant was sympathetic and polite, it still took them over an hour to tell a slightly altered version of what had happened and complete the necessary paperwork.

It was after five by the time they arrived at the park where the Fourth of July celebration would be held. The place was a madhouse already: acres and acres of humanity, some milling around or playing games, others sprawled out on blankets they had spread over the grass, eating, sunbathing, or taking an Independence Day snooze.

Laura and Dusty pulled their hats down low on their foreheads and plunged right in, assessing the crowd. The closer they got to the grandstand where the President was to make his speech, the harder it was to wedge themselves into the mass of people. Here the general mood was less that of a festive holiday than of barely controlled insanity. There were demonstrators aplenty, calling for—in some cases, screaming for—everything from nuclear disarmament to an immediate first strike. It was impossible to make any sense of it all, let alone pick out one group more likely to make trouble than any of the others. In Laura's opinion, they were all loons.

The area around the grandstand itself had been roped off to provide a buffer zone. But it was far from empty. There were television crews swarming all over, setting up their cameras and microphones.

"Good Lord!" She had to put her mouth close to Dusty's ear to be heard. "I knew it would be bad, but not this bad!"

"Let's get out of the center of it!" Dusty agreed.

They made their way back to the edges of the park where they could breathe, narrowly avoiding several fistfights as they went. But, as Lloyd had said, security was plentiful, so none of the melees got far before being broken up.

Policemen were everywhere, roving in pairs. Patrol cars and paddy wagons lined the roads on all sides of the park, mixed with other emergency vehicles such as ambulances and fire trucks. Laura imagined the latter were there not so much to put out fires as to hose down the crowd should things get out of hand.

"This is a waste of time," she said. "Even if we knew who or what we were looking for, we couldn't find it in this zoo. What are we going to do, Dusty?"

He shrugged. "Keep looking anyway, I guess. See that big red-and-white-striped tent on the hill over there? I'll bet that's where the food is. Why don't we head that way?"

"You can't possibly be hungry!"

"No. But the higher ground will make a good place to scan the crowd. Besides, it's closer to the grand-stand, and there's only about an hour till the Presi-dent arrives."

"Damn! Okay, let's get going. It'll probably take us half that long just to get over there," she muttered.

It did. If possible, the park was even more crowded than on their first pass across it. Strangely enough, however, the crowd thinned out noticeably near the food tent. When they got close enough, they found out why.

"Ten bucks!" Dusty exclaimed. "For a wienie?"

"I guess Lloyd decided he'd bankrupt Drucilla if he gave them away." They approached the entrance anyway; at the moment, ten dollars sounded cheap for a place to stand that wasn't already occupied. "Oh, wait. It gets you a whole meal, and it's for charity."

"Peachy." Dusty gave the man at the entrance his last twenty-dollar bill. "Which charity, bub?" he asked him.

"The PORCs."

They took their place in the serving line, waiting

to receive their hot dogs, beans, and potato chips. Dusty certainly hoped this was for a good cause.

"Who the hell are the PORCs?"

"The Party of Oilmen in favor of Reestablishing the Confederacy," Laura replied. "They're an obscure group. I know about them only because I did a term paper on political and charity organizations for a course I took."

They got their so-called meals. Dusty looked ruefully at his plate. "I think I want my money back."

"It's worth it just to have a place to sit down," Laura said. "But otherwise, I agree. The PORCs are hardly a true charity. It's made up mainly of businessmen who feel they were unfairly denied profits during the oil crisis. Their aim, I believe, is to secede from the United States."

"Lloyd chose them to give the concession funds to?"

"Probably Drucilla's choice. I told you her daddy was in oil, y'all."

"Great. And to top it off, my wienie's cold," Dusty complained.

Laura grinned at him. "Want me to warm it up for you?"

"Later, my sweet sexual obsessive. Let's find a place to sit and—oof!" Dusty's back went ramrod stiff. "Uh-oh."

"What's wrong?"

"Either someone was listening to our conversation and became excited, or there's a gun pressed against my ribs."

She looked behind him. Her eyes went wide. "It's—"

"Chester Finch is the name," the big, muscular man told her. "Hell of a party, ain't it? Let's go over there and have a seat. Talk about a few things."

The man was standing so close to Dusty that Laura couldn't tell whether he had a gun or not. But the look on Dusty's face was enough to convince her it was a definite possibility. They both went in the direction he indicated with a nod of his head.

And there, waiting for them at a cozy corner picnic table with a nice view of the grandstand, was Pline himself. He smiled at them as they approached, but it was not the sort of smile that warmed either of their hearts.

"Won't you join me?" he asked in a velvety voice.

"Do we have a choice?"

"No. Chester's gun is silenced. If anyone noticed, which is unlikely, they'd just think you were having a gas attack." Pline shoved his untouched meal a bit farther away from him. "I doubt you'd be the first of the day either."

They sat down. Chester took a seat right beside Laura. It was her turn to feel cold, hard steel against her ribs. She didn't like it. "Please, you don't—"

"Dr. Laura Newton," Pline interrupted. "The Ultraviolet Wacko. Unusual moniker. That is undoubtedly why I remembered where I'd seen your face." He looked at Dusty. "I assume Hiney is not your real name, nor are you a television producer."

"The name is Cantrell," he told Pline. "I'm an archaeologist. I'm also very confused. What's your part in all this?"

"That," Pline said, "is precisely the question I came all this way to ask the two of you. I received a very disturbing phone call from Drucilla Farnsworth, informing me that you are in possession of evidence detailing Chester's little foray into the Four Corners area."

"His looting, you mean," Laura corrected. "And your subsequent sale of stolen artifacts." Suddenly, her mouth dropped open. "Wait a minute! Why would she call and warn you? Her PR man has it all set up for her to publicly accuse you and denounce the looting. Unless . . . ye gods!"

"Accuse me? I'm sure you're mistaken." Pline frowned at her. "What on earth is wrong with this young woman? She seems to be in a trance or something."

Dusty turned to look at her. "Oh, no," he muttered. "Not another brainstorm. Laura! Snap out of it!"

"Huh?" She gazed at Dusty for a moment. Then she smiled. "Good grief! I've got it! You're here for the evidence. Right, Mr. Pline?" she asked him.

"Quite. It hardly takes a genius to figure that out."

"But you don't have anything to do with the curse."

He sniffed in disdain. "Of course not. Ms. Farnsworth practically accused me of the same thing when she—"

"Bought the pot," Laura completed. "I know. We were there." Pline's eyebrows shot up. "We also heard you issue what we assumed was a threat. You said she'd get everything she paid for, and you didn't say it very nicely."

"Naturally. I despise the woman."

"But we thought you planned to make her the next victim of the curse. That's why we followed her, and then we found out about the President's visit. In a way, Mr. Pline, we have you to thank for leading us into the middle of this assassination attempt."

Pline stared at her for a moment, then shifted his stare to Dusty. "Is she insane?"

"Decidedly eccentric," Dusty replied. "But I love her anyway. And she happens to be telling it like it is. The curse is a smoke screen to cover up an attempt to murder the President of the United States. We were almost killed three times in twenty-four hours because of our snooping. That wasn't you or Chester, was it?"

"Hell, no!" Chester cried. "I'm not a hit man!"

"You're holding a gun on the woman I love."

"Oh." He shrugged. "Nothing personal."

"What Chester is trying to say," Pline interjected, "is that we have no reason to kill anyone over a fine for looting. Maim, yes. Kneecaps or elbows, perhaps. Now, if you would be so kind as to take us to that evidence, we—"

"Would you three shut up!" Laura bellowed. They all looked at her, mouths agape. There was so much hollering going on all around them that no one else even noticed her outburst. "Excuse me. I love you too, Dusty," she told him. Then she glanced at the big man with the hidden gun. "Please don't shoot my kneecap off, Chester. And Mr. Pline, I don't give a damn about your stupid evidence right now."

Pline sighed. "I can certainly see how you came by at least part of your nickname. What, Miss Wacko, do you give a damn about?"

She looked at each of them in turn. "I care about what every American here should care about. No matter what your occupation, whether you use capitalism or abuse it, what you should be thinking about right now is how to stop Drucilla Farnsworth and her plot to assassinate the President!"

"Drucilla Farnsworth!" they exclaimed in unison.

Some people at the table next to them took up what they assumed was a cheer. "Three cheers for Drucilla Farnsworth! Hip hip hooray! Hip hip . . ."

"She's taking us all for a ride," Laura continued, leaning in close to them so they could hear her. "But especially you, Pline. Us she'll kill just as soon as she's done whatever she's going to do to the President, but you're her scapegoat. She called you because she knew you'd come right away; she *needs* you here. What do you think will be the first word out of anyone's mouth when they put what happened together with the presence of an Anasazi pot on the podium?"

"The curse!" Chester exclaimed.

"That's right. And who provided that pot?"

Pline gasped. "Me!"

"Correct again. Drucilla said she needed something fresh, remember? That's because she wanted solid proof it had been looted, proof she would then use to claim that you started the curse rumors as a means of increasing business."

"But that's preposterous!"

"Is it? The prediction she made that night on the patio will undoubtedly come true," Laura said. "If she pulls this off, after tonight the market will go crazy. You'll look guilty as hell."

"And we were going to provide the proof she

needed," Dusty said, his eyes wide. "But how did she know about us?"

"She knew because we were not the only pawns in her game. It was Flemming who told you where to find the stuff, wasn't it?" Laura asked Pline. He nodded. "I thought as much. He also pointed out Chester's position to me."

"Damn," Pline muttered. "I knew I shouldn't have told her who my supplier was. But a woman with that much wealth can be particularly persistent. Drucilla wanted to know it all, right down to the exact origination point of every artifact. Except for this last one," he added, his eyes narrowing. "Because she knew perfectly well where it came from, didn't she? She and Flemming were in cahoots."

"Not quite," Laura said. "You see, Carl had it in mind to carve out a niche for himself in black-market artifacts. Someone, probably a spy she managed to place on his team, helped him come up with what he thought was a plan to put you out of business so he could grab *your* spot."

"And I fell for it. I even paid him for the information," Pline admitted bitterly. "He told me he couldn't loot the site himself because he would soon be under investigation for looting his own dig. In actuality, he was going to finger me for the deed."

"Thereby playing an integral part in Drucilla's scheme to make you the prime suspect," Laura told him. "But Carl had his own scheme. He was going to try to clear himself of suspicion by telling his university that he had been selling artifacts from his dig as a means of catching you, a major dealer. To his credit, Carl realized he would need help."

"Enter the Ultraviolet Wacko!" Dusty exclaimed. "No offense, my love."

She smiled at him. "None taken. It was the Newton luck rearing its ugly head. I was in the wrong place at the right time. Carl is a boastful man; I'm sure Drucilla found out what he was planning via her student spy. She probably approved. After all, she would be getting two scientists working on her proof for the price of one. But when Carl failed to persuade me to join him, he panicked and took off."

"I'll bet that gave her an uncomfortable moment or two."

"If I did, it lasted only until she found out I was doing Carl's work for him," Laura said. "How she found out, I don't know. Since she needed someone close to the site to make sure you did, in fact, have it looted, Mr. Pline, it may have been through yet another spy." She looked at Dusty with raised eyebrows. "Remember little Cindy Blake on the team that took over Carl's dig? The one with the cute IQ?"

"You have your flashes and I have mine, Laura," he said.

She scowled at him. "Anyway, Drucilla found out," Laura continued. "Maybe she was planning on using Carl for the publicity-grabbing accident she needed all along. Or maybe she just decided he would look better on the hood of a car than whoever she originally had in mind. Either way, she had him hit, and her plan was rolling again."

"But if we were unknowingly doing her bidding, why would she attack us?" Dusty asked.

"Because we'd done as much as she wanted us to," Laura replied. "Secret agents we're not. While we were listening in on the patio conversation, the man in the black sedan was evidently nearby, observing us. Hell, for all we know, she staged that conversation for our benefit."

Pline nodded. "As a matter of fact, she did show an unusual desire to complete our business outside that evening," he informed them. "I say unusual because she doesn't like Santa Fe air. According to her, it stinks. Imagine!"

"At any rate, I don't think either of the first two attacks was meant to be fatal," Laura said. "The sedan made a hell of a racket before it came at us, and the fire was mostly smoke. What Drucilla wanted was to scare us into going to the police with what we had. That way, her proof against Pline would be a matter of record."

"But we didn't scare. Or I should say, *you* didn't scare," Dusty corrected. "Still, she was willing to let us go on breathing, even after we went to the White House advance team. When we walked right into her house, though, and told Lloyd our story, she decided enough was enough."

Laura nodded. "Another miss, thanks to you, my love. But any moment now, the President's motorcade is going to come down that street out there. If this change of plans and the insane activity here tonight haven't scared her off, she must be pretty sure of herself. Whatever she has planned for him won't miss, unless we can do something to stop it."

Pline stood up. "Well," Pline said, "thank you for a most enlightening discussion."

"Wait!" Laura exclaimed. "Aren't you going to help us?"

"My dear girl, I didn't even vote for the man," he replied. "No, the Lord helps those who help themselves, and right now Chester and I are going to go help ourselves to that pot. Come along, Chester."

Pline turned on his heel and moved away from the table. The big man shrugged as if in apology, then stood up and joined him. As an afterthought, Pline turned back to them and said, "Oh, and please don't get in our way. Chester's a terrible shot. He might kill you by accident."

They disappeared into the crowd. Now that the President's arrival was imminent, even the food tent was overflowing with people. Ten dollars for a good view of the grandstand was the best deal going. The sky had started to turn a deeper blue, signaling the coming evening.

"That selfish bastard!" Laura grabbed Dusty's arm. "What are we going to do?"

"You've laid it all out. I believe it. But nobody else will," he replied. "For one thing, we don't even know why she would do this."

"For the PORCs, of course! What better time to make a bid for secession than during the total governmental chaos that would follow an assassination?"

"Okay, I'll buy that too. It's been tried for less reason, heaven knows. But we're still not going to get close enough to anyone who could help us," Dusty said. "The second we approached the security team they'd drag us off. And nobody, not even the media, is going to notice a couple more nut cases amid this teeming horde."

Laura watched a very handsome man walk by their table, carrying his ten-dollar wienie. He had deep blue eyes, a full head of sandy-blond hair, and teeth so white they sparkled. His face was darkly tanned, with just the right amount of character lines.

She stood up, pointing at him. "Oh, my God!"

Dusty was incensed. "This is no time to go chasing after a movie star, Laura," he chastised. "Besides, what's he got that I haven't?"

"A membership in OOPs," she replied, tugging on Dusty's hand. "Come on, I've got an idea."

"OOPs?"

"The Organization of Oppressed Primitives. They're a radical splinter group composed mainly of guilt-ridden rich white folks who claim to support Native American causes," Laura explained. "Their hearts are in the right place, but they seem more intent on flashy publicity than justice in the courts and suitable compensation."

"So?" Dusty asked.

"So this place is virtually oozing television crews. And Pline has a point. Take away the pot and you take away the curse, and with it Drucilla's smoke screen."

Laura walked boldly up to the man. "Excuse me. I hate to bother you while you're eating, but a serious matter has come to my attention concerning the pillaging of Native American burial grounds. Can I have a minute of your time?"

He looked at her with his blue eyes and said, "Damn right."

24

Their intention was to give Drucilla a problem she couldn't handle. What they got was chaos. After Laura told the rugged movie star about the looted pot, he went to tell every OOPs member he could find. There was a large contingent of them in attendance, staging a rowdy demonstration and posing for reporters alongside a bewildered-looking group of Native Americans they'd latched onto.

Full of indignant outrage, the group formed a scrimmage line and started marching toward the grandstand, intent on grabbing the pot and teaching the ersatz New Confederate Army the same sort of lesson Custer received at Little Bighorn.

The police could have handled fifty OOPs, no problem. But as the scrimmage line advanced it grew in strength, adding zealot after zealot until it became a human tidal wave. Some had a cause and a feverish chant; others were just looking forward to a good holiday brawl.

As the wave rolled on, Americans of every color and creed were swept along with it. Women in bikinis linked arms with scruffy vagabonds; pink-haired punks joined hands with little old ladies in sturdy shoes. Together, united now by the sheer pleasure of unbridled patriotic fervor, they flooded across the park, flags waving and banners flying.

Their first major obstacle was the symphony orchestra. It didn't stand a chance. Clarinets squealed, violins screeched, and sheet music fluttered through the air like giant snowflakes. The wisest and quickest members of the band joined the parade, striking up a military march. Roaring, the wave rolled on, now fifty thousand strong.

Trapped in the buffer zone between the advancing army and the grandstand, television crews bravely stood their ground, pointing their cameras as if they were cannons. They fired, sending a live-feed of hysteria to their networks.

By order of the men in dark blue suits, a fire crew directed a high-pressure hose into the midst of the crowd. But it was far too late. Those who stayed on their feet simply lifted their fallen comrades and marched on. In fact, most of them seemed to enjoy the bracing blast of cool water.

"Save the whales!"

"Free the chickens!"

"Screw the chickens! Free beer!"

From their vantage point atop the grassy knoll near the grandstand, Laura and Dusty looked on as the first defensive column of police was overrun. Hopelessly outnumbered, not about to use their guns on what was now approaching a third of the population they were sworn to protect, they could do little but separate the flood of people into several streams. The end result was that each stream gained force and focus as it passed, like water through a garden sprinkler.

"What have I done?" Laura cried in horror.

Dusty put his arm around her. "Just offhand, I'd say you've started a riot, my love."

"This is terrible!"

"On the contrary," he told her. "It's brilliant. Look at 'em all! Different ideas, different needs, but all working together to achieve a common goal."

"But they don't have the slightest idea what it is!"

"That's America!" Dusty yelled. "Just like you and me, we always seem to pull through when we have to. Look!"

Down on the grandstand, William Lloyd was hollering into a microphone. "People! Please! Calm down!"

Beside him was a padded display case containing the Anasazi pot. Right beside that was Drucilla Farnsworth, dressed in a red, white, and blue sequined gown. She was a pretty woman, but at the moment her rage had turned her into a florid-faced harridan.

"Lloyd, you're fired!" she cried. "You and your stupid publicity coup. By inviting the great unwashed, you've spoiled it all. Give me that thing!"

She grabbed the microphone from Lloyd and hit him on the head with it, sending a booming echo through the loudspeakers. Stunned, he staggered across the stage, knocking over folding chairs as he went. Those chairs, formerly occupied by her friends and public officials, had long since been vacated. Lloyd tumbled off the end of the grandstand, landing on a cameraman. Another cameraman filmed it all.

Drucilla was alone onstage. "Idiots!" she bellowed into the microphone. "Stop this asinine behavior at once, you ungrateful slobs! You're ruining everything!"

Her strident voice carried across the park. Rather than stemming the human tide, however, it gave them a target. They surged toward her, sending television crews scrambling for safer ground. The grandstand started to shake.

"Commoners! Filthy beasts!" Drucilla was pacing back and forth in front of the display case, practically foaming at the mouth. "You . . . you stupid little taxpaying morons! How dare you defy me? I'm rich! Richer than you'll ever be in your wildest dreams!"

If there was a more disgusting sound than fifty-thousand juicy raspberries being delivered at once, Laura had never heard it. The grandstand was pitching and heaving now as the crowd surrounded it, pushing at the supports.

Even as insane with fury as she was, Drucilla could see the futility of further argument. She threw the microphone down and stomped on it. An ear-splitting electronic screech echoed over the park. Then she grabbed the pot from its display case, ran to the back of the stage, and disappeared behind a star-spangled curtain.

Seconds later the grandstand collapsed. People

poured over the wreckage. Laura couldn't see what happened to Drucilla. But she did see a very large man, head lowered like a bull, forcing his way out of the melee. There was a car waiting for him on the street directly behind what was left of the grandstand. He got into it and the car sped off.

"I think Chester got the pot," Laura said.

Dusty shrugged. "We've still got the evidence. Pline won't be able to do anything with it. At least it'll be in safe hands until this is over."

"That may take a while."

Now that they had reached their objective, however, the crowd lost most of its momentum. The band exhausted its repertoire of marches. And as twilight deepened in Colorado Springs, a confused silence descended upon the park.

Then they all heard it: the *whop-whop* sound of an approaching helicopter. All eyes turned skyward and a wild, rippling cry of excitement rose into the air.

The President had arrived!

"If there's one thing I learned from my predecessor," the President of the United States said, "it's to keep 'em guessing."

"Yes, sir," one of the men in the dark blue suits agreed with him. "Now, as soon as we land, we'll get out first. Usual drill. Two in front, two behind, you in the middle with your head down. Then we'll . . ." He trailed off, pressing one finger to an earphone he had stuck in his ear. "Wait a minute. I'm getting some strange reports from the park."

The other Secret Service men had heard the same reports through their own earphones. They were suddenly even more tense and alert than was their norm. The one closest to the helicopter pilot tapped him on the shoulder and indicated he was to maintain altitude and circle the park.

"Holy . . . You'd better take a look down there, sir. The ground team is saying there's been some kind of a riot."

The President looked. He shook his head. "Sad."

"It's your call, sir. Should we land?"

"That's another thing I learned from my predecessor," the President replied. "When in doubt, don't. I'll issue a statement from the airfield instead."

"Yes, sir. We'll find out exactly what happened and brief you on the way. They're saying something about a pot being the cause."

"Damned drugs!"

"Not marijuana, sir. An Anasazi pot. Evidently it was looted from a Native American burial ground."

"Remind me to look into it when we get back to D.C."

Just then, there was a loud explosion, and a brilliant flash of sparkling blue stars blossomed in front of the helicopter. The pilot swerved to avoid its fiery center, only to find himself confronted with another flash, this one a beautiful red with sizzling white tracers.

"Good Lord! They're shooting fireworks at us!"

"Get the hell out of here. Now!"

"Hold still, you son of a bitch! I'm going to give you a green starburst enema!"

From her hiding spot beneath the wreckage of the grandstand, Drucilla Farnsworth peered skyward and punched another button on the hand-held computerized fireworks controller. From the staging area, where even now a swarm of security men were busy snipping wires, another rocket ignited and went sailing into the air.

"Whoosh!" she cried gleefully. The explosion followed, accompanied by the appreciative oohs and aahs of the crowd. *Boom!* "Yee-ha! The South is gonna rise again!"

She pushed the fire button. This time all she heard was a click. Then she heard another click, this one inches from her ear. Drucilla looked, and saw that a man in a dark blue suit had found her. In one hand he held a gun, in the other a pair of handcuffs.

"The only thing that's going to rise is you, lady. Right up out of there and into these."

He pulled her, kicking and screaming, out of the wreckage. Laura and Dusty, who had finally spotted her just before she started sending missiles toward the Presidential helicopter, were there to watch the police take her away.

"This is all your fault!" she yelled at them as the police stuffed her into a paddy wagon. "If you hadn't stuck your noses in, I'd have got him! Got him, do you hear? Long live the Confederacy! I shall return!"

"Not for a hundred years or so you won't," one cop said as he closed the paddy-wagon doors on her.

"Well," Laura said, "I guess that does it."

Dusty nodded. "Now can we quit?"

"You betcha." She linked her arm through his. "We've done enough good deeds. And I'm through chasing after a security that isn't real. Right now all

I want is to go back to the desert and be alone with you."

"I'm all for that. But Scheherazade won't be ready for two weeks," he reminded her.

"Dusty," Laura told him, "I'd happily spend the rest of my life in a sleeping bag, as long as you were in there with me. That's all the triumph I need. Or am I being too primitive?"

He swept her into his arms. "I'll show you primitive."

"Dr. Newton! Dr. Newton!"

They looked up to find themselves surrounded by a herd of television cameras and reporters. Standing off to one side, giving her the thumbs-up sign, was William Lloyd.

"How long have you known about the assassination attempt, Dr. Newton? Did someone try to silence you? How does all this tie in to the looting of Indian ruins?"

"Could you describe how it feels to have saved the President of the United States? Were you scared?"

"Is it true you have a world-famous theory concerning global crime and the greenhouse effect? Tell us more!"

"Yes! More! Were ultraviolet waves responsible for Drucilla Farnsworth's insanity?"

"Dr. Newton! How does it feel to be a hero?"

At last they gave her time to answer, holding a bouquet of microphones in front of her. All across America, people were waiting to hear her words. Laura took Dusty's hand in both of hers and pressed it to her heart.

"It feels great to be a hero," she told them. "It

feels even better to be taken seriously. But let me tell you, ladies and gentlemen, the greatest feeling in the world is to be in love. Happy Fourth of July, everyone!"